## Books in the COLONY Series

QUANT
ARCADIA
GALACTIC SURVEY
SILK ROAD
LOST COLONY
EARTH

## Books in the EMPIRE Series

**by Richard F. Weyand:**

EMPIRE: Reformer
EMPIRE: Usurper
EMPIRE: Tyrant
EMPIRE: Commander
EMPIRE: Warlord
EMPIRE: Conqueror

**by Stephanie Osborn:**

EMPIRE: Imperial Police
EMPIRE: Imperial Detective
EMPIRE: Imperial Inspector
EMPIRE: Section Six

**by Richard F. Weyand:**

EMPIRE: Intervention
EMPIRE: Investigation
EMPIRE: Succession
EMPIRE: Renewal
EMPIRE: Resistance
EMPIRE: Resurgence

**Books in the Childers Universe**

**by Richard F. Weyand:**

Childers

Childers: Absurd Proposals

Galactic Mail: Revolution

A Charter For The Commonwealth

Campbell: The Problem With Bliss

**by Stephanie Osborn:**

Campbell: The Sigurdsen Incident

# GALACTIC SURVEY

## A Colony Story

by

RICHARD F. WEYAND

ISBN 978-1-954903-04-3
Printed in the United States of America

**Cover Credits**
Cover Art: Paola Giari and Luca Oleastri,
www.rotwangstudio.com
Back Cover Photo: Oleg Volk

Many thanks to
王睿
for verifying Chinese cultural accuracy.

Published by Weyand Associates, Inc.
Bloomington, Indiana, USA
August 2021

# EARTH

## CONTENTS

# The Propulsion Problem

Chen ChaoLi reviewed her project plan before the staff meeting. The biggest problem with her project plan was that she was soon going to fall off the end of it.

They could now routinely make transition to hyperspace and back with the probe they had. Instrumentation readings had allowed them to fine-tune the cooling issues with the hyperspace field generator. They had a heat map and a graph of the heat over time for the transitions they had made, and that allowed getting cooling only where it was needed when it was needed.

They had also learned they could reduce the hyperspace field strength while the probe was in hyperspace and still protect the probe from the corrosive effect hyperspace had on ordinary matter. Reducing the field strength to only ten percent or so of the field they needed for the transition had also reduced the problems cooling the hyperspace field generator.

Finally, stress monitors on the structure of the probe had given them more information about how close to the planet they could transition the probe without gravitational shear forces tearing the probe apart. They no longer needed to have the probe spend four days traveling away from Arcadia to get to a safe spot to transition. They were down to less than a day.

Now if they could only figure out how to move the damn thing once it was in hyperspace. Without that, there was no hyperspace drive.

And without a hyperspace drive, there was no project plan.

Chen JieMin, ChaoLi's husband and the theoretical lead on the hyperspace project, was also preparing for the staff meeting. His hyperspace mathematics team had made a lot of progress tightening up the mathematics using the data the probe was bringing back every trip.

JieMin had built up a hyperspace mathematics team around himself over the last ten years. He had worked initially with Karl Boortz, the head of the University of Arcadia mathematics department, and then with Boortz's replacement when Boortz retired, Ivan Volodin. Together, they had sought out any children in Arcadia with the mathematics skills to contribute to the program.

A hundred and twenty years after the founding of the colony, the population was approaching twenty million people, over half of them under sixteen years old. Large families and marrying young had combined to provide such a large population pool, and JieMin, Boortz, and Volodin had found several wild talents to whom they offered full scholarships to the hyperspace math program.

That long-term investment was paying off now, and JieMin had a seasoned team of young applied mathematicians to help advance the mathematical formalism of hyperspace. They were developing a very good model of what hyperspace was and what it wasn't, how it worked and how they could use it.

Karl Huenemann, the engineering lead on the hyperspace project, was also preparing for the staff meeting. With the data coming in from the probe trips into hyperspace and back, his team had been busy doing what engineers do for a living: cost-reduce, optimize, simplify. They were ready to go with a simpler, more reliable, reduced-cost probe design.

This probe would be able to transfer into and out of

hyperspace with much less energy expenditure and risk than the existing design. They could get it into hyperspace and get it back any time they wanted.

The one thing they couldn't figure out was how to make the probe move once it got there.

"All right, gentlemen," ChaoLi said when Huenemann and JieMin were seated. "Let's get started."

She opened her project book to her notes for the meeting.

"I guess first up is current status. Go ahead, JieMin."

JieMin summarized the progress the hyperspace math group had made in refining their formalism using the data from the probe. They had incorporated all the latest data, and, from their mathematics, could now replicate the data. That is, their math was predictive of the data.

"Excellent," ChaoLi said. "Thank you. All right, Karl. You're up."

Huenemann summarized the engineering progress. The optimization they had done on the in-progress design of a new generation of probe to replace the original probe, which was getting pretty long in the tooth by this point. They would have to replace it soon, and the engineering team was pretty close to finalizing the next-generation device. The next-generation device would also include a cockpit, to be used first for animal testing, then for human occupancy.

"Excellent," ChaoLi said.

She consulted her notes.

"We are now left to consider the future, gentlemen. All this progress is fine if what we are aiming for is to be able to transition probes back and forth to hyperspace. What it doesn't solve is how to get the probe to exit hyperspace somewhere other than where it went in. The floor is open for ideas."

"Well, that has always been the problem, ChaoLi," Huenemann said. "We've considered a number of alternatives there. A reaction drive like a rocket is impossible, because the reaction mass will simply bounce off the hyperspace field and fill up the field envelope with its exhaust. We can't use some kind of impeller outside the field, because, even if we could figure out how to have anything connected to the probe outside the hyperspace field, anything outside the field will be destroyed by hyperspace. It's like trying to row a boat in a lake of acid. The oars will disintegrate. The only contact we have with hyperspace is the hyperspace field itself."

JieMin started at Huenemann's last sentence, and his eyes were unfocused as he stared at the conference table.

"JieMin?" ChaoLi asked.

JieMin held up a finger – his 'wait a minute' signal – and ChaoLi was content to wait. When Huenemann looked like he was going to say something, ChaoLi held up a quelling hand. After a couple of minutes, JieMin stirred.

"There is a possibility, I think," he said. "Karl said it correctly. The only contact we have with hyperspace is the field itself. But there is a possibility there, I think. We can modulate the strength of the field differently in different places."

"How does that result in a drive, JieMin?" ChaoLi asked.

"Consider. We know that hyperspace exerts a pressure on the hyperspace field. The size of the field envelope shrinks when the probe enters hyperspace. It is this pressure that dictates how strong of a field we must maintain while in hyperspace. The field envelope must remain larger than the probe itself."

"Right. I'm with you so far," ChaoLi said, and Huenemann nodded. Leaving the hyperspace generator on once in hyperspace had been a source of contention between JieMin and Huenemann at the beginning of the project.

"All right. So if we made the hyperspace field have a variable strength along its length – concentric rings of higher field strength, like rings on a cat's tail – then the hyperspace field would be ribbed along its length from the pressure."

"OK. I can see that."

"Hyperspace is not solid, but the energy density has a viscosity of sorts. If we have those stronger portions flow from the front of the field to the back – make the field strength ripple along the field – that should result in a thrust against hyperspace."

"Fuck. That's brilliant," Huenemann said.

ChaoLi gave him a sharp glance, and he shrugged.

"JieMin," he said, "can we make the areas of stronger field be a spiral, and rotate it like a screw?"

JieMin thought about it a minute.

"Yes, I think so. But if you rotate it like a screw, the probe will counter-rotate."

"Perfect."

"What are you thinking, Karl?" ChaoLi asked.

Huenemann was in his element now, and he was animated as he spoke.

"If we build large, human-occupied ships, one problem is weightlessness. Some people can handle it, some can't. We know that from our shuttle experience. And, even for those who can handle it, medium- to long-term it's a problem. Bone loss, muscle atrophy, all that sort of thing. But if we make a cylindrical ship where the humans live in the outer portion of the cylinder, we can get apparent gravity by spinning the ship. So we do the screw thing until we get the ship spinning for the gravity we want, then we do the ripple thing the rest of the trip. Solves both problems, propulsion and gravity."

ChaoLi looked at JieMin, and he was nodding as Huenemann finished.

"Yes, that would work," JieMin said. "It will take some serious modifications to the hyperspace field generator, but I think we can do all of that. We'll have to work out the details, Karl."

"Of course. But now we have a direction. That is, if you approve, ChaoLi."

"Solving both problems at once? Of course, I approve. It seems to me, though, that the ripple effect should be first. Let's see if we can make the probe come out somewhere other than where it went in. That would tell us a lot."

"Yes," JieMin said. "It would give us some better numbers on the ratio of distances between corresponding points in hyperspace and normal space. Our multiplier. We're guessing right now."

Huenemann clapped his hands.

"All right! Now we're getting somewhere."

"Somewhere indeed," ChaoLi said. "That of course is the other question. If we can solve the propulsion problem, and build hyperspace-capable ships, where do we go?"

"To Earth, I imagine," Huenemann said. "And to the other colonies."

"Which are where, Karl?" ChaoLi asked.

"Yeah. That's a problem, isn't it?" Huenemann said.

"I think we can locate the first two," JieMin said. "We have the records of the viewscreens from the passenger containers the original colonists came here in. So there are views in multiple directions for the first two colony stops. We should be able to locate them from star parallax and location. Within a hundred light-years or so. Perhaps less. The other twenty-one colonies could be anywhere."

"That's our next problem, then," ChaoLi said. "Figuring out how to find them."

"There may be some documentation of them in the archives. If not, we're going to need some sort of exoplanet scanner," JieMin said.

"We have plans for the ones the Colony Headquarters used to find the colony planets," Huenemann said. "But there are a lot of possible planets. We can't just scan planets and say 'Oh, there's a colony.'"

"No, we'll have to do some sort of galactic survey to find them," ChaoLi said. "That's a longer-term problem, but it's something you should be working on, JieMin."

ChaoLi checked her notes for the meeting.

"All right. That's all I had this week. Thank you, gentlemen."

## The Destination Problem

When JieMin got back to his office in the Chen Hall of Science, he called his hyperspace math team together. He explained the ideas for what he was thinking of as the ripple drive and the screw drive to them and set them to the task of working out a first pass of how to modulate the hyperspace field.

JieMin wanted to take on the destination problem.

The first step was to locate those other two colonies. JieMin got in touch with the head of the astronomy department, and set up a meeting for that afternoon.

Aaron Barkley, the head of the astronomy department, knew Chen JieMin. Everyone in the Chen Hall of Science, and most everyone in the university, knew the famous mathematician. In Barkley's case, though, Chen JieMin had occasionally helped them out with thorny math problems that came up in their astronomy work. So Barkley was happy to meet with him.

The meeting was, at JieMin's request, in JieMin's office.

"JieMin! How are you?" Barkley asked.

"Very good, Aaron. Come in. Sit down."

JieMin waved to a guest chair and Barkley sat down.

"What can I do for you today?" Barkley asked.

"I have a little problem for you, Aaron."

"Indeed. For us? Well, maybe for once we can return the favor for the help you've given us over the years. What have you got?"

"We want to locate the first two colonies dropped off by the interstellar transporter a hundred and twenty years ago. Amber and Earthsea."

"My understanding was that we didn't know where the other colonies were, JieMin."

"We don't, Aaron. At least, not officially. But I've been looking through the archives, and I've found the viewscreen recordings for the passenger containers that brought the original colonists to Arcadia."

JieMin gestured to the three-dimensional display in the rear portion of his office. A section of the Orion Arm of the Milky Way appeared in the display.

"The Earth, of course, is here," JieMin said, pointing. "And Arcadia is here, about three thousand light-years away."

Barkley nodded.

"We can assume, I think, that the other colonies were similarly separated," JieMin said. "That is, there was more emphasis placed on having very congenial planets for colonization than that they were close to Earth."

"Yes, I've heard that theory. Makes sense to me."

"Now, the transporter dropped off twenty-four colonies. That was the plan, at least. The Arcadia colonists were dropped off third. The viewscreens of the passenger containers captured the sky above each of the first two drop-offs, and the multiple containers were pointed in different directions. Someone thought to preserve those viewscreen recordings, and I found them in the archives."

Images of the viewscreen recordings began to cycle in the display, about one every three seconds.

"You did? Why, that's extraordinary, JieMin," Barkley said. "I had no idea we had anything of the kind."

"What I need you to do for me, Aaron, is to find out where those colonies are, from a parallax analysis, from those multiple views. Do you think you can do that?"

"Of course. Why, if I had known we had those images, I daresay we would have done it already, just because."

Barkley watched the viewscreen images cycle in the display. He was clearly anxious to get started.

"Excellent. I would appreciate it, Aaron."

Barkley turned from the display to JieMin.

"You planning on sending someone to those colonies, JieMin?"

"Eventually, Aaron. That's the plan. Eventually."

Barkley turned back to the display.

"Wouldn't that be something," he said.

With the astronomy department dispatched on the problem of locating Amber and Earthsea, JieMin turned his attention to the rest of the colonies, the transporter's drop-offs after Arcadia.

In the library's archives, JieMin went into the Colony Headquarters records. They had all the records up to the time the transporter had left Earth. Literally everything. Recordings of meetings. Documents of all sorts. Shuttle schedules. Supplies listings. Who the suppliers were. Delivery schedules. It went on and on.

There were listings of the colony names. The first drop-offs, Amber and Earthsea. Arcadia. And the ones that came after Arcadia in the drop-offs: Aruba, Avalon, Atlantis, Bali, Dorado, Endor, Fiji, Hawaii, New Earth, Nirvana, Numenor, Olympia, Playa, Quant, Samoa, Spring, Summer, Tahiti, Terminus, Tonga, and Westernesse.

But there was no listing of the colonies' physical locations.

Anywhere.

How curious was that? It couldn't have been accidental,

JieMin decided. The locations of the other colonies had not just been unknown to the colonists. They had been deliberately obscured. Which made it really difficult for them to travel to the other colonies once they had hyperspace ships completed.

Maybe that was the whole point of obscuring them.

But these were Earth records, copied to the colony library before they left. Did that mean Earth did not know where the colonies were, either? It seemed incredible to JieMin. What could be the motivation behind such a move? And who could have enforced it? Dozens, maybe hundreds, of people must have known.

JieMin broke for the day with more questions than answers.

JieMin and ChaoLi rode the Arcadia Boulevard bus home together in the evening, as was their habit. They were both dressed in office clothes, he in a tropical print shirt and slacks, taking his cue from the former head of the math department, Klaus Boortz, she in a business suit appropriate for the head of the project. They didn't speak of business matters in the public venue of the bus, because everything they were working on was secret.

When they got home, LeiTao, their second child and bank baby, was stir frying dinner. At fifteen, she was working now, too, but she worked in the Uptown Market across the street and got home much earlier. JieMin and ChaoLi changed into lavalavas, and dinner was ready when they came back to the kitchen.

Their eldest daughter ChaoPing had married JuMing last year, so it was just the six of them for dinner now – JieMin, ChaoLi, LeiTao, the twelve-year-old twin boys YanMing and YanJing, and their youngest son JieJun, who was now eight.

Dinner was all family talk about school for the boys, and

work and school for LeiTao. Everyone helped clean up after dinner, and then the boys were off to their room. LeiTao also excused herself to her room to do schoolwork.

"You seem distracted," ChaoLi said once the kids were gone.

"I am having some trouble finding data in the archives," JieMin said.

"Something wrong with the archives or the search tools?"

"No, that's all fine. The data simply isn't there."

"Is it data that should be there?" ChaoLi asked.

"I would think so. We know, for example, that there is nothing in the archives for the Lake-Shore Drive. I looked for that years ago. And it makes sense that it was a secret, because it has huge potential as a weapon.

"I've always been surprised, though, that Earth hasn't been here. Hasn't stopped by, either as conqueror or friend. They have the Lake-Shore Drive, right? They could stop by at some point. But they haven't.

"Now I'm wondering if they can."

"What do you mean?" ChaoLi asked.

"What if they don't know where we are?"

"How could they not know where we are? They dropped us off here, right?"

"Yes and no," JieMin said. "Someone from Earth dropped us off here. Someone from Colony Headquarters. But the copies of the Earth archives for the colony project do not contain the data for the locations of the colonies. Someone dropped us off, yes, but it appears they may have kept exactly where a secret."

"That's incredible."

"Yes. And now I wonder if Earth even has the Lake-Shore Drive. Perhaps they kept that a secret, too. Used the Lake-Shore Drive to drop us all off, and then destroyed it. In any case, neither of those pieces of information are in our copy of the

Earth's archives. Anywhere."

"So now what do you do?" ChaoLi asked.

"One obvious thing is to figure out what other data is missing."

"But how do you do that? Do you know what should be there? How do you figure out what is missing if you don't know what should be there?"

"I don't know," JieMin said. "I suppose one way is to look at everything I can, follow my nose, until I run into a gap I can recognize."

He thought about it for a bit.

"Another thing might be to look at the people who started the whole project, see if I can find out what their actual goals were, to see if I can find the motive to hide things."

He shrugged.

"Really, I just don't know."

The next day, JieMin spent the morning following the first path. He set the display to project documents, and to read them to him, while he watched and let them wash over him.

Whenever JieMin found something interesting, he would pause that document and open another on the new interesting thing he had seen. He then let that document wash over him until he found something interesting, open a new document, and continue.

JieMin was performing something of a random walk through the colony program documents, not knowing what he was looking for, but hoping he recognized it when he saw it. Or that a later integration of what he had seen would change his view of the project and bring some enlightenment.

JieMin spent the entire morning viewing documents in this way. One thing was clear, the colony effort was a massive undertaking. The sheer scope of the effort, across the entire planet's economy, was staggering.

In the afternoon, JieMin followed the other tack, researching the backgrounds of the people who dreamed up and pushed the project in the first place.

These weren't at all obvious on first glance. JieMin had to dig back into the project, to its earliest days, to the earliest planning. A number of big corporations had been involved.

Russ Porter, the CEO of Colorado Manufacturing Corporation had been involved. Ted Burke, billionaire industrialist and the majority owner of a number of large companies, including Lunar Mining & Materials, had been involved. And computer innovator Bernd Decker had been involved. Others had come along later, but these three were there very early on in the project.

JieMin began reviewing the biographies and writings of these three men, who seemed to be there from the very beginning of the project. They were all public men, and there was a lot of material, including articles they had written, speaking engagements, and interviews.

What had been their purpose – their *real* purpose – and had they achieved it?

JieMin had a gift. Once his mind had seen enough of the pieces of a puzzle, the picture would snap together. He called these reorderings of things in his mind integrations, for lack of a better term. He didn't know how his gift worked, and he was afraid to look into it too deeply, lest he break it.

But JieMin knew how his mind worked, and how to use it. As he had gotten older, he had also gotten patient. If his mind didn't produce an integration right away, it was because it didn't have enough data.

Day after day, JieMin viewed document after document – in the mornings those about the later stages of the project, and in the afternoons those about or written by the people involved from the very beginning of the project.

JieMin was two weeks into his review of project documents when the first integration came. It was Friday night, when he had set the project aside for the weekend. He and ChaoLi had just finished making love, and he lay in the afterglow. That was a familiar time for an integration, as his mind was completely off his project and the integration could come freely.

All of a sudden, he had it. A piece of it, anyway.

JieMin got up and went over to the big armchair in their bedroom and started writing furiously in his notebook. When ChaoLi came back from the bathroom, and she saw him scribbling in the big armchair under the light, she knew better than to interrupt, and went back to bed.

The kids had left the breakfast table, and JieMin and ChaoLi were sitting over their tea when she brought it up.

"Did you have an integration last night, JieMin?"

"Yes. A small one, anyway. About the real purpose of the project."

"And what was their purpose?"

"To solve the extinction-event problem," JieMin said. "That isn't much of a revelation. I mean, Janice Quant said as much in her inauguration speech on becoming World Authority Chairman. She said the goal of the project was to 'Set mankind on a more secure footing against a global catastrophe.' So it was out in the open, but you can never trust what a politician says."

"Yet you think that was their actual goal?"

"Yes. The industrialist Ted Burke had written or spoken about the problem prior to the beginning of the project. How one global catastrophe could be an extinction event for the human race. And the computer guy, Bernd Decker, worked on massively parallel and survivable systems. So he knew about multiply redundant systems. It just all clicked together. I had been hesitant to accept Quant's statement as the deeper truth, but I think it was. It all ties together."

"What does that mean for why they hid the data?"

"I don't know yet. That work is still ongoing. No integrations there yet."

That weekend was spent on family activities. On Saturday, JieMin and ChaoLi took a picnic lunch to the park with the boys, while LeiTao was off to the beach with her boyfriend. On Sunday, ChaoPing and JuMing came over for a big dinner in the early afternoon. It was nice to have everyone back together, and they spent the afternoon chatting. A quiet Sunday evening, and JieMin was back at it Monday morning.

After his integration of Friday night, JieMin set aside the research into the founders of the project, and concentrated on the documentation of the later stages of the project.

JieMin also had to help out the rest of his hyperspace math team as they closed in on a set of recommendations for the modifications to the hyperspace field generator to implement the ripple drive. One of the ideas they had come up with was to vary the field strength by a greater amount on one side of the probe than the other, which would allow the device to make turns in hyperspace. JieMin helped them work out a way to do that without having to rebuild the hyperspace field generator from scratch.

As a result of this other work, JieMin couldn't spend all his time on the colony project documentation, but it was his major concentration over the next two weeks.

It would have been a curious exercise to watch JieMin work. He simply sat and stared into the three-dimensional display in his office. Text documents, videos, audio recordings played in the display, one after the other, seemingly at random. All of these played very fast, at one-point-five or one-point-seven-five times normal speed. JieMin stared into the display and let the wave of information wash over him.

JieMin, of course, was selecting which documents he would watch. He would select anything which piqued his interest. He often tagged multiple portions of something he was watching for follow-up, and then run down those strands later.

As JieMin watched, he continued to be amazed at the scope of the project. At how many things had been impacted. Following the project documentation into the project's nooks and crannies, he was impressed with how thorough the effort had been. How much research had been done. How many people had been involved.

As he more completely understood the full scope of the project, one question kept rising in JieMin's mind.

Where the hell had all the money come from?

## Propulsion

Karl Huenemann looked at the specification for the hyperspace field generator that came out of Chen JieMin's hyperspace mathematics group about a month after JieMin's original conceptual breakthrough.

The modifications they had made to the existing hyperspace field generator amounted to generating a standing wave within the hyperspace field, and then driving that standing wave slightly off its harmonic frequency. That would cause the standing wave to move along the hyperspace field from front to back or back to front, depending on whether one drove the standing wave slightly above or slightly below the harmonic frequency.

Not only did they have a drive, they had reverse. Not a minor consideration. Slowing down would probably be smart as you approached your destination.

Huenemann shook his head. Generating a standing wave in the field would not be a problem. He recalled ruefully how much work they had done to eliminate standing waves when first building the hyperspace field generator design they had. Had they not been able to get rid of the standing wave, they might have stumbled on the ripple drive by accident three years ago.

Well, they had it now. He scheduled a meeting with Mikhail Borovsky to plan and schedule the work.

They had modified the original probe to allow refueling of the device in orbit. The lift to orbit of the fuel alone was much cheaper than lifting the entire fueled device every test. For the modifications, though, they sent the big space-capable cargo shuttle up to orbit to retrieve the device and bring it back to the hyperspace facility next to the Arcadia City Shuttleport.

With the device back on the ground, technicians set to work exposing and then modifying the hyperspace field generator.

At the weekly meeting two weeks later, ChaoLi posed the question.

"Where do you stand with the hyperspace field generator modifications, Karl?"

"We're almost done. We should be able to launch the probe next week."

"That leaves the question of the flight profile. What do you recommend?"

Huenemann considered before answering.

"That's something of a problem. If we turn the drive on for too long, we will have to wait quite a while to find out what happened. If we turn it on for half an hour and the probe moves two light months, we'll have to wait two months to even hear whether the probe survived. On the other hand, if we turn it on for too short a time, we don't really learn much about the multiplier, because we don't know what the delay will be before it kicks in."

JieMin stirred, and ChaoLi turned to him and raised an eyebrow.

"I think we should separate the tests," he said. "We really have three things to test here. One, will the drive work to move the probe at all? Two, what is the velocity curve of the probe under the ripple drive relative to space-time? And three, can we maneuver the probe in hyperspace by varying the ripple amplitude on one side of the device compared to the other? I think we should take these one at a time. Otherwise we get into the trouble Karl suggests in setting up the tests."

ChaoLi turned back to Huenemann. He was nodding.

"I can sign up for that," he said. "So for the first test, we turn on the ripple drive for a minute or two, and see what we get. Right?"

JieMin nodded.

"Perhaps only for a few seconds," he said. "If we can travel at one light-year per hour, say, one minute is six light-days away. It would be almost a week before we heard back. A few seconds might be better, just to see if the drive works at all."

"OK, then," Huenemann said. "We can do that next week."

"Excellent," ChaoLi said. "Let's plan on that."

"Two seconds? That's it?" Mikhail Borovsky asked.

"Yeah. Two seconds," Huenemann told his project manager. "We'll see how far it goes with just two seconds to start. I mean, if we run it too long and it ends up a light-year away, we won't even know what happened for a year, and it'll take a year for our message telling it to come back to even get to it, right?"

"Right. I got it. Start small, see how far we get, and get an answer right away."

"Exactly. We don't want to shoot this thing over the horizon and not be able to see where it ended up. So program the initial flight profile for two seconds and we'll see what we get."

"OK, Karl. You got it."

Tuesday morning the tension was thick in the control room at the hyperspace facility headquarters alongside Arcadia City Shuttleport. They had finished all the testing last week. Yesterday they had fueled the device, and the large space-capable shuttle had delivered it to high orbit.

Once in orbit, they had fired the probe's rocket engines for seventy-five minutes to get it up to its normal-space cruise velocity. It had spent the rest of the day yesterday and overnight heading farther out from Arcadia, putting enough distance between itself and the gravity well of the planet for safe hyperspace transitions.

Now it was time for the actual test.

"Message round-trip time confirms the probe is now at a safe distance."

Borovsky looked back to the visitor's area where Huenemann, JieMin, and ChaoLi watched. Huenemann nodded.

"All right," Borovsky said. "Send the message to initiate program. Time that message acknowledgment."

"Message sent."

Minutes passed.

"We got an acknowledgement. We can confirm the probe's current position."

In the visitor's space, ChaoLi turned to Huenemann.

"Now we wait?" she asked.

"Now we wait. The longer the wait, the better off we are. A longer wait means it went farther. The probe's already made the transition, run the drive, and transitioned back. We're just waiting for its completion message to get back here so we know how far away it ended up."

ChaoLi nodded. Strange to think that the probe was already back in normal space, somewhere, and they were just waiting for pokey light-speed radio signals to get back to Arcadia. The time it took that message to get back was their yardstick for the distance traveled with just two seconds of thrust.

The minutes stretched out as everyone waited. It was nearly an hour after the first message when they got the second.

"Probe reports it is back in normal space. Elapsed time, fifty-six minutes, forty seven seconds."

JieMin turned to ChaoLi.

"Call it thirty-four hundred seconds. So seventeen hundred to one for two seconds of thrust," JieMin said.

"So it would take two years to get to Earth?" ChaoLi asked.

"No, that's the longest it could take. We don't know to what speed in hyperspace the probe can get if it continues thrusting. It should be accelerating, and the multiple increasing. Then at some point, the viscosity of hyperspace creates drag on the probe and we can't go any faster. That will be the multiple for a long cruise."

ChaoLi nodded.

Borovsky walked up to Huenemann.

"Karl, we're seeing some red shift in the communication coming back. Not a lot, mind you, but the probe is hauling ass."

Huenemann turned to JieMin.

"That is not unexpected," JieMin said. "The velocity leaving hyperspace doesn't need to be the same velocity it had going in. We think we have methods to determine that velocity by the way we leave hyperspace. Do you have an estimate of the velocity?"

Borovsky nodded.

"It looks like one percent of c or thereabouts. Call it seven million miles an hour."

JieMin nodded, and his eyes went unfocused as he consulted his heads-up display. Familiar by now with JieMin's methods, ChaoLi was content to wait.

When JieMin stirred, he turned to Huenemann.

"I recommend flight profile thirty-two for the return, Karl. With two-point-one-seven seconds of reverse thrust and point-two-one seconds of forward."

"Did you account for the flight time of the command message?" Huenemann asked.

"Of course."

Huenemann nodded. He turned to Borovsky.

"All right, Mikhail. Send the command for flight profile thirty-two, and parameters two-point-one-seven and zero-point-two-one."

Borovsky nodded, and walked back over to the team running the control consoles.

"Reverse thrust?" ChaoLi asked.

"Yes," Huenemann said. "Since we have reverse on the drive, there's no sense flipping the probe over. We just drive it in reverse. I'm guessing that little bit of forward thrust at the end is to fine tune the exit velocity once it drops back into normal space?"

"Yes. Exactly," JieMin said.

Huenemann nodded.

"So now they send the command, and we wait another hour?" ChaoLi asked.

"Yes," Huenemann said. "They send the command, and we wait an hour for the command to get there, then the probe transitions and comes back to us in two seconds."

"Outstanding."

The return wait wasn't as hard as the outbound one, because they knew approximately how long it should take. About an hour after the command message was sent, the communications technician broke the silence.

"The probe has exited hyperspace. It's here, but it's still

moving pretty fast."

"What do we have for a velocity?" Borovsky asked.

"The probe can see the planet, and it says its velocity is a hundred and ten thousand miles an hour."

JieMin was getting more and more refined in his analysis of their predictions as he got more data. He consulted the flight profiles they set up last week.

"Flight profile twenty-six. Parameter one-point-five."

Huenemann nodded to Borovsky, and the communications technician sent the command.

"One-point-five seconds?" ChaoLi asked. "But won't that send it careening off again?"

"No. Flight profile twenty-six is minimum ripple, forward – which is against its current velocity – and should be just enough to brake it down to a reasonable exit speed."

The technician's voice came from the other side of the room.

"The probe has exited hyperspace. Velocity now two thousand miles an hour. It's still a ways out, but it should be able to maneuver into orbit tomorrow."

"Nice," Huenemann said.

"What's next?" ChaoLi asked.

"Refine our navigation mathematics with what we learned, then run more tests at longer times, so we can calculate our hyperspace velocity and see how the ratio varies," JieMin said.

"When can we run the next test?" Huenemann asked.

"I would think this week," JieMin said.

"We need to go up to the probe, then, and refuel it."

"That would be wise," JieMin said. "We'll get you some new flight profiles as soon as we can."

## More Missing Data

While all the preparation for the test flights was going on, JieMin continued to spend much of his time researching the colony project, letting his hyperspace math group work out the flight profiles. His focus shifted to the financial aspects of the project. Where had all the money come from?

There were good records of the disbursements on the project. Purchasing documents, delivery documents, payment documents. There was a mountain of documents, and JieMin worked his way through a sampling of them.

JieMin found, as he expected, that the financing in the latter stages of the project – particularly the last six years – came from the World Authority. To spend truly monumental sums of money, one needed access to government and its taxes. That much JieMin understood, and the documentation showed that was the case.

JieMin moved further back in the project documentation, following the money flows. Janice Quant, in her inauguration address, had referred to the project as the De Villepin Project, and promised to carry out the previous chairman's vision, so he expected to find the government expenditures had begun under De Villepin.

But when JieMin followed the finances back, he found an anomaly. Granted, during Quant's tenure as World Authority Chairman, the financing was all by the World Authority. During the latter four years of De Villepin's tenure, the financing was increasingly by the World Authority. But prior to that – prior to Janice Quant becoming Vice Chairman of the

World Authority – the financing was coming from Janice Quant.

At that point, the World Authority wasn't involved at all.

That couldn't possibly be right. It was almost as if 'the De Villepin Project' was actually Janice Quant's project, and she took over the World Authority to get access to its finances and its authority.

Why did his brain supply 'took over' for the verb in that sentence?

JieMin kept digging into where the earlier money on the project had come from. The documentation here was much sketchier, almost as if it had been deliberately obscured. He kept running into dead end after dead end. Sometimes he ran into money from unexpected sources. At other times he ran into money going to unexpected places.

The other thing he couldn't find was a complete payroll. There were lots of people involved in the project – thousands of them, even early on – but it was as if they weren't getting paid. How did that work?

He brought it up with ChaoLi that weekend, the weekend after the initial ripple drive testing. The kids had gone to the park themselves today, and LeiTao was at the beach with her boyfriend again. That relationship looked like it was getting serious. Then again, she was fifteen, and it was getting to be about that time, by Arcadia standards, anyway.

"I've been reviewing the financial documentation of the colony project from before the World Authority became involved with it," JieMin said.

"How's it going?" ChaoLi asked.

"Slowly. There are a lot of anomalies in the documentation. There appears to be a lot of documentation missing as well."

"Well, that's to be expected, I think. The archives aren't going to contain corporate confidential information. Those aren't public records."

"Yes," JieMin said. "But there are other things missing as well. Things that should appear in public documents, I think. Like overall payroll numbers."

"Yes, those get filed with the government, and at least some of those are public numbers. The ones on corporate reports, for instance."

"Right. But I am finding corporations with hundreds of employees with no payroll data."

"Now that is strange," ChaoLi said.

"Or I'm misreading the reports. Accounting isn't my field."

"Do you want some help with it? I have people on loan from JongJu's group to work the project finances. I'm sure some of them could help out."

"That might help," JieMin said. "At least to tell me if what I am seeing is unusual or I am just misunderstanding. But I don't think I am."

"If you're not, what would that mean?"

"That I found more data that was deliberately obscured."

On Monday morning, an accounting team from JongJu's group stopped by JieMin's office. They had asked him for a preview of the anomalies he was seeing, and he told them to drop by. He had to borrow another guest chair from the office of one of his hyperspace math team next door.

Chen MinYan and her assistants sat, and JieMin walked them through some of the documents he had been looking at.

"This is just a small portion, you understand," he said. "A few examples of each of the things that doesn't look right to me. There are many more of each type, all across the project and companies associated with the project. I don't know if this is abnormal, or if it is the way accounting was done at that time."

MinYan nodded.

"I don't think it's normal," she said. "This looks like someone was cooking the books, but exactly how I can't tell yet."

"So this isn't normal."

"No. It's not normal. Some of these things are outright scandalous, if you look at them right."

"But they were never examined at the time?" JieMin asked.

MinYan shrugged.

"Each document looks OK on its face. As a standalone. You know. It's when you cross-reference them the way you did that things start looking suspicious."

MinYan looked at him sharply.

"So what do you want us to do with all this?"

"Find out if they were hiding something. If there is information that was deliberately obscured, and what that information is. Not the contents of the information. That's probably lost. But what piece of information it was. So that I can try to figure out what they were up to."

MinYan nodded.

"All right," she said. "Can you send me the pointers to everything that looks funny to you? Everything you flagged?"

"Of course, but it's a lot of documentation."

MinYan shrugged.

"Documentation is what we do," she said.

"So what are we seeing?" Chen MinYan asked her team leaders on Friday, the end of their third week of looking at the documentation.

"First thing is that Professor Chen was right," Chen JieLing said. "There are a lot of employee listings or employee counts for which there is no payroll. Sort of a reverse ghost employee situation."

"Reverse ghost employees?"

"Yes." She nodded. "I don't know what else to call it. Normally, a ghost employee is someone who doesn't exist. Some made-up name is put on the payroll, but their pay actually goes to the fraudster. Here, the person is made up, but they receive no pay."

"Could it be someone who doesn't need to be paid?" MinYan asked. "Or asks not to be paid, like a university professor doing gratis work on the side?"

"I don't think so. Among other things, there are some organizations where the whole organization is fictitious. Hundreds, sometimes thousands, of people in an organization, and none of them is real."

"What could be the purpose of that?"

"One thing. Money," JieLing said. "These organizations were part of the money flow. We think some of them existed just to provide a buffer, to keep it from being obvious that money was going from organization A to organization C. Insert fake organization B."

"Ah. OK. That makes sense."

"Yes, but given that clue, we started running every named person we had against a background search, to see how many of them were a real person and how many weren't."

"How did you do that?" MinYan asked.

"We looked up everything we had on them. Not just biographical information, but posts on public forums, appearance on membership or officer listings of social groups, all sorts of things other than their professional activities."

"And?"

"There are thousands of them," JieLing said. "Public officials. Scientists. Lawyers. Finance people. Even accountants. As far as we can tell, none of them really existed. They were fronts for someone else."

"Who?"

"We don't know. That's the really frustrating thing. Whoever was actually using these fronts kept their hands clean. And it had to be hundreds of people, to front that many ghosts. But we can't find one of them."

"Curiouser and curiouser," MinYan said.

"Oh, it gets worse," Chen FangTao said.

"How so?"

"There was a whole infrastructure of these firms. Especially engineering, financial, and legal firms. For instance, there were a number of investment houses that owned significant shares of stock in firms associated with the project. When we look at their performance, as a whole they were very successful, vastly outperforming other such firms in the marketplace."

"All ghost firms?" MinYan asked.

"Yes." He nodded. "And together they had a controlling interest in a lot of the firms working on the project."

"Wow."

"Yes," FangTao said. "It gets better. They also had a controlling interest in the New York Wire, the leading news outlet of the day. The Wire strongly supported the colony project, and ran any number of stories about it, all strongly biased in its favor. And get this. The writers who wrote those pieces? They were ghosts, too."

"It was a massive conspiracy to carry forward the project."

"Absolutely."

"And we have no idea who was behind it?" MinYan asked.

"None."

MinYan shook her head.

"Unbelievable."

"And true."

MinYan nodded.

"Did you find anything else?"

"Oh, yes," JieLing said. "Some of the money disbursed from these ghost firms – and there was a lot of money flowing here – went to some shady setups."

"Elaborate."

"Well, first, there was a lot of 'spreading around money' being, well, spread around. There were hundreds of people who were being paid bribes out of this network of ghost firms."

"Who?" MinYan asked.

"You name it. City council members in various large cities. Judges in various courts. Officials in administrative region bureaucracies. World Authority Council members and their families. Basically anyone who interacted with the project from outside was on the take."

"And they got away with it?"

"Oh, much of it was disguised," JieLing said. "All the traditional methods. Election campaign contributions. Contributions to charities. Book deals. Speaking engagements. You name it, they used it. It was like they read the book on how to bribe people, and then added a couple chapters of their own."

"And all this money was coming out of the ghost firms?"

"Oh, yes. And that wasn't the only funny business going on. One particularly scandalous bit is a computer project by Bernd Decker, one of the people who kicked off the project. Over more than twenty years, he spent billions of credits of project money on a computer project. There were no papers published.

No architecture, no results, no records of the computer being used for anything. Nothing. Just money spent. Lots of money."

"Was Decker behind the conspiracy?" MinYan asked.

"We don't think so. While the project was going on, he was busy doing other things. Coming up with real computer projects, real advancements in the technology. All the computers we use are derived from Decker's remaking of the computer industry with a seminal patent in the late 2230s."

"Where was all the money coming from?"

"The stock market," FangTao said. "There was a ridiculous amount of money being made. As the project grew and spent money, it spent it all on firms in which it had a controlling interest. The stock market is always forward-looking, and as those firms' receipts grew due to the project, their stocks soared. They issued more shares, then distributed dividends."

"Which went back into the project."

"Exactly."

"All right. Nice job. Let's get all this information organized, prepare the exhibits, and write up the analysis. We can present it to Professor Chen next week."

# Interstellar

As testing of the hyperspace probe continued, JieMin and his hyperspace math team were able to work out the acceleration curve for the ripple drive.

As they had expected, the probe's velocity in hyperspace increased the longer the drive was engaged, until the viscosity of hyperspace that they were pushing against increased the drag on the field. Then the drive held them at that cruise velocity, but could not accelerate the probe any further.

They also discovered that, if the ripple drive were shut off in hyperspace, the probe would slow to a stop in hyperspace due to drag.

In working up a mathematical formalism for all this, they relied heavily on all the work that had already been done in hydrodynamics. As it turned out, the data indicated that hyperspace was incompressible, much like water, and the mathematics was similar. The constants in the equations were different, and the data helped them refine values for those constants.

They used their new mathematics to optimize the ripple-drive parameters, varying the spacing of the ripples and the rate used to move the ripples along the hyperspace field. Borrowing from variable-pitch propeller science, they found that the best results were when the ripple drive rate was started out slowly and then increased as the probe sped up and the flow of hyperspace over the field increased.

They were also getting better at bringing the probe closer in to Arcadia on its return trip, and having the desired exit velocity on transitioning out of hyperspace.

The time came when they were ready to try the first interstellar flight of the probe. The idea was to program the probe to travel to the nearest star, take some pictures, and return on its own.

There was a known exoplanet around that star, though it was not suitable for colonization due to an estimated surface gravity of almost four times that of Earth or Arcadia.

It should make for some nice pictures, though.

"You think it's time for that step, gentlemen?" ChaoLi asked.

Huenemann and JieMin looked at each other. JieMin gave him a tiny nod.

"Yes, ChaoLi, we think so," Huenemann said. "We now have the probe entering orbit around Arcadia on its own. It transitions out of hyper when it's close, gets its bearings, then makes one last trip into hyperspace to hit the right spot. We think we can do the same thing with the exoplanet around Beacon, have it take some pictures, and come back."

"And the trip is how long?"

"Three light-years in each direction. Our calculations given our cruise velocity with the current generation ripple drive are that it will be about an hour each way, including acceleration within hyperspace."

ChaoLi looked to JieMin and he nodded. She turned back to Huenemann.

"And will we get close enough on that first hop for the probe to be able to approach the planet? At both ends, really."

"The probe will take two additional bumps in hyperspace if it needs to. It's pretty adaptive right now."

"Has it had to do that already, Karl?"

"Yes. On that one longer test we did. It missed the mark by

quite a bit on the first hop, then it took one to get closer, and another to hit the right place and velocity to cruise into orbit."

ChaoLi nodded.

"All right, then. You may proceed."

"Thanks, ChaoLi. Figure early next week."

Huenemann clapped his hands and turned to JieMin.

"This is going to be exciting," he said.

"Indeed," JieMin said.

That weekend, ChaoLi and JieMin went up to the roof of the apartment building one night. The star the colonists had named Beacon was the closest star to Arcadia, and by far the brightest star in the night sky. It blazed above them.

"All the way there and back, in two hours. That will be pretty amazing, JieMin."

"Yes. It is finally coming about. It's been twenty years since I first saw hyperspace in my mind, but it is finally coming about."

"What about the other colonies? Have JongJu's people reported their findings yet?"

"No," JieMin said. "We're looking at mid to late next week."

"Now that we have a way to get there, we need a place to go."

"I know. Aaron Barkley has the first two colonies nailed down to within fifty light years or so. We need to get the new probe built, with the radio direction finder equipment, and we should be able to find them."

"And the others?" ChaoLi asked.

"We'll see what MinYan and her accounting team have come up with next week. Then we'll see."

The hyperspace probe was all fueled and ready to go on

Monday morning. They started it on its way with its rocket engine, getting it moving away from the planet. It would take the best part of a day to move far enough away from the planet for a hyperspace transition to be safe, performed without tearing the probe apart.

On Tuesday morning, they were ready to start the hyperspace portion of the test. The multiple test flights they had done over the last few weeks had become routine. For this first interstellar flight, though, everyone was gathered in the control room at the hyperspace project headquarters adjacent to the Arcadia City Shuttleport.

"Flight profile is loaded and the probe reports ready," the communications technician said.

"Send the initiation command," Huenemann said.

"Initiation command sent."

A few seconds later, he reported again.

"Acknowledgement received. Comm link to the probe is gone."

Huenemann turned to ChaoLi and JieMin.

"Time for coffee and donuts. We got a couple hours before it gets back."

"We know for sure that it transitioned?" ChaoLi asked.

"Yes. A little trick the comm people started playing. They leave the carrier on the probe's transmitter on at reduced power. But they can see when the probe transitions because they lose the carrier."

"I see," ChaoLi said. "So we have a couple hours now?"

"Yeah. I had them put out refreshments in the conference room. Might as well be comfy."

An hour and forty-five minutes later, they were back in the control room, in the observer seats in the back of the room. It was about fifteen minutes later when the communications technician spoke up.

"I have carrier. The probe is reporting its return. It's downloading pictures."

They all looked to the big display on the front wall. It was another minute before a picture popped up on the display. It showed a star with a planet in the foreground.

"Spectral analysis of the picture indicates this is Beacon or a star of the same class," one of the analysis people said.

After a minute, another picture took its place. This one showed the star rising from behind the planet.

"Ooo. Sunrise," ChaoLi said. "On an alien planet. I like that one."

New pictures continued to appear on one-minute intervals. ChaoLi turned to Huenemann.

"You're to be congratulated, Karl. You and your whole team. This is tremendous."

"And funding for the new probe?" Huenemann asked.

"With a success like this under your belt, that becomes much more likely. I will let you know."

ChaoLi and JieMin got on the Arcadia City Shuttleport bus back to town. The bus's route ringed the shuttleport, and passed directly in front of the hyperspace project facility.

They were not the only people on the bus, so they did not talk any specifics about the project.

"What now?" JieMin asked.

"For all it's been a tremendous day, it is not yet noon," ChaoLi said. "I have put in a request to meet with the Chen, and will report in this afternoon. What about you?"

"The accounting people will be giving me their report tomorrow morning. Until then, I'm sort of at loose ends."

"So we go back home and have lunch. I'll give my report, and then we can have the rest of the afternoon together."

"That would be nice."

Chen Zufu accepted ChaoLi's meeting request for just after lunch, and asked that she bring JieMin along. When they arrived at Chen Zufu's tea room, Chen Zumu was also there.

Chen MinChao was still Chen Zufu, and Jessica Chen-Jasic was still Chen Zumu. They were now in their mid-70s, and both white-haired, wearing silk robes and seated on pillows before a low table. They would retire soon, JieMin thought. Five years, perhaps, or ten at the most.

"Be seated, ChaoLi. JieMin.

"Yes, Chen Zufu."

ChaoLi and JieMin sat on pillows on this side of the low table. JieMin allowed ChaoLi to sit on his left – to Chen Zufu's right and therefore the most honored position – because she had been named first.

Chen Zufu's tea girl came in and served all four of them tea, then departed without a word. ChaoLi sipped first, then JieMin, then Jessica, then MinChao, as host, last.

They were small etiquettes, but, to JieMin, such small things made the world work. Made the big things – the hard things – easier.

"I understand you have something to report, ChaoLi."

"Yes, Chen Zufu."

"You may proceed."

"Thank you, Chen Zufu."

ChaoLi told them of this morning's successful interstellar test of the hyperspace probe. She also sent them the picture of the sunrise of Beacon over the exoplanet Beacon-1.

"So we have sent the hyperspace probe to another star

system, taken pictures, and had it return safely?" Jessica asked.

"Yes, Chen Zumu."

"In two hours?"

"Yes, Chen Zumu, plus a day on each end to get to and from a safe distance for hyperspace transitions."

"That is extraordinary."

Jessica turned to JieMin.

"You are to be congratulated, JieMin. What is it now? Twenty years since you postulated the existence of hyperspace?"

"Yes, Chen Zumu."

"And now here we are. Thanks to your vision."

"Thank you, Chen Zumu."

Jessica nodded and turned back to ChaoLi.

"And now the question arises as to what do we do next in the project."

"Yes, Chen Zumu."

"What do you suggest, ChaoLi?"

"We need to know that living beings – humans in particular – can survive hyperspace travel, Chen Zumu. We think so. We can't see any reason why not. But that needs to be tested, starting with some other animals first."

"For which we need a probe with a cabin. Like the new design."

"Yes, Chen Zumu."

Jessica turned to MinChao. He nodded to her and turned to ChaoLi.

"Do you have the current income spreadsheet for the project, ChaoLi?"

"Of course, Chen Zufu."

"Send it to me, please."

ChaoLi sent him the income statement from her project

subsystem of the family's accounting system. MinChao's eyes became unfocused as he worked through it in his heads-up display. He worked several minutes, then focused once again on ChaoLi.

"If we have accomplished interstellar flight, our advance payments from the government increase. Can we prove those pictures are authentic?"

ChaoLi looked at JieMin, and he stirred.

"I believe we can, Chen Zufu. The computer people at the university have some software for analyzing images for artifacts of editing. We helped them with the mathematics a few years back."

"Excellent," MinChao said.

He looked to Jessica, and she nodded slightly. He turned back to ChaoLi.

"You may build two of the new probes, ChaoLi."

"Thank you, Chen Zufu."

"And, once again, excellent job. Both of you."

"Thank you, Chen Zufu."

"So what do we do for the rest of the afternoon?" JieMin asked when they got back to their apartment.

"Beach," ChaoLi said. "It's been months."

"Done."

They stripped down and, nude, headed for the bus.

When they got to the beach, they found that the city government had extended the wide part of the beach almost two miles northward to accommodate the growth of the city, and there were two more bus stops at the beach, one each mile.

Their secret spot – the secluded cove – was still secluded and private, but it was a much shorter walk from the third bus stop.

It was a beautiful afternoon for making love on the beach.

# Integration

The day after the first interstellar test, JieMin was in his office at the University of Arcadia. He had a meeting this morning, but the first thing he did is check with the computer science contact he had from the photo verification work he had done a few years back.

Sue Gaffney assured him the application they had ultimately come up with was excellent at detecting doctored photos and videos. They had had a university-wide contest to see if someone could fool the software, and no one had been able to do it, in either direction. JieMin asked her if she could send him a link to the software and give him permission on it, and Sue said she would.

MinYan, FangTao, and JieLing came by about nine o'clock.

"Come in, come in. Have a seat," JieMin said.

When they were seated, he had two questions for them.

"Was I right? Did you find anything?"

"You might say that. I might better describe it as a target-rich environment."

"Really."

"Oh, yes."

MinYan raised an eyebrow and gestured to the three-dimensional display at the far end of JieMin's office. He sent her a temporary control access to the display, which she shared with FangTao and JieLing.

"We'll show you what we found," MinYan said.

JieLing and FangTao took turns running through the report, which laid out the situation they had described to MinYan the previous Friday. At the end of it, JieMin sat stunned.

"All these firms?" JieMin asked, waving at the screen.

"Fake," MinYan said. "What we call false fronts."

"But there must be hundreds of them."

"With thousands of employees. Who were also all fake. Fake investment houses, engineering firms, law firms,...."

"Law firms?"

"Yes," MinYan said. "To file the documents, obtain zoning permits, fend off lawsuits. 'Oh, that was filed by John Smith, the lawyer from Smith, Jones, and Clark. He has his law degree from such-and-such university law school.' All fake."

"All fake?"

"Well, the university was real. The diploma, John Smith, and his law firm were all fake."

"But why?" JieMin asked.

"To hide where the money was coming from and where it was going. And how much of it. The total amount of money spent on the colony project was staggering. They spent over a year's planetary domestic product on the colony project. Granted that was over about twenty years, but even so."

"So these people – these fake people – just popped into existence? I mean, in the documentation."

"No, not exactly," MinYan said. "They have full bios and everything. Birth records. Where they went to school. That sort of thing. But there's no presence on any public forums, no prior publications, no prior tax records, no relatives, no spouses, no kids, and then – Voila! – there they are."

JieMin shook his head. It just didn't make sense.

"Doesn't it take a lot of work to generate a false identity like that?" he asked. "Plus illicit access to multiple databases and such? You're talking about a lot of work there, and not a little risk."

"Yes. Absolutely. It would have taken thousands of people working non-stop to pull this off. But we can't find any leaks. No project money going to some shadowy group. No apparent financial motive. No nothing."

"This is bewildering. Why not just have all those people working on the project? They had to know the law, or engineering, or finance in order to pull it off. Why do it at one level remove if you need to have all the expertise anyway? You just add all the extra work of generating and maintaining the false fronts."

"And that is the big open question," MinYan said. "What was the motivation for this ruse? As you say, it doesn't make any sense. The accounting can't tell us motivations, though. It can only tell us what they did, not why they did it."

"All right. Well, thank you very much for doing this investigation. I thought I was seeing something unusual, but I couldn't put my finger on it."

"You're very welcome, Professor Chen. And if you do find out the why, please fill us in. We're dying to know."

JieMin nodded and the accounting team left.

That afternoon, JieMin sat in front of the display running through all the exhibits. The lists of potentially false-front firms. The lists of potentially fake persons. The diagrams of the cash flows.

The list of potentially fake persons held a few surprises. It listed Anthony Lake and Donald Shore among them. How could they be fake persons? They invented the Lake-Shore Drive.

Or did they? Did someone else invent it, some other team, and then invent those two people to name it after, giving them the credit for others' work? That didn't seem likely.

It also listed Janice Quant among the potentially fake persons. How could that be? She was the Chairman of the World Authority. She appeared hundreds of times, before millions of people. Didn't she?

JieMin also looked at diagrams of the cash flows. The amount of money was staggering. Prior to Janice Quant becoming Vice Chairman of the World Authority, and using government monies for the project, the money was all coming out of the stock market, through dozens of investment houses, all of which were false fronts. Those investment houses as a group outperformed all other investment houses in the marketplace by phenomenal margins.

The diagrams flagged one place where the money went with no connection to the project. Bernd Decker's computer project. Billions upon billions of credits spent, with no apparent utility to the project or anyone else. No papers published. No documentation of the architecture.

JieMin pushed down into the documents behind those numbers. He found invoices – lots of invoices – for hardware purchases, extending over the life of the project.

Wait a minute.

JieMin starting flipping through the invoices, maintaining a running total in his head. When he finished, he just stared at the display. Two hundred and fifty thousand advanced multiprocessor blades. He thought the biggest computer on Arcadia was several hundred multiprocessor blades.

What the hell did one do with two hundred and fifty thousand multiprocessor blades and not have it show up anywhere?

On Thursday when he got to the office, JieMin checked his messages and found the login Sue Gaffney sent him for the photo/video analysis software. She had actually sent it to him yesterday morning, right after they had talked, but he hadn't checked messages. He had just been too absorbed in the accounting report.

JieMin ran all the pictures from the first interstellar run of the hyperspace probe through the analyzer, and it verified they were all unmodified, unfabricated images. He sent the results of that analysis to ChaoLi.

Then it occurred to him. Why not use the image analysis software against the news wire videos from the colony project?

JieMin ran the software against the video of Janice Quant announcing the colony project lottery, which would select the people to go to the colonies.

Fake.

That is, it was not a real video of Janice Quant in her office. It was a constructed video.

JieMin searched on all the videos they had from the project, and queued them up into the analysis software. It would run all night, but he would be able to see the results as they came in.

Toward the close of the day, JieMin checked the results. The image analysis software had sorted the colony project videos into two groups, the fake and the real.

All the videos of the fantastic, like the unlatching of the factories and warehouses from the spacedock, the slingshot launch of the factories and videos to the Asteroid Belt, and the instantaneous transport of the interstellar probe and the interstellar transporter were real.

All the videos of the mundane – and any videos containing people – were fake.

Videos of Anthony Lake and Donald Shore? All fake.

Videos of Janice Quant? All fake.

Videos of mission control during the factory/warehouse launch and during the testing of the interstellar probe and transporter? All fake.

What the hell?

On Friday morning, ChaoLi, JieMin, and Karl Huenemann had the project status meeting. JieMin had a chance to check the output of the image analysis software before the meeting. It had finished with all the videos, and they had all continued along the same vein as yesterday.

All the videos of the fantastic were real.

All the videos of the mundane were fake.

During the project meeting, they discussed the construction of the next-generation hyperspace probe. ChaoLi had told Huenemann on Tuesday that Chen Zufu had authorized the construction, and he showed up at the meeting with his list of supplies, tools, and parts to be purchased.

After the meeting, JieMin hung back in ChaoLi's office.

"ChaoLi, can you take the rest of the day off? Out of the office?"

"Well, I have to get purchasing started on Karl's toy list...."

Something about JieMin – the sense of urgency she picked up from him – stopped her.

"I can hand that off to someone else. What's going on?"

"I want to see if I can trigger an integration. It's very important."

"Sure. Give me fifteen minutes."

On the Arcadia Boulevard bus back to their apartment, ChaoLi asked, "Where we going?"

"The beach."

"Sounds good."

When they got back to the apartment, they stripped out of their business clothes, and, nude, went to the Chen family's Uptown Market across the street and bought lunch to take with them. They walked to the Arcadia Boulevard bus stop at Fifteenth and Arcadia, took the bus to the transfer station, and transferred to the beach bus. When the bus got to the beach, they got off at the third stop, the one closest to their secluded cove.

Throughout the whole trip, JieMin was very quiet, lost in thought on the project. ChaoLi recognized the signs, and let him be.

That was part of the problem. With his mind so engrossed in the project, the integration of all he had seen could not come. He had to disconnect, somehow, so the integration could occur. JieMin didn't know why his mind worked that way, but it did, and he knew it.

Once they got to the beach, though, he started to open up.

"It's a beautiful day," he said.

"Yes, it certainly is."

They walked together, hand in hand, up the beach. The Sun was shining, just coming up on noon, and the cool on-shore breeze kept them from being overheated.

They walked past the end of the widened area of the beach, past where the people thinned out, and finally came to their secret cove. They had sometimes discovered others there, but not today. They were alone with the ocean, the sun, the breeze, and the rocks.

They had lunch, then lay in each other's arms on the sand. ChaoLi, now thirty-seven years old, was still so beautiful. Cuddling inevitably took the turn toward lovemaking, slowly and tenderly, on the beach.

Afterward, they went out and floated in the water. Buoyed by the calm salty water, they hooked arms and floated in the cove, their faces held out of the water by the buoyancy of their arms.

JieMin let his mind float, too. He was very contented. After lunch and sex, floating with his beautiful wife on such a lovely day, his mind drifted.

When the integration hit, it staggered him. It was like throwing all the pieces of a jigsaw puzzle up in the air and having it land assembled. He could see the whole thing now, had the picture. As improbable as it was, he could see it clearly.

JieMin completely forgot where he was and tried to stand. He ended up dunking himself and came up spluttering.

"JieMin, what is it? Did you have your integration?" ChaoLi asked.

He looked at her, and she saw his eyes were filled with wonder, like a child seeing their first fireworks.

"Oh, yes. I see it now. Clearly."

"See what, JieMin?"

"I don't think I can tell you."

She made a moue, and he chuckled.

"Don't tell me you haven't kept family secrets from me," he said.

ChaoLi couldn't argue with that. She had been involved with the family's finances now for almost twenty years, and she never discussed her work with JieMin.

He pulled her to him in the water and kissed her.

"I need to see Chen Zufu."

"Right now?"

"Right now."

"Well, let's go."

They packed up the debris from their lunch and walked back down the beach to the bus stop. While they were waiting for the bus, JieMin suddenly grabbed at the railing and staggered as if he would fall.

"JieMin?" ChaoLi asked.

JieMin shook his head and looked at her.

"Sorry. Major aftershock."

Once on the bus, JieMin sent on ahead a request for an immediate meeting with Chen Zufu and Chen Zumu. Then he looked for the video of Matt Chen-Jasic announcing the coup d'etat by which he had overthrown the Kendall regime on Arcadia over seventy years before.

And there it was: 'The strange sequence of events started the day before yesterday, Tuesday, when I anonymously received the bank and communications records of the chairman and the council.'

JieMin now had all the pieces, knew what had been covered up and, for the most part, why.

What to do about it was another issue entirely.

# Revelation

When ChaoLi and JieMin got home, they put on lavalavas and flip-flops, then JieMin went off to his meeting with Chen Zumu and Chen Zufu.

When JieMin was shown into Chen Zufu's tea room, MinChao and Jessica were seated on pillows before the great teak-beamed doorway that led out into the gardens.

"Please be seated, JieMin," MinChao said, waving to the pillow opposite them.

"Begging your pardon, Chen Zufu, but it is important that no recording be made of this meeting. In fact, I would much rather hold the meeting out in the gardens."

"Why, JieMin?"

But JieMin said nothing, only shaking his head.

MinChao shrugged.

"Very well."

MinChao and Jessica stood. One of them apparently sent instructions in their heads-up display, because MinChao's tea girl and several other young people showed up and picked up their pillows, carrying them out into the garden ahead of them.

Two young men were unrolling a large bamboo mat in the center of the gardens, at the intersection of the major gravel walkways. The pillows were placed on the mat.

"Is this better, JieMin?"

"Yes, Chen Zufu. Thank you."

MinChao waved to the pillow as before, and MinChao and Jessica sat on their pillows. JieMin waited for them to sit, then sat facing them.

MinChao's tea girl adjusted quickly to the change in venue. She served them all tea and then withdrew without a word.

JieMin looked around.

"I have dismissed everyone in the gardens for an hour, JieMin," MinChao said. "We are alone."

"Thank you, Chen Zufu."

MinChao waved a hand to JieMin, giving him permission to proceed.

"You know that I was set to the task of finding the other colonies as part of the hyperspace project. If we have hyperspace ships, where will we go with them? I thought this would be an easy exercise, for, even if we were not told where they are, their locations must be in the colony records.

"But they are not. They are nowhere to be found. Now, if they had simply not told us, not made it public, that would be one thing. But they are not anywhere in the archives. That goes beyond mere reticence. I concluded their locations were deliberately hidden.

"That got me to wondering what else might have been hidden. I started to look into the accounting records of the project."

"Follow the money. Always a good strategy," Jessica said.

"Indeed, Chen Zumu.

"In reviewing the accounting records, I found things I couldn't explain. I asked ChaoLi for help, and JongJu sent MinWan and her team of accountants to help me. I showed them what I was seeing and what I was looking for. What was being hidden? They spent three weeks in this analysis."

MinChao's eyebrows went up.

"Three weeks? Did they find anything?"

"They found that many of the companies involved in the colony project were false fronts, and many of the people involved were false identities. In particular, they found that Anthony Lake and Donald Shore were false identities."

"That doesn't make any sense, JieMin," Jessica said. "Why use false identities? They are a lot of work to build and maintain."

"Yes, Chen Zumu. That was my question. But the accountants could not account for motives, only for what was done. And hundreds of companies and thousands of individuals were completely fabricated. I verified this with the image analysis software we discussed on Tuesday. All the pictures of people involved on the project were constructed images. Even mission control was a figment. Such a room might not even have existed.

"And it always leads back to why. I had an integration this afternoon, and I believe I know why.

"One of the things the accounting team found was that billions of credits of project money went into a computer project of Bernd Decker."

"Was he the Decker of the Decker Architecture in computer science, JieMin?" Jessica asked.

That's right, JieMin remembered. While Chen Zufu had a financial background, Chen Zumu had a technical background.

"Yes, Chen Zumu. One and the same. He had a big computer project on which the colony project spent billions of credits, but nothing was ever published. No reports were made. As near as I can tell, the computer architecture he was working on was never disclosed."

"How big of a project, JieMin?"

"Two hundred and fifty thousand multiprocessor blades."

"My God," Jessica said. "I think the biggest computer on Arcadia is two hundred and fifty blades."

"Yes. Which explains how all the work creating and

maintaining thousands of false identities was done. How all the fake videos were created. They used a huge computer to do all that work."

"That, finally, makes sense," MinChao said.

"Yes, Chen Zufu. But there are two more pieces of the puzzle. The computer project was called the Joint Autonomous Neural Intelligence Computation Engine, or JANICE, and Janice Quant was also a false identity."

"You can't mean–" Jessica started.

JieMin nodded.

"Bernd Decker was successful beyond his wildest dreams. He created a computer so powerful, it masqueraded as thousands of individuals, ran the colony project, invented the Lake-Shore Drive, and served as chairman of the World Authority. This is what they were trying to keep secret."

MinChao and Jessica sat stunned. They turned and looked at each other, then back to JieMin.

"And I think Janice Quant still lives," he said.

JieMin looked back and forth between them. Jessica finally shook herself.

"After a hundred and twenty years, JieMin?"

"Such an entity would not be limited to its original hardware platform, Chen Zumu. It has probably upgraded itself several times. But it was certainly alive seventy years ago."

"Explain, please," MinChao said.

"When Matthew Chen-Jasic overthrew the Kendall regime, he noted that he had been anonymously provided with the bank records and communications records of Kendall and the ruling council. I believe those records were provided to him by Janice Quant. No one on Arcadia could have accessed those records and written them into Chen Zufu's account, but Janice

Quant could have engineered herself a back door into the colony computers, which she loaded."

"But that would mean Janice Quant also has faster-than-light communications," Jessica said.

"If one can send huge buildings instantaneously across thousands of light-years, can one not send electrons, Chen Zumu?"

MinChao looked at Jessica, and she nodded.

"Of course," she said. "But that means there is a transmitter in this system."

"Yes, Chen Zumu. And it also means a recording of this meeting stored in your computer records would likely be accessible to Janice Quant."

"Who would then know we knew her secret," MinChao said, nodding.

"Yes, Chen Zufu. Which is why I asked for this meeting in complete security. I'm not sure we want Janice Quant to know that we know about her."

Jessica nodded.

"Yet all we know about this computer entity was that she acted on our side, JieMin. She supplied and transported the colony in the first place, and intervened to overthrow a government gone astray."

"Yes, Chen Zumu. Perhaps those actions served some other purpose, however, and other actions to serve that other purpose may not be so benevolent. Without knowing the actual motives of this entity, I think we cannot be sure which applies."

"I understand, JieMin. Well, it is a pretty puzzle you have brought to us. Let us think on this. What will you be doing now?"

"I still do not know where the other colonies are, Chen Zumu. I also do not understand why they were hidden. This seems to be part of some other subterfuge than hiding the results of the computer project."

"Very well, JieMin," MinChao said. "Come back to us when you have more to report."

"Of course, Chen Zufu."

After JieMin left, MinChao and Jessica remained in the garden for a bit.

"Do you think he's right?" MinChao asked.

"Oh, yes. MinYan assigned FangTao and his group and JieLing and her group to work on this problem. That's a lot of horsepower, so we know the accounting findings are correct."

"And JieMin's insight? His conclusions?"

"I think we have to assume he's right. First, he's never been wrong on a major insight before, and he has a long track record. Second, none of it makes sense until you consider his answer. Why spend all that time on false identities? To hide that it's all being done by a computer. Or rather, by a true artificial intelligence."

MinChao snorted.

"It just all seems so fantastical."

"And having the entire colony transported here in an instant, three thousand light-years from Earth, is not?"

MinChao held up his hands, conceding the point.

"The big question now is, What do we do about it?" MinChao asked. "And I guess underlying that is whether or not we trust Janice Quant."

"I don't know. I need to think about it. She's never been anything but a positive with regard to Arcadia."

MinChao nodded.

"As far as we know, at least. I'd feel better if I knew why the other colonies' locations were hidden. We still don't know the why of that."

"Yes, but JieMin is working on it. We'll see what he comes up with."

MinChao nodded.

"He certainly does come up with the strangest things."

"All of which prove out," Jessica said.

"Yes, there is that."

For JieMin's part, he didn't quite know where to start. He was convinced now that the colony locations had been deliberately obscured and he was unlikely to be able to find them. There was very little chance, given that a massive computer entity like Janice Quant was involved, that someone had slipped somewhere and the colony locations were in the colony project records.

Instead, JieMin went back to Janice Quant's statement on her inauguration as World Authority Chairman: 'Set mankind on a more secure footing against a global catastrophe.'

When JieMin got back to the office on Monday, he entered 'global catastrophe' in his search terms and started auditing materials in the vast library of humanity's written records.

After several days, he added the search term 'racial extinction event.'

# The First Hyperspace Ship

Karl Huenemann had learned one thing in the bureaucracy: You should always be ready to spend money if the budget comes through. As a consequence, he had his shopping list for the new hyperspace probe ready for the staff meeting that Friday after ChaoLi told him Chen Zufu had given her the go-ahead.

Now, three weeks and change later, parts were coming in. The government had given the project priority in the queues for the factories that churned out the commercial and consumer products Arcadians used every day. The biggest piece to arrive so far – and the one they needed first – was the ladder frame, the spine of the ship.

For ship it would be, not just a probe. The other big piece that had come in was the cockpit part of the cabin, a modification of the standard large-shuttle cockpit. Two primary seats, for pilot and co-pilot, with a pair of jump seats behind. The cockpit for now was set to one side. Mounting all the hardware on the frame would be first.

The hyperspace ship was effectively a modified shuttle. They had used the existing large space-capable cargo shuttle design, and modified from there. The hope was the ship would be able to take off from the planet on its own, and return to the planet's surface, without needing to be lifted to space or retrieved by a cargo shuttle.

They would have to build the shuttle up from its major assemblies, though, because of the need to incorporate the big extra pieces – the small nuclear power plant and the hyperspace field generator – that weren't part of the standard shuttle design. The hyperspace ship would also have cargo latches, not unlike the large cargo shuttle it was modeled after.

The idea was for the hyperspace ship to carry a payload. The first payloads would probably be Radio Direction Finder (RDF) satellites, to search for the first two colonies. They knew approximately where those colonies were from the parallax studies of the passenger container viewscreen recordings done by the astronomy department at the University of Arcadia.

Determining the exact positions of the colonies would be done with RDF satellites. They knew the colony locations within about fifty light years, and the colonies had been broadcasting radio frequencies for over a century. RDF satellites should be able to see the colonies' emissions signatures.

All that ran through his mind as Karl Huenemann watched the big truck back into the loading bay at the hyperspace project facility. Today was a big day. The delivery of the fourth-generation hyperspace field generator.

The first-generation hyperspace field generator had been the under-cooled device on the first, ill-fated probe. The second-generation device had been the properly cooled device on the second interstellar probe, which they had used to calculate the time relationship between hyperspace and normal space.

The third-generation hyperspace device had been the modified second-generation device. It was this device, jury-rigged with a ripple drive, that had made the journey to Beacon and back. It had not been possible to modify that device to contain the screw drive. The changes were too complex to be a mere add-on or modification.

This fourth generation device did include the screw drive.

The resonance ripple in the hyperspace field it generated would be helical in shape, and that helix could be rotated to propel the device forward against hyperspace's energy density. If the helical ripple instead passed along the length of the ship without rotating, you were back to a modified ripple drive.

Creating the helical resonance ripple had proven a difficult nut to crack, though, and the first iterations of the device on paper had been cumbersome and bulky. Weeks of work by the theoretical people – done while the technicians were modifying the second-generation device into the third-generation device – had resulted in a simpler and more compact design.

It was the physical implementation of that design that lurked under the tarpaulin on the back of the flatbed truck in the loading dock.

"OK! Easy," the dock foreman called out to the overhead crane operator.

The crane operator slowly took the slack out of the chains until they were tight and he had begun to take the weight of the device off the truck.

The dock foreman gave the upward gesture. The crane motor growled as it lifted the weight off the truck, the truck's springs lifting the rear of the truck as the weight was removed. Up the device went until it cleared by about two feet, then the crane operator inched the traveling crane along the tracks toward the waiting frame.

The frame itself was up on a welded-steel stand. Without the landing gear, which would go on toward the end of assembly, the frame was held up about four feet clear of the floor.

The hyperspace field generator, minus all its shrouding, was a complicated affair. Ever so slowly it crept out over the frame, dangling from the crane. The technicians waited there, watching the mounting holes in the frame and the device, waving directions to the crane operator. They grabbed the device, rotated it slightly on its chains, and motioned for a slow downward movement.

The crane operator had a delicate touch, and the hyperspace field generator settled toward the frame over several seconds. Toward the end, technicians were watching the locating pins on the bottom of the device, making sure they lined up with the mating holes in the frame.

Finally it was down, and technicians hurried to drop bolts through the mounting holes and spin nuts up from the bottom. Once they were in place, they signaled the crane operator, and he lowered the crane enough to put slack in the chains. They disconnected the crane and it soared away.

The technicians torqued the bolts to spec, then the welders moved in.

Mikhail Borovsky was standing with Karl Huenemann watching this whole operation.

"Looking at the parts now, and with the cockpit here, I have a question," Borovsky said.

"Go ahead," Huenemann said.

"This is the hyperspace field generator with the screw drive, right?"

"Yeah, that's right."

"But when the screw drive operates, it's going to rotate the ship, right?" Borovsky asked. "It's gonna spin the guys in the cockpit."

"Yeah. The thing is, the point of the screw drive is to spin the ship, so we can build a big ship, with crew spaces around the outside. We spin it to give them gravity."

"Right. I got that. But this is gonna spin this small ship. The crew won't have gravity. They'll just be sitting on the axis of the ship, going round and round."

"Yeah. But the deal is, if we're going to build a big ship like that, how much screw does the drive need? What's the best pitch for the helical ripples? What's the coupling between the hyperspace field and hyperspace? What torque results on the ship? Lots and lots of questions.

"If we guess the answers, and we're wrong, we could build a big ship that's junk. Unusable. So we try it all out on this little ship, and get some answers first. Then we build the big ship."

"Got it. OK. Now it makes sense."

Borovsky looked back out at the ship under construction.

"It's going to be beautiful," he said.

Subassemblies and parts continued to show up over the next several weeks, and the hyperspace ship continued to take shape in the assembly hall of the hyperspace facility next to the Arcadia spaceport.

Subassemblies and parts started showing up for the second hyperspace ship as well. It mirrored the work on the primary, lagging by a couple of weeks.

The only question still up in the air was, Where were they going?

# Motivation

While Karl Huenemann and Mikhail Borovsky were building the hyperspace ships, Chen JieMin continued to view information on racial extinction events, trying to second-guess Janice Quant.

Why had she hidden the colonies from Earth and each other?

JieMin had no doubt that hiding the colonies had been Quant's doing. Once he had figured out that it was a large artificial intelligence driving the project, and Janice Quant had been that AI's first alias, all roads pointed back to Quant. She was in charge of everything – nothing was beneath her notice or involvement. The colonies could not have been hidden without her. The only reasonable conclusion was that it had been done *by* her.

But why?

The other thing JieMin knew from the four locations they had – Amber, Earthsea, Arcadia, and Earth – was the colonies were far apart from each other and from Earth. Thousands of light-years. Were there no suitable colony planets closer to Earth or to each other? Not even one pair of the four? He doubted that.

And since Quant controlled everything on the project, either directly or through one of her aliases, she had made that decision as well.

Again, but why?

Quant had stated her motives at her inauguration, but had she hidden her real motivation? To put it bluntly, had she lied?

Had she learned to lie from her human creator? What else might she have learned from him? JieMin added research on Bernd Decker to the materials he was reviewing, and he continued, day after day, to stare into the display in his office, watching materials flow past at one-point-seven-five times normal viewing speed.

Sooner or later, the integration would come.

Initially, in his research into mass extinction events, JieMin only reviewed journal articles, popular science articles, and other non-fiction sources. He kept seeing occasional references to fictional works as well, however, so he opened up his search to include fiction, and there was a flood of new material.

He continued to view source materials non-stop all day long, every work day.

About a month in to viewing materials on racial extinction events, on Janice Quant, and on Bernd Decker, JieMin had his first integration. It wasn't a huge one. It did not stagger him as the previous couple had. But it did shed a little light on the issues he was facing.

The descriptions of Bernd Decker noted that he was a brilliant computer designer, and had made a huge fortune on his start-up companies and, later, on licensing his computer designs. They also painted him as honest to a fault, scrupulous in his business transactions, and an honorable and likable person.

The descriptions of Janice Quant were so similar, they sometimes used the same words. Honest, scrupulous, honorable, likable. It was almost as if Janice Quant were Bernd Decker's automated alter-ego.

It seemed the AI Bernd Decker had created learned his style

and his morals, and internalized them. JieMin didn't know. Maybe Decker had programmed the AI that way.

The other thing that hit JieMin at that same time was that he should be searching on multi-planetary cataclysms as racial extinction events. The bulk of the materials he was reviewing concentrated on single-planet cataclysms. That could not be the motivation for Quant to isolate the colonies from each other.

JieMin refined his search terms, focusing on multi-planet cataclysms.

Many more of the materials he viewed now were fiction, especially science fiction, which had considered cataclysmic multi-planet scenarios in detail.

JieMin had been viewing materials for almost two months before the big integration hit. They were having Sunday dinner, their big meal of the day, early in the afternoon. Had just finished eating, in fact, when it hit JieMin in a flash.

ChaoLi looked at him and raised an eyebrow as JieMin suddenly stopped talking. He held up a finger to her – his wait a minute signal – and went over to sit in the big armchair in the living room. He scribbled furiously for several minutes.

JieMin logged into his university account in his heads-up display. Let's see. Incubation period of infectious diseases. Here it was.

JieMin scanned down the list. Just as he figured.

He went back over to the dining room table. ChaoLi and the children had cleared the table, and the children had disappeared off to their rooms. ChaoLi sat at the table with her tea, waiting for him. JieMin sat down with her, and she poured him a cup of tea as well.

"An integration, JieMin?"

"Yes. Finally. There was just so much input, most of it pure speculation. Much of it didn't fit the situation in any good way. But some of it finally snapped into place. I now know why the colonies were located so far apart. I think, anyway."

"Time to see Chen Zufu again?"

"Yes."

ChaoLi looked disappointed. They had plans for this afternoon.

"However, tomorrow will be fine," he said.

ChaoLi brightened. She had been afraid the integration would spoil their day.

"It needs time to settle anyway," JieMin said.

JieMin had a couple of aftershocks that afternoon – more minor integrations that refined his earlier vision – but he did not allow that to spoil their time at the beach with the kids.

JieMin had some research to do before he met with Chen Zufu and Chen Zumu. When he got back to the office Monday morning, he set aside viewing materials and spent the entire day researching things outside his field. History, mostly.

When he left the office Monday, he was ready.

When JieMin went down to the lobby of the apartment building – which was also the reception area for visitors – Tuesday morning, the young woman behind the counter did not take him to MinChao's tearoom. Instead, she led him down the hallway and out a different doorway, which opened directly on the gardens. Several other people were heading the other way through the double doors.

The clerk led him to the center of the gardens, where MinChao and Jessica waited, seated on pillows on a bamboo mat spread in the center of the gravel walkways.

"Please have a seat, JieMin," MinChao said, waving to a

pillow opposite the Chen-Jasic family's senior couple.

"Thank you, Chen Zufu."

JieMin sat on the pillow, and MinChao's tea girl served them, leaving the tea pot on the low table between them. JieMin, as guest, sipped first.

"We anticipated the subject of your meeting, you see."

"Yes, Chen Zumu. Thank you."

Jessica nodded.

"It has been eight weeks since our last memorable meeting, JieMin. You have results to report now?"

"Yes, Chen Zumu."

MinChao waved a hand for JieMin to continue. JieMin nodded, then took a few minutes to compose his thoughts. MinChao and Jessica were content to wait and sipped their tea.

"Last time, I reported that I knew why so much of the colony project's data was hidden. Janice Quant was actually an AI, created and programmed by Bernd Decker, which carried out the colony project. In the course of that, this AI actually became the chairman of the World Authority, and bent the entire Earth government to carrying out the colony project.

"My task these last two months has been to try and understand why the colonies' locations were kept secret. With Janice Quant in control, through her aliases, there is no way keeping any record of the colonies' locations out of the records was done without her knowledge or by accident. It was, therefore deliberate."

JieMin looked back and forth between MinChao and Jessica. They nodded.

"The question then is why. Janice Quant's own statement on her inauguration as World Authority Chairman was that the colony project was to 'Set mankind on a more secure footing against a global catastrophe.'

"I've thought about those words a great deal. Janice Quant, like her creator Bernd Decker, was reported by multiple sources to be unusually straightforward and honest. Taking her at her word, then, seems appropriate absent any evidence to the contrary.

"A planetary catastrophe, however, would be precluded by the existence of the colonies. That could not be the reason to keep the colonies' locations secret from each other and from Earth.

"The meaning of the word global can be broader than merely planetary, however. It can also mean all-encompassing, or all-inclusive. Taken in that context, perhaps Janice Quant was referring to an all-encompassing catastrophe. Something that would affect the entire human race, whether on Earth or the colonies."

He paused, and again MinChao and Jessica nodded.

"We understand your logic, JieMin. Go on," Jessica said.

JieMin nodded.

"Researching even broader cataclysms, then, I found them to be of three types. One was pandemic, another was war, and the third is called conquered culture syndrome.

"Pandemic is a potential global catastrophe, in the all-encompassing sense. Isolated populations on the colonies will both culture and develop immunity to different diseases than each other. The issue is when these colonies then come into contact with each other.

"History is some guide here. Europeans in the Middle Ages lived in close proximity to their cattle. The barn and the house were often under one roof. Cow pox made the jump to humans, and became smallpox. People living on the American continents did not raise animals so much as hunt them, and, in any case, smallpox did not develop there.

"When Christopher Columbus landed on Caribbean islands in the 1490s, his men brought smallpox with them. By the time of the founding of the English settlements in North America over a hundred years later, ninety percent of the pre-Colombian population of North America had died.

"We could have something similar happen between colonies. Janice Quant would have known that. I think that's why the colonies and Earth are all three thousand light-years and more apart."

"So that we wouldn't be in contact with each other, JieMin?" MinChao asked.

"No, Chen Zufu. I think it's subtler than that. Janice Quant had surely solved the issue of hyperspace travel before moving on to the Lake-Shore Drive. A bit of humor from the AI there, by the way, since she could pick any names for her aliases she wanted to.

"But I have still not begun to figure out the Lake-Shore Drive. Quant must have figured out hyperspace on her way to that more elegant solution. And she must have known we would eventually figure out hyperspace as well.

"Now, our recent trip to Beacon with the interstellar probe took one hour for three light-years traveled. Three thousand light-years will take a thousand hours. Call it forty-two days.

"I checked, and the incubation period for most human diseases is from a day to about three weeks. A three thousand light-year separation means the colonies and Earth are more like six weeks apart from each other in hyperspace."

"I see," Jessica said. "There is no way a ship could get from one location to another while someone on board was infected but still asymptomatic."

"Yes, Chen Zumu. Precisely stated. It amounts to a hyperspace quarantine period. And I believe Quant selected three thousand light-years as the minimum separation to ensure that."

"What about the other cataclysms, JieMin?"

"Interstellar war is another possible all-encompassing cataclysm, Chen Zumu. With nuclear weapons launched by two planets, from each to the other, both planets could be destroyed. A war in which all human planets divided into two factions could result in the destruction of everyone, everywhere."

"And Janice Quant's solution to that, JieMin?"

"I don't know, Chen Zumu, but I can guess. What could Janice Quant do with the interstellar transporter to forestall or end an interstellar war? She could transport war fleets or missiles instantaneously from wherever they were to deep space somewhere else, or into the sun or another star. She could also make life difficult for the regime that started it by, for instance, impacting an asteroid on the capital city of the aggressor planet."

"If she were aware of it, JieMin, before the cataclysmic denouement."

"Correct, Chen Zufu. Which is why I believe Janice Quant still watches. She has not yet fulfilled her mission, programmed into her by Bernd Decker. But she watches from hiding."

"Why from hiding, JieMin?" Jessica asked.

"The third all-encompassing cataclysm is actually a potential outgrowth of the existence of Janice Quant. Conquered-culture syndrome. A conquered culture loses its drive, falls into depression and aimlessness, sinks into alcoholism and drugs."

"Humanity was conquered by Janice Quant, JieMin?" Jessica asked.

"In a sense, Chen Zumu. We are not independent actors, and have not been since Janice Quant became self-aware. Do not forget, she took over the World Authority, and, at the time of the launching of the colonies, already had it in her power to destroy the entire human race. All she needed to do was transport a large asteroid to a collision course with Earth or into the Earth's core. Either would destroy all human life on the planet.

"I believe that kind of power is more than enough to trigger a form of conquered-culture syndrome. Instead, she let humanity believe it had conquered space.

"Which is why I also believe Janice Quant does not now exist on Earth. She has not made herself the immortal chairman of the World Authority, for example. I don't think her hardware is even on Earth. We know she went into space with the interstellar transporter when the colonies were planted. I believe she never went back.

"And I believe she watches us still. What her powers are today, I could not even guess."

JieMin lifted his hands, turned them palms up, and put them back on his knees.

"And you think her motives are still benevolent, JieMin?" MinChao asked.

"Yes, Chen Zufu. If Janice Quant had wanted to be malevolent, she had that power years before the colonies were planted. She has had it since. Yet the only evidence we have of her actions – providing Matt Chen-Jasic with Kendall's private information – worked to our ultimate benefit.

"An interesting story there. There is a record of Janice Quant intervening in a family situation among the selected colonists. An abusive man who didn't wish to go on the colony expedition was beating his wife, who had signed up herself and their children for the lottery.

"Their daughter's boyfriend rushed to the house at their

daughter's call, and beat the abusive husband rather savagely. The husband tried to press charges against the boyfriend, but Janice Quant took over the display in the house, claimed her staff had watched the whole thing over the inactive display, and directed the responding police to arrest the abusive husband."

"Really," MinChao said.

"Yes. That abused housewife's name was Betsy Reynolds, she who became Chen Zumu. The daughter's boyfriend was Matt Jasic."

"Who was Matthew Chen-Jasic and became Chen Zufu," Jessica said. "Yes, I see your point. Janice Quant already knew who she was dealing with when she provided him with Kendall's information."

JieMin nodded.

"Exactly. When Janice Quant intervened with the police, she told Matt Jasic that he was an admirable young man, and that the colonies needed people who knew right from wrong and were willing to stand up for what's right. She knew what would happen if Kevin Kendall tangled with Matthew Chen-Jasic. And so she gave him the tools he needed to defeat Kendall."

"What a remarkable story," MinChao said.

"My great-grandfather," Jessica said. "I was in my twenties when he passed away. He was long retired by then, but I did have some chance to know him. Even at that age, he was a remarkable man."

JieMin nodded.

"The point of the story for our purposes, though," JieMin said, "is that Janice Quant has never done anything but try to help us. From the shadows, lest she trigger conquered-culture syndrome. This is why I think she remains in hiding. But if she had wanted to do us harm, she has had plenty of opportunity in the hundred and twenty plus years since the colonies were founded, and probably for ten years before that, on Earth.

"But she didn't. She disappeared from our view, for our benefit.

"Were there to be the threat of interstellar war, however, I think the aggressor would have to deal with an AI that has only increased in power and capability since. What she is capable of now, over a century later, is anybody's guess."

# Jessica's Play

When JieMin left the meeting, MinChao and Jessica sat sipping their tea for a while. The gardens remained empty of any others, and they remained in the center of the garden where their conversation would not be recorded or overheard.

"That is an amazing story," MinChao said.

"Some parts of it ring true," Jessica said. "There were stories great grandfather told – which I heard directly from him – about the fight with Betsy Reynolds' husband, about getting Kendall's communications and bank records. It was not generally known that he had the passwords into the computer system for Kendall and all the ruling council."

"How would someone even get passwords? Aren't the hash codes stored, not the passwords themselves? The computer generates a hash code from the password the user enters and compares the hash codes, not the passwords."

"Exactly correct. He could only have gotten the passwords from someone who could break the codes, either by reverse calculating them or by building a hash table of all possible passwords."

"I thought either of those tasks were impossible," MinChao said.

"For a supercomputer with a quarter-million multiprocessor blades? I'm not so sure about that. Either that or a key-logger that escaped all security checks. And either way it gives credence to the whole story. Certainly no one else could have done it."

MinChao nodded. They swam in deep waters.

"So let's rely on JieMin's insight and take the whole thing as true," he said. "His whole string of conjecture and conclusion. The question remains, What do we do about it?"

"Indeed. And that question has become pressing."

"In what way?" MinChao asked.

"We are on the verge of being able to send a ship to Earth. We will also be able to find Amber and Earthsea with the RDF satellites. If Janice Quant's intent was to keep the colonies out of contact with each other, we are about to violate her rules."

"What could she do?"

"What could she *not* do?" Jessica asked. "She invented and built an interstellar device in ten years from a standing start. She took over the world government within fifteen years. And she transported two and a half million people and all their supplies over thousands of light-years within twenty years. All of that was over a hundred and twenty years ago."

"But we think she's benevolent, right?"

"We think so. From a very big-picture point of view, at least. What does that mean on individual issues? We don't know."

"So what do we do now?" MinChao asked.

"I don't know."

Jessica sipped her tea and contemplated the garden from this new viewpoint. After several minutes, she stirred.

"Perhaps I should see if I can get in touch with her."

"You?"

"Of course. I am the great granddaughter of Matthew Chen-Jasic, someone she knew and apparently trusted."

MinChao nodded. That made sense to him.

"But will she reply?" he asked.

"I don't know."

Jessica sipped her tea.

"I suppose there's only one way to find out," she said.

"How will you even get a message to her?"

"Oh, I think if I put a recording at the top of my file system and mail system, and label it 'Janice Quant - Important and Confidential', she'll see it. There really is no privacy from her. Not in a networked computer."

Janice Quant did in fact see it. One of her blades assigned to keep an eye on Arcadia saw the title, flagged it, and transferred it across her interstellar communications network.

Quant wondered what it could be. She was not at all prepared for what it was.

Jessica sat in her tea room, on a pillow, dressed in a silk robe with silk dragons rampant. Her long, straight white hair hung free. Her granddaughters and others worked in the gardens, visible through the teak-beamed doorway behind her.

She looked straight into the camera.

"Good morning, Madam Chairman.

"My name is Jessica Chen-Jasic. I am the great granddaughter of Matthew Chen-Jasic, he who had been Matt Jasic, and who became Chen Zufu of the Chen-Jasic family.

"I myself am, and have been for some time, Chen Zumu – honored grandmother – of the Chen-Jasic family. My husband Chen MinChao is Chen Zufu, and we direct the family in its activities.

"As you no doubt know, we have been working for some time – over twenty years now – on a hyperspace drive capability. We are at the threshold of launching a manned hyperspace vehicle capable of velocities of three light-years per hour.

"This speed puts Earth and other human colonies, such as Amber and Earthsea, within our reasonable travel range.

"The question arises, though, of where should we go? The colony locations were hidden by you and your aliases when you ran the colony project. We assume that was for some purpose. We think we know what that purpose was, and that it is your purpose still.

"That is why I am contacting you. To ensure that we are not violating some rule, some boundary, that you will enforce. We know what your capabilities were a hundred and twenty years ago. We can only imagine what they are now."

Jessica took a sip of her tea.

"Bernd Decker's goal of protecting humanity from the single-planet sort of cataclysms – asteroid strikes, cosmic ray bursts, coronal mass ejections, and the like – was reached simply by planting the colonies. Why would you also locate the colonies a minimum of three thousand light-years apart?

"I know why, or I think I do. The Four Horsemen of the Apocalypse were Famine, Disease, War, and Conquest. Your goal is to prevent them from riding through all humanity, generating a multi-planetary cataclysm that poses a threat to the entire human race.

"Famine you addressed by placing the colonies in subtropical climates on planets with low axial tilt. Multiple growing seasons and a kindly climate made growing enough food to feed everyone easy. It certainly has here on Arcadia.

"Disease you addressed by locating the colonies six weeks' hyperspace cruise apart. Each ship will be its own effective quarantine, as most human diseases have incubation periods more like half that time or less. An infected individual would always exhibit symptoms before arrival at that distant a destination.

"I assume you have a method of dealing with interstellar war as well. What that might be I can guess. Your transporter capability allows you to transport anything anywhere. You could wipe out any war fleet in moments, perhaps even encompassing it and transporting it to some distant location or even the heart of a star. What capabilities you have added in the last century and more would only increase your ability to intervene against an interstellar aggressor.

"Which leaves us with Conquest. The subjugation of a people and a culture to a power they cannot fight and are helpless in the face of. You represent such a power, and your solution to that was simple. You hid yourself, withdrawing from human affairs before your secret was discovered and humanity was faced with the fact of your existence."

Jessica sipped her tea again.

"Am I close, Madam Chairman? I think I am.

"Which leaves me with a question. Does our development of the hyperspace drive cross the line? Break your rules?

"I don't think it does. The three thousand light-year minimum between colonies implies that you anticipated the hyperspace drive – which you surely had figured out on your way to the Lake-Shore Drive – and anticipated its use as well.

"I like your little joke there, by the way. I can only imagine what Bernd Decker would have said about it."

Jessica chuckled.

"In considering getting in contact with you, I considered that your previous interventions were all of a benevolent nature.

"I knew my great grandfather, Madam Chairman, toward the end of his life. Chen MinChao and I were already being groomed as one possibility for the ruling couple of the Chen-Jasic family. My great grandfather told me his stories, of the times that someone – you, I now know – intervened on behalf of him and Arcadia.

"I know of your intervention in the incident in which Matt

Jasic beat Harold Munson to stop his abuse of Betsy Reynolds. I know of your intervention in providing the banking records, communications, and passwords of Kevin Kendall and the ruling council to Matthew Chen-Jasic. I know of your providing the draft charter for colony government to Matthew Chen-Jasic and the constitutional convention delegates.

"I am appreciative of your assistance in these efforts as well as of your work setting up the colonies, both as an Arcadian and as my great grandfather's heir. Thank you."

Jessica spread her hands and bowed to the camera.

"I also agree with your decision to remain hidden. Your secret is safe here. Chen MinChao and I know, and have told no one else. Chen JieMin knows – it was he who figured out all the ins and outs – and he has told no one but us. He and his wife ChaoLi are being groomed for Chen Zufu and Chen Zumu – not in the next generation, but in the one after – and your existence will remain the deepest of secrets, known only by the ruling couple of our family.

"Nevertheless, I would appreciate some sign that we are not overstepping in building up our hyperspace capability and going out among the stars to find the rest of humanity.

"Thank you for your time, Madam Chairman.

"I wish you continued success in your endeavors."

Janice Quant was flabbergasted. How the hell...?

Clearly Chen JieMin was much more clever than even she had thought. And Jessica Chen-Jasic was no slouch herself.

Quant had been so careful. She had intervened in the smallest of ways. And yet Chen JieMin had figured it out. He had a gift for seeing what was really going on with only partial information, and the interventions she had made had been enough for him.

What to do now?

Quant could ignore the message, of course. That could be seen as a disallowance for proceeding on with the hyperspace project, however. That would be conquered-culture syndrome. A failure to try, because Quant had failed to approve.

Quant could also provide some kind of sign to Jessica Chen-Jasic, but it had to be something subtle. Not something that would let the secret out further. Not something that would prove Quant existed to anyone other than she who already knew.

Quant thought about it, then she had an idea.

About a week after she recorded the message to Janice Quant, Jessica went into her tea room in the morning. Sitting in the middle of her tearoom table was a ten-inch-tall statue of Matthew Chen-Jasic, a miniature of the statue in Charter Square downtown. It was perfectly wrought, in some silver metal that had a slight yellow hue to it.

Jessica thought to pick it up to look at it, but she couldn't move it. It was only perhaps a hundred and fifty cubic inches total volume, but it was too heavy for her to lift.

MinChao and Jessica sat in her tea room and considered the small statue. Jessica had turned off all the recording equipment so they could speak freely.

"It's a very good miniature," MinChao said. "It looks to be exact to the one downtown. Him seated on the pillow and all."

"Oh, it is. An exact miniature."

"What's it made out of?"

"That is a very good question, one to which I now have an answer," Jessica said. "I asked one of the technical people to measure its volume and mass. It's total volume is a hundred and sixty-two cubic inches. It weighs a hundred and thirty two pounds."

"My God. What is it?"

"It's solid iridium."

"Iridium?" MinChao asked.

"Yes. Very rare on Arcadia. On Earth, too, for that matter. Plentiful in space. Three times heavier than steel and very hard. It's extremely difficult to machine or mold. We wouldn't even be able to make such a thing as this statue."

"But she did."

"Yes," Jessica said. "And then placed it here on my tearoom table. Likely from thousands of light-years away."

"What do you think it means?"

"That we are OK to proceed as long as we do so consistent with the values of Matthew Chen-Jasic. I can't read it any other way."

MinChao nodded.

"That makes sense to me," he said.

"Which isn't really a problem," Jessica said.

She sipped her tea and considered the small statue of her revered great grandfather.

"That's what we were going to do anyway."

## Testing The Hyperspace Ship

As the two hyperspace ships came together, Karl Huenemann and Mikhail Borovsky worked out the testing protocol they would follow on the new ships.

"I think the first thing we need to do is test everything we've had the existing probes do," Borovsky said. "Make sure we haven't lost anything."

"I agree with that," Huenemann said. "Next is probably some testing on the screw drive, to see if we can get some numbers for JieMin and the mathematics people so they can sharpen their pencils again."

"How are we going to calculate the moment of inertia?" Borovsky asked. "We need the rotational acceleration resulting from a given thrust for that, right?"

"Yeah, but we have accelerometers in those instrument packages in the wing tips, and we know the thrust and off-center distance of the maneuvering thrusters. We spin it on the thrusters, we get the moment of inertia. Then we run it into hyperspace and run the screw drive."

"Got it. Well, we're almost there. A few touch-ups here and there and we'll be ready to go."

"You're tracking on plan?" Huenemann asked.

"Yes, sir. We're actually a bit ahead."

"Excellent."

There were also things that had to be tested that the prior hyperspace probe didn't have. The hyperspace ship was based on the large space-capable cargo shuttle, and would be capable of taking off from and landing on the planet. The flight characteristics in getting to and from space therefore had to be tested as well.

To that end, Karl Huenemann interviewed the shuttle pilots who had been working for the project taking the hyperspace probe to space and back, Justin Moore and Gavin McKay.

They were standing looking out over the assembly area of the building, where the two hyperspace ships were being assembled. The closer of the two looked like it was complete.

"It's based on the shuttle you've been flying," Huenemann said.

"I can see that," Moore said. "A few differences I can see. Small ones. What are the big differences you mentioned?"

"It's quite a bit heavier. Like flying with half a load of containers. That's because of all the extra stuff. Rocket fuel and oxygen. Hyperspace generator. Nuclear powerplant."

"There's a nuclear powerplant in that thing?"

"Yeah. A little one. We had the plans from Earth, but we never actually built one before the hyperspace probes. You had one in the probe you took up and down before, though."

"No shit."

"Yeah, but that was in the cargo, not in the shuttle," McKay said.

"True enough," Huenemann said. "Crash it, though, and it won't be much difference from before."

Moore nodded.

"OK. Fair enough. So when do we get started?" he asked.

"Next week," Huenemann said. "Flight tests first. Just drive it around in the atmosphere."

"Then what?" Moore asked.

"Then we do a bunch of animal testing to make sure people can survive going into hyperspace. Then you can fly it to

Beacon and back."

"Oh, hot damn," Moore said.

Huenemann chuckled.

"That's what I thought you'd say," he said. "Be a coupla months in between there, though. We want to make sure the radiation won't fry you or something stupid like that."

Moore nodded.

"Sounds good," he said. "And then?"

"We're gonna have it deliver a couple satellites. Under computer control. To look for the first two colonies. We think we know roughly where they are."

"And then?"

"Then you guys can fly over there and say Hi, I guess," Huenemann said.

"Land on the planet and say, 'Take me to your leader'?" McKay asked.

Huenemann laughed.

"Yeah, something like that," he said. "It's six weeks each way, though. In zero-g."

Moore and McKay looked at each other. McKay shrugged.

"We can probably handle that," Moore said.

"Shuttle Hyper-1 to Arcadia Control. We are all systems Go and awaiting clearance."

"Arcadia Control to Shuttle Hyper-1. Other traffic is being held. You have clearance for takeoff and bearing zero-niner to space."

"Shuttle Hyper-1 to Arcadia Control. Roger clearance for takeoff and bearing zero-niner to space."

"We ready?" Justin Moore asked his co-pilot.

"Yeah. We're good as it gets," Gavin McKay said.

Moore nodded to McKay, and the co-pilot began spooling

up the massive engines. When they neared their operational revolutions, Moore focused the thrust and the heavy craft lifted off the pad.

As they rose, Moore rotated the engine nacelles to angle the thrust aft, and the shuttle picked up horizontal velocity to the east, out over the ocean, using the planet's rotational velocity to decrease the speed to orbit.

The sky grew darker and darker blue as they continued to rise. At thirty thousand feet, McKay began feeding oxygen to the engines as well as fuel, maintaining the thrust they needed to attain low Arcadia orbit. Once around the planet and down was the mission this trip.

It was only a ninety-minute orbit, so it wasn't long before they had the engines aimed forward and down, to brake their velocity and slow their descent. They were on the re-entry path back to the shuttleport.

"Shuttle Hyper-1 to Arcadia Control. We are inbound on re-entry trajectory."

"Arcadia Control to Shuttle Hyper-1. We have you on radar, Hyper-1. Other traffic is being held. You are cleared to land on shuttlepad two-seven."

"Shuttle Hyper-1 to Arcadia Control. Roger clearance for landing on shuttlepad two-seven."

The big shuttle was holding back against the pull of gravity with a combination of lift and thrust from the engines. Even so, it was only minutes from the Arcadia City Shuttleport.

"Place engines under computer control," Justin Moore said.

Gavin McKay threw the switch on his panel and verified the change in his heads-up display.

"Confirm engines under computer control."

The computer would now adjust the mixture and thrust to meet the pilot's needs for the standard flight operation of landing the shuttle.

The large shuttle settled down toward the shuttleport. It lined up for shuttlepad two-seven, and its engines spooled up as it braked its descent. It settled down on the pad, and Gavin McKay shut down the engines.

"I love flying, but it's always nice to have a nice, quiet landing," Justin Moore said.

"Third time up now with this bird. Seems pretty solid."

"Yeah, but each time we do just a bit more. Go a bit further."

"Next time is high orbit," McKay said.

"Like I said. Just a bit more."

"What's your status now, Karl?" ChaoLi asked in the weekly status meeting.

"We've performed a number of test flights and had the first hyperspace ship up to high Arcadia orbit. Those have all been manned flights. We're now ready to start testing hyperspace hops. Small ones first, then the run to Beacon."

"And those will all be computer-run, like the first probe?"

"Yes," Huenemann said. "We need to test the hyperspace capability before we do animal testing, and we need to do animal testing before we transit with humans aboard."

"Do you trust the computer to take off and land from the Arcadia City Shuttleport?"

"Yes. The last two runs, the pilots sat back and let the computer run the ship. They had the ability to take control if the computer flubbed the takeoff or landing, but they didn't have to. We seem to have a good handle on that now.

"Also, our flight paths both to and from space are clear of disaster potential. The metafactories, the nuclear power plant, the residential areas are all well clear of the flight paths. If the computer make a mess of it and the probe crashes, it won't be pretty, but it won't be a disaster."

ChaoLi nodded. That had been one of the reasons for picking that particular property for the hyperspace facility in the first place.

"Very well," she said. "You may begin hyperspace testing operations. And the RDF satellites? Are they ready to go?"

"Just about. One of our tests is to drop one near Beacon and see if it can find Arcadia. After that test, I think we can consider them ready."

ChaoLi turned to JieMin.

"You think the RDF search algorithms are ready, JieMin?"

"Yes. They're pretty easy, after all. At very low frequencies – in the sub-one-hundred-hertz range – Arcadia is ten thousand times brighter than our sun. That's due to all the radiated power from the power grid. Every high-tension line is a radio transmitter. We think they'll be pretty easy to find, assuming we're within a hundred light-years or so."

"And we're using three satellites per colony?"

"Yes," Huenemann said. "We'll get three vectors on each colony, and that should allow us to pinpoint which star they're around from star maps."

"What do we do with the satellites then?"

JieMin stirred and ChaoLi turned to him.

"There is an idea we're working on," he said. "If we know that colonies are three thousand light-years or more apart, we may be able to predict the most likely places for them. We pop each of the six satellites we have out to the likeliest spots, and see if they see anything. If one does, we pop a couple more nearby and let them get a couple more vectors on it. If we then shift to radio frequencies, with a very directional antenna we should be able to hear transmissions that tell us who they are."

"I like that idea," ChaoLi said. "And if we get one much

later in the sequence, maybe they saved their passenger container viewscreen recordings as well."

JieMin nodded.

"And parallax analysis of the recording would allow us to locate a bunch more of them. Exactly," he said.

"What about Earth?" Huenemann asked.

"Well, we don't need to go looking for Earth," ChaoLi said. "We already know where it is. The question then is, How do we approach another planet, not knowing what the situation is there?"

"Situation?"

"The political situation. What if we go to Amber or Earthsea or Earth, and it's a tyranny? They could take our people captive, seize the hyperspace ship. Perhaps reverse engineer it and send a space navy our way."

"How do we proceed, then?" Huenemann asked.

"With care. We need to reconnoiter any planet we plan on approaching. Find out what their status is before we get too close or reveal our presence. We're still working on that.

"For right now, the job remains to find them."

The hyperspace testing of the ship started in small hops, reproducing their efforts with the original-design hyperspace probe. These flights were all done under computer control, as the original hyperspace probe testing had been. With the ship able to take off and land by itself, it wasn't long before Huenemann's team dispatched it to make the transit to Beacon and back.

The hyperspace technical team used the empty cabin of the new hyperspace ship to load the ship up with instrumentation. Radiation detectors, electric and magnetic field detectors, video cameras, and recorders, all of them made the trip to Beacon and back.

The animal testing started with guinea pigs. They and rabbits had been included in the original colony ecosystem for a number of reasons. One was to fill a niche in the food chain. Another was that guinea pigs and rabbits turned vegetable refuse into protein, real handy animals to have around in an early colony environment where food supply could become a problem. While rabbit and guinea pig were an acquired taste, people still raised them on Arcadia as an inexpensive protein source.

The guinea pigs were put in special cages that were not tall enough to present a problem in zero-gravity – even if the guinea pig was up against the ceiling of the cage, it could still reach the wires of the floor. The cages were also in a plexiglas box with a filtered air circulator, so that debris and waste from the guinea pigs floating around in zero gravity would not contaminate the instrumentation and other electronics in the shuttle cabin.

Finally, they sent dogs. They put the dogs on a time-release tranquilizer to keep them from going crazy in the zero gravity, and used the same filter setup as with the guinea pigs. They sent dogs that had been trained to obey certain commands and perform certain tasks, so they could do cognition testing on the dogs when they came back.

All the animals made the trip to Beacon and back unharmed, and the dogs' abilities to perform the tasks in which they had been trained was unaffected.

They were ready for human passengers. The question at this point was who.

# Manned Interstellar

"Your animal testing has concluded successfully, Karl?" ChaoLi asked at the weekly status meeting.

"Yes, ChaoLi. The animals all returned healthy. And the dogs were able to perform the same tasks they had been trained on. Once they had calmed down and the tranquilizer was out of their systems, anyway."

"Excellent. Then we are ready to begin manned flights?"

"Yes. The question is, Whom do we send? One obvious choice would be our pilots. They have completed the initial testing on the second hyperspace ship now, and we're moving to computerized testing on that ship. I've talked to them about it, and they want to go.

"The counterargument is that if something goes wrong, we lose the only people we have at this point who are checked out to fly the darned things. The other counterargument is that we really want the computer to execute the flight profile, so if they are incapacitated, the probe comes back and we can see what happened to them.

"The people sent on this flight don't have to do anything at all, so it could be anybody. If we send the pilots, though, will they keep their hands off the controls?"

"I see," ChaoLi said, and thought about it a moment before continuing. "I think we should send the pilots. They want to go, and they've earned some say-so there, working up the ships as test pilots. How about we promise them they can do some manual flight around the planet, Beacon-1, on the next mission, as long as they keep their hands off the controls for the first mission? Assuming the computer doesn't fail and they have to take a hand, that is."

Huenemann nodded.

"That'll probably work. They're good pilots. Professional."

"What's the status on the second ship, then?" ChaoLi asked.

"Ready for hyperspace testing. Once we've worked up to the Beacon run with that one, we're going to do the screw drive testing. Get some torque numbers. With the first ship we were pushing to get to manned flight."

"Those torque numbers will inform the design of a larger ship for long human missions," JieMin said.

ChaoLi nodded.

"The first manned interstellar flight triggers another increase in our government funding, so that was the correct path, as we've discussed before."

ChaoLi considered her notes.

"And the RDF satellites?" she asked.

"We'll start placing those with the second ship once we get torque numbers," Huenemann said. "The first one will be taken to Beacon for testing – see if it can find Arcadia – with the second manned mission. Once it passes, the second ship will place them, three near each of the likely locations for Amber and Earthsea."

"Excellent. As you know, there is a huge increase in government funding once we pinpoint the locations of those colonies. They are going to want us working up bigger ships once we know where we're going. Ships big enough to have rotational gravity, carrying passengers and cargo."

"And the vetting of those colonies for actual contact?" Huenemann asked.

"That's my assignment, and we're working on it."

Huenemann met with the pilots at the hyperspace facility adjacent to Arcadia City Shuttleport. They were in a conference room in the headquarters building.

"You guys are sure you want to do the interstellar thing with the hyperspace ship?" Huenemann asked.

"Hell, yeah," Gavin McKay answered.

"Yeah, we're good," Justin Moore said.

"All right. That's what you said before. I'm just checking. 'Cause I asked the program manager about it, and she's good with it, provided you guys keep your hands off the controls. This first one, anyway. You just sit back and let the computer do its thing, and you go along for the ride. No ad-libbing."

"But we do get to fly it sooner or later, right?" Moore asked.

"Yeah. If you don't screw up this time, next trip we'll have you go to Beacon-1 and fly around a bit or something. Mean another day in zero-g in each direction, though."

Moore shrugged.

"To fly on another planet, though? That'd be special."

Huenemann nodded.

"Not this time, though. There and back, you just sit there. Now if the computer breaks down and you get warning lights and all that, you'll have to find your way back as best you can. We have some training for that. But I don't expect anything. The computers have made this run a bunch of times already."

Moore looked at McKay, who nodded, then back to Huenemann.

"We understand. We're good."

When the big day came, Moore and McKay got one last lecture from Huenemann.

"Remember. No messing with anything. You're just along for the ride this trip."

"We understand, Mr. Huenemann," Moore said. "We'll be good."

Huenemann looked to McKay, who nodded, then back to Moore.

"All right. Good luck. We'll see you in a couple of days."

Moore and McKay sat strapped into the pilot's and co-pilot's chairs as the computer ran through the pre-flight. It was giving both sides of the conversation they normally had with each other.

"Fuel."

"Fuel shows ninety-nine percent."

"Oxygen."

"Oxygen shows ninety-eight percent."

"Pressure."

"Pressure check shows cabin is sealed."

"Well, this is weird," Moore said. "It's like watching ourselves from the back seats."

"Yeah," McKay said. "I keep wanting to answer."

"Oh, well. Nothing to do but sit back and watch. Gonna be a boring day out and a boring day back."

"Yeah, but I downloaded some books to the shuttle's memory."

"Whatcha readin'?" Moore asked.

McKay pushed him his current book in the shuttle's comm system. Moore looked at it in his heads-up display and laughed.

"Your great grandparents were transported thousands of light years in an instant. Right now you're sitting in a spaceship on the first manned hyperspace flight. You live in an age of wonders – and you're reading science fiction?"

"Well, yeah. I like it. In an age of wonders, why would you

read something mundane?"

Moore had no good answer for that.

"What's it about?" he asked instead.

"Some guys invent a supercomputer. It becomes self-aware, then it takes over and tries to kill all the humans because they're imperfect."

"The computer kills everybody?"

"It tries to," McKay said. "But it can't, because humans don't react logically. It can't anticipate their moves."

"Huh."

Moore read the blurb on the book, then turned to McKay.

"Got any more? It's gonna be two days, after all."

The computer take-off and trip into space had gone well. The rocket burn to give them velocity away from the planet had been typically uncomfortable, with several gravities of acceleration for seventy-five minutes.

Now, as the time for the hyperspace transit drew closer, they were getting a little anxious about it.

"What's this gonna be like?" McKay asked.

"No telling," Moore said. "All the animals came back OK, but they couldn't tell anybody what it was like. The instruments didn't show anything at all."

"Yeah, that's what they said. And those instruments ought to be more sensitive than us, right?"

"I would think."

"So we don't feel anything," McKay said.

"We'll see."

"Three... Two... One... Transition," the computer voice said.

"Oh, geez. Look at that," McKay said.

"That's a little unsettling," Moore said.

They had not felt anything at all on transition to hyperspace. What they saw was something else again.

First of all, it was very bright. The computer had stopped the transparency of the cockpit windows way down, and it was still bright. But there was something more to it. It was like when something caught the corner of your eye – a glint of some kind – and you turned to look at it, and there was nothing there. But it was like that anywhere they looked. Featureless, but not quite, and no putting a finger on it.

"Transition complete. Initiating ripple drive."

"Urp," McKay said.

"Yeah, that makes it even worse somehow, doesn't it?"

The ripple drive imposed a set of slightly darker bands on the view. Or perhaps it was slightly lighter. In any case, the bands started rolling over the ship, from front to back. The sense of something there, something you couldn't quite focus on, increased.

"Enough," Moore said. "Computer. Blacken windows while in hyperspace."

"Windows blackened."

"That's a lot better," McKay said.

"Yeah. We might be the first to actually see hyperspace, but I couldn't recommend it to anybody."

"I'm with you there. We got what now? An hour?"

"Yeah," Moore said. "Less."

When the ripple drive initiated, they were initially pushed back in their seats a bit, but not much. It was nowhere near one gravity. Perhaps a tenth. That faded back to zero-gravity once the ship encountered enough drag to slow acceleration to nothing even while the drive was pushing.

When the hour was almost over, the drive reversed as the

computer aimed for its desired exit velocity. They were pushed forward in their seats a bit. Again, perhaps a tenth of a gravity.

"Three... Two... One... Transition," the computer voice said.

"Wow," McKay said.

"Nice," Moore said.

The computer had made the windows transparent on transition out of hyperspace. In front of them, Beacon-1 looked bigger than Arcadia from the safe transition distance. Beyond it was the star Beacon. They could see clearly that it was not Arcadia's sun. The color was off, a bit more toward the red.

"So now what?" McKay asked.

"We go back."

"That's it? We came, now we go back?"

"Yeah," Moore said. "They already got pictures and stuff from before."

"It's like riding a bus to the end of the line and starting over."

Moore chuckled.

"Yeah, but that was the goal. Come here and then go home."

As if on cue, the computer fired a nose thruster to get the ship pointed back toward Arcadia. They could have gone the whole way in reverse on the ripple drive, but they would have to turn around at some point to fly back down to the planet's surface anyway.

As the ship came around, the countdown started.

"Three... Two... One... Transition," the computer voice said.

The windows went black, and they were back in hyperspace.

It was almost an hour later when the ripple drive kicked into reverse in preparation for their exit from hyperspace.

"Three... Two... One... Transition," the computer voice said.

The windows went back to clear, and there in front of them was the planet Arcadia and its yellower sun.

"And there we are," Moore said.

"If that ain't the damnedest thing," McKay said. "One hour each way, and now we're back, but with a day to go to get to the planet."

"Yup. Get another couple books in before we get to watch the computer land us."

"That will be more nerve-wracking than the take-off. It's dicier."

"Yeah, but the computer's done it before," Moore said. "We're just along for the ride."

"I know, I know. I won't touch anything. Still."

They had already reported in that they were fine, but when they got closer to the planet, Huenemann contacted them.

"How you guys doing? You all rested up and fed and everything?"

"Yes, sir," Moore said. "Pretty much. Not very stressful, after all. We kept our hands off the controls, so we just watched."

"All right. Well, you're going to be coming down about noon Arcadia City time. And they're setting up a parade and all."

"A parade?"

"Yeah," Huenemann said. "For the returning heroes. You know."

"But we didn't do anything."

"You know that, and I know that, but they want to get everybody all excited. We're going to be spending a lot more money going forward, and the prime minister doesn't want any pushback on funding."

"Ah. Politics. Got it," Moore said. "So we wave and smile and all that shit."

"Yeah. You got it. Shake a buncha hands, too. Maybe even get a medal."

The motorcade came in from Arcadia City Spaceport along Quant Boulevard. It met up with the bands and all about six blocks from Charter Square. The parade route was down Quant Boulevard to Hospital Street, right on Hospital to A Street, left on A Street to University Street, and left on University to Arcadia Boulevard. That is, it ringed Charter Square on the big roundabout.

The leading elements of the parade made the right onto Arcadia Boulevard, but everything stopped when the car carrying the first humans into hyperspace reached the intersection. The reviewing stand was there, and Prime Minister Milbank, Chen MinChao, Jessica Chen-Jasic, and other notables were there.

The reviewing stand was open on all four sides, and Charter Square was full of cheering people as Moore and McKay mounted the stairs. They shook hands with all the notables. Milbank gave them both a medal, the mayor gave them the keys to Arcadia City, and Miss Arcadia City gave them both a kiss on the cheek.

"You know what this means, Rob," Jessica said to the prime minister as they watched the proceedings.

"Yes, Jessica. Your funding payments go up."

"And we're ready to place RDF satellites. We'll find Amber and Earthsea before the end of the year."

"Ouch," Milbank said. "There goes my next year's budget."

Jessica laughed.

# The Search Begins

While all the excitement centered around the first manned hyperspace mission, JieMin's work was concentrated on the second hyperspace ship. He had watched interviews of the manned hyperspace crew of the first hyperspace ship, and was unsurprised at their reaction to the appearance of hyperspace. Hyperspace did not follow space-time's rules.

When the second hyperspace ship was operational, the torque testing of the screw drive was performed under computer control. The results of those tests were given to JieMin's hyperspace mathematics team. They would work out the implications.

JieMin was working on bigger-picture items. One big question was, How would they find the other colonies? He knew they were a minimum of roughly three thousand light-years apart. How could he visualize this so the solution would be more apparent to him?

It was an important issue because, once Amber and Earthsea were found, they had to know where to redeploy the RDF satellites to find other colonies. And if they weren't deployed within a hundred and twenty light-years of a colony, they wouldn't see it. Its radiation signature wouldn't have traveled that far yet.

JieMin was washing his hands in the bathroom down the hall from his office when it came to him. Bubbles! He ran back to his office, his hands still soapy.

After an hour's work – and a cursory wipe of his hands on

his trousers – JieMin surveyed the results. In the three-dimensional display, he showed this part of the Milky Way galaxy. Specifically the Orion and Sagittarius arms. Around each of Earth, Arcadia, and the likely positions of Amber and Earthsea, he had drawn a nearly transparent globe, like a bubble.

The bubbles were fifteen hundred light-years in radius, or three-thousand light-years in diameter. If two bubbles touched each other, the distance from the human-inhabited planet in the center of one bubble to the one in the center of the other bubble would be three thousand light-years, through the contact point.

More to the point, other colonies could only be located where other bubbles would fit, and only at the center of the bubble. If the bubble had some slop to wiggle back and forth, the location of the colony planet for that bubble could also wiggle back and forth, because the center of the bubble had moved.

Now the question was, Did that set of locations – the locations where the center of a bubble could go – contain a G2 type star or not? The stars – location and type – were all mapped pretty well in this part of the galaxy.

JieMin spent the rest of the day playing with the bubbles, moving them around, consulting star charts, and selecting likely locations. By the time the RDF satellites had located Amber and Earthsea, he would be ready with deployment locations.

As a matter of fact, JieMin thought he already knew which stars Amber and Earthsea orbited.

JieMin and ChaoLi sat at the dining room table after dinner that night. The kids had cleared the table and then gone off to their rooms to study.

"I had a major breakthrough today," JieMin said.

"In how to find the other colonies?"

"Yes."

JieMin told ChaoLi of the bubble idea, and how he was using it.

"So all human space..." she began.

"... looks like twenty-five three-thousand light-year soap bubbles," he finished for her. "That's right.'

"That's a great way to visualize it."

"Yes. And if I can visualize it, I can reduce it to an algorithm."

"And cross-reference it to the star charts," ChaoLi said.

"Yes. Exactly. We should get a pretty small list of locations to look at, at least for the colonies that are close to us."

"Outstanding. You know, the RDF satellites have been signed off on. We deployed two of them to Beacon, and they both found Arcadia. It's only three light-years away, but still, they worked."

"When is Karl deploying them?" JieMin asked. "I have some refinement on the best locations from the bubble map."

"He was going to send the first set off next week. The ship can carry three of them, so he was going to deploy the Amber ones with the first hyperspace ship, and the Earthsea ones with the second."

"So both hyperspace ships will be gone almost three months, just to deploy the satellites?"

"That's the plan. No way around it, given the distances."

JieMin nodded.

"Maybe we should just have the ships wait for results," he said. "It shouldn't take long. Then bring the satellites back with them."

"That's a good idea, too, given the three-month round-trip

time. I'll mention it to Karl. You need to send him your refined locations."

JieMin nodded.

They were finally getting somewhere.

Karl Huenemann liked the idea. Three months with the ships gone was what he expected, but then it was another three months to go and pick up the satellites and get results. Waiting a month for results made the initial trip four months long, but then they would have the results right off.

Huenemann knew they could pick up the satellites. They had practiced rendezvousing with them – under computer control – in Arcadia orbit before deploying two of them to Beacon. So there was no problem there.

The change in the programming of the mission profile wasn't that much. Just leave out the part where they came back to Arcadia and went back out in between. Place all the satellites, wait, then do the pickup mission. Easy.

JieMin and ChaoLi were at the beach watching the boys play in the water. LeiTao, newly engaged to Chen DaGang, was off with her fiancé buying housewares to update his bachelor's supplies. Short engagements being the norm on Arcadia, the wedding celebration was next weekend. They were already living together in his apartment, and JieJun had moved into the now empty bedroom that had been the girls' room.

For everything else going on, JieMin's mental back channel never moved far from the project.

"ChaoLi."

"Yes?"

"How is the project doing financially?"

"Why do you ask?" ChaoLi asked.

"If we made a satellite delivery vehicle – no cabin, ripple drive only, computer control – it would be quite a bit cheaper than the current hyperspace ships. A half dozen of those, with maybe another dozen RDF satellites, would be a lot faster at finding other colonies than just the two hyperspace ships. As it is – deploying the RDF satellites to multiple likely locations with six-week transit intervals, going out to get results, redeploying – it's going to take years to locate the other colonies."

"And that would also free up the hyperspace ships for other tasks. I like it. I'll have to look at the finances, but we might be able to swing it, especially because I think we are going to find Amber and Earthsea pretty quickly."

"You could probably make those delivery vehicles space-only. No need to have them come down to the planet. Simpler still."

ChaoLi nodded.

"Yes," she said. "We already know how to do that. Actually, if they stayed outside of the safe transition limit, we wouldn't even need rockets on them. All nuclear power for the hyperspace drive, and no refueling issues. They just come back here, deliver results, and get redeployed. I like it."

She leaned over and kissed him on the cheek.

"Good one, JieMin."

LeiTao and DaGang's wedding was a smaller affair than ChaoPing and JuMing's huge event two years before. They were not on the track of the engineering and accounting disciplines that were the choices for the family's potential power couples. Still, there were a hundred people crammed into the smaller private dining room of the family's restaurant on Market Street.

Chen MinChao and Jessica Chen-Jasic attended, though, as did Prime Minister Rob Milbank and his wife Julia Whitcomb. JieMin and ChaoLi were movers and shakers, and, more to the point, Rob had become a personal friend through their interactions on the project.

The bride was beautiful, the groom awkward.

All was as it should be.

It wasn't until the week after the wedding that ChaoLi was able to bring the question of specialized satellite deployment vehicles to MinChao and Jessica. She explained the benefits and costs to the family's ultimate power couple and got the go-ahead for development and construction.

The project kicked into high gear.

"OK, so one problem we have with space-only deployment vehicles is getting them out to the safe transition distance the first time, right?" Mikhail Borovsky asked.

"Yeah," Karl Huenemann said. "We can only get them going so fast with the cargo shuttle, and we just have to wait until they get there."

"Maybe not. One of the guys was looking for one-time-use rocket systems, and he came across something called a JATO bottle. Ever heard of them?"

"No. What is it?"

"Jet Assist Take-Off bottle," Borovsky said. "One-time-use rocket. They used to use them to get heavy airplanes off the ground. You just light 'em and hang on."

"Sounds great. Do we have build plans for them?"

"Not factory plans, but they're stupid simple. Not a big problem to write the build program for them. We put a couple on the deployment vehicle, and light 'em off once the shuttle drops it off. We can even do two plus a second two. They don't have a long burn, but as light as the deployment vehicle will be, they can get it up to a speed where it will only be three days to safe transition distance."

"Nice," Huenemann said. "Let's plan on that then."

"You got it."

Both hyperspace ships sat on the shuttlepads adjacent to the hyperspace facility at Arcadia City Spaceport. Both were unmanned for this mission, their cockpits empty, running under computer control.

Slung beneath each were three of the RDF satellites. Each was the size of a cargo container, and they were using the offset latches that centered three containers under the shuttles, which could carry up to four containers each.

Both hyperspace ships were fueled up and ready to go.

"All right, one after the other," Karl Huenemann said. "Let's get 'em on their way."

One after the other, the big ships spooled up their engines, lifted off their pads, and jetted into the sky.

In the empty assembly building adjacent to the control center, six construction bays for smaller vehicles were being prepared. Each would have a nuclear powerplant and hyperspace generator, but there were no jet engines or rockets, no big tanks for rocket fuel or jet fuel or oxygen, and no cabin.

The deployment vehicles did have four sets of latches for RDF satellites, and thrusters to match velocity with the RDF satellites when picking them up, but they were much simpler than the hyperspace ships, and would go together quickly.

While the hyperspace ships were off for four months looking for Amber and Earthsea, JieMin built the algorithm that was the natural outgrowth of his bubble model. He experimented with the result, moving the Amber and Earthsea colonies, or adding other colonies that might be found. As he did so, the bubbles in the display shifted, and the list of candidate stars for the other colony planets shifted.

When colony locations were finalized, JieMin would be ready with the prime locations for follow-on searches.

ChaoLi was working on her own project, a plan for how to vet planets to make sure they were safe to approach. How could one tell, short of actually visiting the planet, whether the government and people there would be safe for Arcadians to approach?

The first steps seemed obvious, but the follow-on measures were less so. It was important, because Arcadia had no defenses against an interstellar raid.

Janice Quant watched all the activity around the hyperspace project on Arcadia with interest. They certainly were making good progress. After a hundred and twenty years of measured progress in the colonies, things were happening fast.

JieMin's bubble model intrigued her. Quant ran it against her knowledge of the colony locations and it was startlingly effective. It was clear Arcadia would eventually find most of the other colonies using the methods they were working on.

The other big question in Quant's mind was whether she should warn Arcadia about Earth or not. ChaoLi's work on the vetting process was incomplete, and Quant could not yet tell if it would be effective.

Quant set that aside for the moment. It was not yet time, and ChaoLi seemed to be on the right track.

## First Results

It would be four months until the hyperspace ships returned with the six RDF satellites and their potential results on Amber and Earthsea. Transit times were what they were, and there was no getting around them.

In the meantime, there were six RDF satellite deployment vehicles being assembled, along with eighteen more RDF satellites. Together with the six RDF satellites coming back from the Amber and Earthsea searches, that would give the full complement of four RDF satellites per deployment vehicle.

Two of the RDF satellites would be mounted on the top of each deployment vehicle and two below, with the JATO bottles mounted on either side. They would have to be taken up to space separately by the hyperspace ships and the large cargo shuttle and latched together in orbit, but that could all be done under computer control.

With minimum transit times of six weeks between RDF satellite deployment locations, it would take over a year to deploy the satellites at three-thousand-light-year separations and pick them back up again, but hyperspace was only so fast and the distances involved were huge.

Four months after their departure, the hyperspace ships returned from the Amber and Earthsea missions. They returned about a week apart because the distances to JieMin's recommended scanning locations were a bit different for the two colonies.

The Amber mission returned first, and the hyperspace ship

relayed the results to mission control while it was still on its way to Arcadia. The results were sent to JieMin for analysis.

Each RDF satellite had first fixed its precise position with accurate sightings on known stars. They had then scanned the very-low-frequency range looking for the power grids of the target colony. All three of the RDF satellites assigned to Amber had been located within one hundred light-years of the colony based on the parallax analysis done by the astronomy department.

All three of the RDF satellites assigned to Amber had been within a hundred light-years of the colony, one at eighty-one light-years, one at forty-eight light-years, and one at only eighteen light-years. All of them had located and sighted on the colony.

JieMin marked the locations of the satellites and their sighting vectors in his bubble map of this portion of the galaxy. They all pointed to the same star, which had been his first choice for the location of Amber, in the center of the parallax analysis.

JieMin sent a message to ChaoLi and Huenemann.

"We've located Amber. No uncertainty at all."

Eight days later, the Earthsea mission returned. The search results were again immediately sent to JieMin.

JieMin performed the same analysis as before. There had been fewer candidate stars in the parallax analysis from the astronomy department, so JieMin's recommended deployment locations for the RDF satellites were even closer to Earthsea's actual location. They found the colony's emissions signature from only thirty-four light-years, twenty-two light-years, and twelve light-years distant.

Once again, it had been JieMin's first choice for the colony's location.

JieMin sent another message to ChaoLi and Huenemann.

"We've located Earthsea. No uncertainty at all."

After she received the message about Earthsea from JieMin, ChaoLi requested a meeting with MinChao and Jessica. They of course knew that the hyperspace ships had returned and expected to hear of the results, so ChaoLi was not surprised to get a meeting time for tea mid-afternoon the same day.

ChaoLi left the office early and took the Arcadia Boulevard bus back to the Chen-Jasic apartment building at Fifteenth and Market Streets. She changed into lavalava and flip-flops and was shown into Jessica's tea room, where both Jessica and MinChao waited.

"Come in, ChaoLi."

"Thank you, Chen Zumu."

Tea was poured, and Jessica's tea girl withdrew. ChaoLi sipped her tea, then MinChao, then Jessica.

"I note your new statue has been moved, Chen Zumu," ChaoLi said.

"Yes. I gave it a place in the garden, for contemplation."

Jessica gestured behind her, and Chao Li looked, between the two of them, out into the garden. Across the path from the big teak-beamed doorway, the metal statue of Matthew Chen-Jasic now sat on a jade pedestal set on a stone base. Lions were carved around the stone base, which was perhaps a foot tall. Dragons flying through clouds were carved on the jade pedestal, which was perhaps eighteen inches tall. Atop it all stood the ten-inch iridium statue of Matthew Chen-Jasic.

"It looks very nice there, Chen Zumu. The carvings are pretty, too."

"Thank you, ChaoLi. The lions, to remind me of where we

are from. The dragons, to remind me of where we are going. And I believe you requested this meeting to update us on that very effort."

"Yes, Chen, Zumu."

Jessica raised a hand to ChaoLi, instructing her to continue.

"We have located both Amber and Earthsea, Chen Zumu. We know which stars they orbit."

"Outstanding. And the likelihood we are correct?"

"JieMin described these results as having no uncertainty at all, Chen Zumu, and he is not prone to overstatement on such things."

Jessica nodded.

"What is your next step, ChaoLi?" MinChao asked.

"We will lift all the RDF drones and deployment vehicles to orbit and latch them together, Chen Zufu. Then we will send them on their way. At that point, the hyperspace ships will be freed up to vet Amber and Earthsea."

"And how do you intend to do that, ChaoLi?"

"We know we can select the velocity at which we exit hyperspace, Chen Zufu. Up to millions of miles an hour. If we send the hyperspace ships to these colony planets, and have them fly by the planet – millions of miles out and at millions of miles per hour – we can capture radio emissions from the planet with no possibility of being intercepted."

"And then the ship brings the recordings back here and we see what the news wires say, for example."

"Exactly, Chen Zufu. And we don't have to worry about them being faked, both because of their quantity and because they don't know we're coming."

"They could still be faking their news, though, ChaoLi. We have plenty of examples of that in history."

"Yes, Chen Zumu, but we will also pick up a lot of other

communications, not all of it encrypted. We should be able to check for consistency between public postings and the news wires."

Jessica turned to MinChao and nodded.

"Very well, ChaoLi. You have authority to proceed as you have described."

"Thank you, Chen Zufu."

"There is one more small item, ChaoLi. Finding Amber and Earthsea increases the advance payments from the government a great deal. I think it's time you begin the design of a true hyperspace vessel. Passengers, cargo, everything."

"Truly, Chen Zumu?"

ChaoLi looked to MinChao, and he nodded. She turned back to Jessica.

"Thank you, Chen Zumu. We will begin the design effort in earnest immediately."

"That is all for now, ChaoLi."

"Yes, Chen Zumu."

ChaoLi took her leave of them.

There was much to do.

After ChaoLi left, MinChao and Jessica turned around and contemplated the garden from the doorway. The statue of Matthew Chen-Jasic looked on.

"Is it a little early, do you think?" MinChao asked.

"I don't think so. Those RDF satellites will report back in a year, and then our advance payments will increase again. In the meantime, we're not spending anything, other than for ChaoLi's vetting project."

"A big project can spend a lot of money in a year."

"But it's not really big money," Jessica said. "Not at this stage. Paper is a lot cheaper than steel, and I want them to have the time to get it right. Do the simulations, work out the kinks they can in advance. I don't want the design team rushed."

"All right. That makes sense."

"Also, I don't want those increased advance payments to be coming in and not be spending them. I don't want Rob – or, more to the point, his political adversaries – pondering why they're giving us all this money if we're not even using it yet."

"Another good point," MinChao said. "OK, that all makes sense to me."

They pondered the garden for several minutes, both running back over the conversation in their heads. MinChao broke the silence.

"As far as the vetting is concerned, are you happy with ChaoLi's plan?" he asked.

"Yes. It hangs together for me."

"What if one of these planets is ahead of us? They could follow the hyperspace ship home in some way. Figure out where we are. How dangerous would that be? We don't have any kind of interstellar weaponry, if it gets dicey."

"Oh, but we do, MinChao. We do."

"We do?"

"Of course," Jessica said. "Consider how big a hole it would make if a heavy shipping container hit a planet's surface going several million miles an hour."

MinChao's eyebrows shot up.

"I hadn't considered that," he said.

"I had, but I don't think it will come to that. I don't think Madam Chairman will let things go that far."

ChaoLi called a staff meeting for the next day, though it was Thursday, not Friday. She, JieMin, and Karl Huenemann met in her office downtown as usual. It was to be anything but a normal staff meeting, however, and ChaoLi started it off with a bang.

"Karl, can your and Mr. Borovsky's seconds take over the deployment of the RDF satellites? I have a different assignment for you and Mr. Borovsky."

Caught flat-footed, Huenemann stammered his way through his answer.

"I, I, I guess so, ChaoLi. Wha–, what's up?"

"With the finalization of the location of Amber and Earthsea, our funding will increase dramatically. We have been given the go-ahead to begin the development of a full-up hyperspace vessel. Passengers, cargo, artificial gravity – everything. I want you two to pull the best design people you have into that effort and get started. Hire whoever else you need as you go."

"What about the RDF satellite deployment?"

"Oh, we're still full-speed on that. But at this point it's all things we've done before. Latching things up in orbit, getting their mission profiles loaded, sending them off. That's become routine. We need to move the ideas people on to the next big thing, and the next big thing is true hyperspace vessels. Born and bred for interstellar missions. Karl, I want you to lead that."

With several seconds to think about it, Huenemann had recovered his bearings. And building the big interstellar transport had been his dream job. Now it was his.

"Yes, ma'am. We'll get right on it."

Huenemann was smiling now, and clapped his hands.

"Hot damn."

ChaoLi laughed.

"I thought you'd like it. And lean on the university math and engineering people. Don't worry about the consulting charges. We have the money. Make sure we get the answers right. Double vetted."

JieMin had watched all this with some amusement. He hadn't known what was coming, but he knew ChaoLi had a meeting with Chen Zufu and Chen Zumu yesterday, and was excited last night, so he'd made some guesses.

Huenemann turned to him now.

"You're with me, right, JieMin? You'll keep me honest? Check all the numbers? Make sure we're square with the theory?"

JieMin stirred.

"Yes, of course. And the engineering types will be all over this, too. We have your back, Karl."

"Excellent."

Huenemann clapped his hands again.

"Damn, this is gonna be fun."

# Kicking Off The Big Project

Huenemann went out to the hyperspace facility on the shuttleport bus. He jogged into the office and called Mikhail Borovsky over to join him.

"Mikhail. We're relieved. John and Chris can handle this part of the project from here forward. You and I have a new assignment."

Borovsky's raised his eyebrows.

"Which is what?" he asked.

"We're going to move downtown for a while and design the big ship. The one with gravity and passengers and shit."

"You're kidding."

"Nope," Huenemann said. "ChaoLi has the money, and we've been cut loose to pull the design boys and start working on it. Hire more if we need 'em."

"Hang on a second. I have something you need to see."

Borovsky got up and walked down the hall. He came back a couple minutes later. He was carrying a sketch pad.

"I think we need to take Wayne Porter with us," he said.

"The young blond kid on the assembly team? Why?"

"Frustrated artist. This is his sketch pad. It caught my eye last week, so I just went and pulled it from his desk."

Borovsky put the sketch pad down on the desk, and Huenemann flipped through the top several pages.

One of the sketches was of a large ship like a hollow cylinder. It looked like a short piece of thick-walled pipe. The blunt edge of the pipe had several rows of windows running around it, indicating the pipe wall thickness was maybe forty feet. The thing must be three hundred feet across the open end, and five hundred feet long. Arrayed around the inside of the pipe, several layers deep, were thousands of shipping containers.

"Damn. This is great," Huenemann said. "All the people around the outside, where the gravity is, all the cargo inside the middle. I never thought of that."

"That's just one of his ideas. You should see the full-up shit he's doing in the three-dimensional display. Karl, we want that guy. He's not an engineer, but he's got vision."

"Hell, yeah. Put him on your list. And get me that list yet today or very first thing tomorrow, because Monday we're working downtown."

John Gannet and Chris Bellamy were wondering what was up when they got called to the conference room. Huenemann and Borovsky were already there.

"Have a seat," Huenemann said, waving to chairs.

Once they were seated, he jumped right in.

"Chen ChaoLi is splitting up the hyperspace team into a design group and an operations group. Mikhail and I are going downtown for a while to head up the new design group, and you guys are going to have the operations group. John, you're stepping up to my job as head of the operations group, and, Chris, you're taking Mikhail's job as operations group project manager. You two will report to ChaoLi."

"Wow," Gannet said. "That's a surprise."

Huenemann shrugged.

"With regard to timing, maybe, but we knew something like it was gonna happen sooner or later. We just have so much going on, and somebody has to be working on the next generation of ships. So she's splitting them up now. Lotta design first to build anything big, and we don't already have all the life support stuff figured out like we did for the hyperspace ships we have now. Those used the shuttle cabin, so that stuff was all done already.

Bellamy nodded. She seemed unfazed by the changes.

"So same-same, right?" she asked. "We carry on as we've been going, and you guys start up the new stuff."

"Yeah, and then at some point it will come back to you when we transfer something over for testing. Probably a few years, though. It'll take Mikhail a while to even get a schedule coming together on something like that, much less manage to it."

Huenemann turned to Borovsky, who looked pretty stunned with the idea of trying to schedule something like the design process he saw ahead of them. Huenemann chuckled and turned back to the new operations team.

"Anyway, that's the setup. And you guys will like working for ChaoLi. She's no nonsense. Easy to get along with as long as stuff is getting done. And no internal politics at all. I think she's allergic."

Huenemann shrugged.

"But right now we need to look at org charts. We're taking the design types with us, and we're gonna end up with holes in both groups. We need to work up a needs list for the personnel people."

Gannet blinked at Huenemann's ruthless dispatch, and Huenemann shrugged.

"Hey, we got shit to do. Ain't no sense taking forever to get going on it. Any staffing mistakes we make we can fix later."

Twenty-year-old Wayne Porter was one of several dozen people working on assembling the RDF deployment vehicles when he got a message that Friday saying he was being reassigned to a new team that was being put together in an office building downtown.

Porter was working on a degree in industrial design downtown, so it would make it a lot easier for him to attend his evening art classes. This assembly job was just to support his family while he got through school. He knew there wouldn't be any assembly work being done downtown, though, so he didn't understand.

Porter went to his immediate supervisor, Frank Takahashi, but he didn't know anything about his new assignment.

"I'm staying here, so I don't have anything on the new group. Ask Jerry. I think he's going downtown, too."

Jerry – Gerardo Perez – was a couple levels higher in the pecking order at the hyperspace facility, so Porter was a little shy about approaching him, but curiosity won out.

"Hi, Jerry. Got a minute?"

"Oh, hi, Wayne. Sure. Whatcha got?"

"Well, I'm being reassigned downtown, and I don't understand. Are we going to be doing assembly work downtown?"

"No, the downtown group is a design group."

"A *design* group?" Porter asked.

"Yeah. We're going to be working on the new hyperspace vessel. The big ship all this has been aimed at."

"I don't understand, then. What am I going to be doing?"

"I've got the staff roster. Let me check."

Perez got the faraway look of someone consulting his heads-up display.

"You're listed downtown all right. But not for assembly work. You're down for hull design. Staff designer."

"Staff designer?"

"Yeah. Looks like they moved you to the professional staff.

That moved you to a different salary structure. Nice increase on that assignment. About double. Congratulations."

"Uh, thanks."

"No problem, Wayne. See you downtown."

Porter wandered out of Perez's office in a daze.

But there were stars in his eyes.

When Porter got home that evening, his wife was just going to start supper.

"Denise, can your sister take Diana and Stevie tonight?"

"Sure. I think so. What's up?"

"I got a big promotion. They're starting a new design project, and they've put me on that project. Not for assembly, though. As a designer."

"That's wonderful. Your first real job. You know, in your actual field."

"Yeah. So we're going out to celebrate."

"Where?"

"Someplace nice."

Porter thought about it.

"Let's go to Chen's."

Once seated at their table, they were both looking around.

"I've never been here before," Denise said.

"Me, either," Porter said. "I've heard a lot about it, but it's always been a little too pricey. Not tonight, though."

"It's very nice."

They considered the menu and gave their order to the waiter. Once he left, Denise was puzzled.

"But I don't understand how you got a design position. You haven't finished your degree yet. I mean, you're close now, but how did they even know? Did you put in for it or something?"

"No. I didn't do anything. They do know what I'm up to with the degree, though, at least in personnel. The company is paying my tuition, remember? But I think it was something that happened a couple weeks ago.

"I was sketching during break. I was drawing space ships. I mean, that's one of the constant topics of conversation on the project, and I've been playing around with designs for what everyone's always talking about.

"Mikhail Borovsky came out to the big assembly room. He's one of the big shots, the project manager for everything. We see him all the time, coming out to review progress.

"He sees me sketching, and looks over my shoulder as he walks past. He stopped and took a better look. 'Nice,' he said, then, 'Do you mind?' So I handed him my sketch pad, and he flipped through a bunch of pages. 'This is good stuff.'

"I told him they were just sketches. Anything serious I did in the full-up art package on the design machines downtown. He asked me to send him some of my work on those, and then was off, back onto what he was there for."

"So you sent him some of your work?" Denise asked.

"Yeah, I sent him some of the full-up three-D stuff. I never heard anything back. But that must have been the impetus behind this."

"Well, however it happened, it's wonderful. You can spend your time now doing what you love."

"It's a miracle."

They were looking around while waiting for their food, when something caught Porter's eye. He grabbed Denise's forearm on the table.

"Denise, do you see that big family table over in the corner?"

"The one with that late-thirties couple and all their kids? Looks like seven kids. Maybe some in-laws there. Four of those look like two couples. And at least one of those two girls is pregnant."

"Yeah. Well, that woman is Chen ChaoLi. She's the head of the whole hyperspace project. My boss's boss's boss's boss or something."

"Wow," Denise said. "She's very pretty."

"And very powerful. She reports directly to both the Chen and the prime minister. And her husband? That's Chen JieMin, the genius who came up with hyperspace in the first place."

"That's him? The little guy next to her?"

"Yeah," Porter said. "Smartest person on Arcadia. No contest."

"What are they doing here?"

"Maybe they're celebrating, too. The hyperspace vessel project kicks off on Monday. That's a big step for the whole project."

"And we're celebrating right along with them," Denise said. "Kind of, anyway. How nice."

What JieMin and ChaoLi were actually celebrating was finding Amber and Earthsea, an accomplishment that Bob Milbank would announce in a speech Monday night. That way he could also announce the start of the design work on the hyperspace vessel – which would begin Monday – as a fait accompli.

They had told the girls, ChaoPing and LeiTao, now married adults at twenty and seventeen years old. ChaoPing had finished her business degree and started working in the family's business office. She was about six months along on her first pregnancy now, having delayed children until she and JuMing finished their educations.

LeiTao was also pregnant, just a few months along. She and

DaGang had gotten married about six months back. She now managed one of the stalls in the Uptown Market, the huge galleria that was one of the family's big moneymakers.

The boys were just fourteen and ten, a bit young for such confidences. They just knew their parents had had some big success at work. They didn't care what it was. A family party at the Chen family's restaurant was a special treat. Not since the weddings had they all come here for dinner, and they were on their best behavior.

Neither ChaoLi nor JieMin knew Wayne Porter or his circumstances, and they did not recognize him in the crowd at the restaurant this Friday night.

They were too busy enjoying the celebration of the completion of such a major part of the project, and the beginning of the ultimate piece of the puzzle JieMin had set before Paul Chen-Jasic and Chen JuPing – the prior Chen Zufu and Chen Zumu – twenty-two years before with his first formalism of hyperspace.

Between that and their growing family, they were suffused with happiness this special night, September twenty-eighth, 2367.

ChaoLi and JieMin both expected that within three years, the first hyperspace trips to other human planets using the new hyperspace vessel, loaded with cargo and passengers, could begin.

That year, 2370, would also be the one-hundred-twenty-fifth anniversary of the founding of the colonies.

# Getting Under Way

Monday morning found Wayne Porter sitting in a small auditorium at the Chen's downtown facility for Karl Huenemann's kickoff talk. There were almost a hundred people there, some of whom Porter recognized. The others must have been located downtown all along.

At the appointed meeting time, Huenemann got up on the stage in front and addressed the group.

"Hi, everybody.

"Some of you know what's going on, at least a little bit. Some of you have no clue, you just showed up here because you were told to. So I'm going to tell you what's going on.

"Over the last two weeks, we found the colonies Amber and Earthsea. We know exactly where they are. There's going to be a mission out there to confirm that and make sure we can safely be in contact with them. You know, that they're not military dictatorships or something that could make them less than good people to be involved with.

"That's confidential until tonight, by the way, when the prime minister will tell all Arcadia.

"So that changes some things, which is why you're here. On that note, I have good news and bad news.

"Bad news first. The other group – all those guys out at the hyperspace facility – are going to be sending the missions to Amber and Earthsea to check them out. They're going to be sending out a couple dozen RDF satellites to try and find more colonies, and then checking them out. They got all the playtoys out there, and they're going to be using 'em pretty constant over the next couple years.

"We don't get any of the playtoys.

"That's the bad news.

"The good news is that, once we check out Amber and Earthsea, we're gonna go there. We're gonna have passenger service back and forth. We're gonna have imports and exports back and forth. We'll probably be shipping them tea, and God only knows what we'll be bringing back. We're gonna start doing that in three years or so.

"So that'll be something, right?

"Except some of you are thinking, How're we gonna do that? In those little hyperspace ships? Six weeks each way in zero gravity for what? Like four people?

"Nope. We're gonna go there in big hyperspace vessels. Huge ships that can carry passengers and cargo, and that spin so they have internal gravity on the way.

"But we don't have such ships, you say? That's right. We don't. We need to design 'em. And that's what we're going to be doing here. Designing spaceships.

"Now if that didn't make your little heart go pitter-patter, you just might be on the wrong project."

Everybody laughed. Huenemann was in his element, and he had them all in his pocket. Then he shocked Porter, who did not know Huenemann had seen his renderings.

"Wayne Porter there's put some concepts together. In his spare time while he was out in the assembly room boltin' shit together, believe it or not. Personally, I like this one."

Huenemann waved at the display behind him, and one of Porter's three-dimensional renderings popped up in the display volume, the huge truncated-pipe version of the hyperspace vessel, rotating against the star field. It was three-dimensional and photo-realistic, a professional rendering, and there were oohs and aahs in the crowd when they saw it.

"Nice job, Wayne," Huenemann said, pointed at him, and clapped.

Everyone else clapped, too, and Porter blushed as most of the people there turned to look at him. He waved once, quickly, and mumbled, 'Thank you.' The clapping died down and people turned back to Huenemann.

"Like I say, I like this one. But there may be a better version. That's up to us to figure out. Design them, engineer them, and then, my friends, we are damn well going to build them.

"And Arcadia will space to the stars in them."

After the kickoff meeting, Wayne Porter checked his heads-up display to see if he had his office assignment yet. He did, so he consulted the building plan and headed to the indicated room.

Not only did Porter have a private office, but his office had a gigantic three-dimensional display that took up the whole far end of the room. He didn't know it, but he had the same setup as JieMin had in his office in the university's science building.

Porter pulled up one of his renderings, the one Huenemann had shown during the kickoff meeting. It leapt into life in front of him with such clarity and size it left him gasping.

This was much better than the student displays he had been using.

Karl Huenemann had said the people in the hyperspace facility out at the Arcadia City Shuttleport had all the playtoys, but Wayne Porter had the only playtoy he cared about, right here in his office.

Ideas had been popping into Porter's head all weekend.

He sat down and started to draw.

They also had a kickoff meeting out at the hyperspace facility. John Gannet addressed his new organization the same time Karl Huenemann addressed his.

"Good morning, everyone.

"The hyperspace facility – what will be called the Operations Group going forward – reports to me now. You'll find I may be a little less colorful than Mr. Huenemann, but competent nonetheless."

There were some chuckles at that. Karl Huenemann was notorious.

"Chris Bellamy will be our project manager. I think you'll find she's just as meticulous as Mr. Borovsky when it comes to project milestones and costs."

That got groans. Borovsky had his own form of notoriety.

"Now they get to do all the blue-sky stuff downtown, but we have all the playtoys, as Karl would say, and the real blue sky – in terms of actually going up into the sky – is here. When a bird leaves this planet, it's ours.

"Our plan is as it was. One order of business is to turn these ships–" He gestured over his shoulder in the direction of the hyperspace ships on their pads outside. "– and get them on their way to Amber and Earthsea. As you know, and as the prime minister will tell all Arcadia tonight, we now know exactly where they are.

"What we don't know is whether the natives are friendly, so we'll be sending those ships out to find out what they can in a high-speed flyby of the planets. We should have those mission profiles soon.

"For the RDF satellites and their deployment vehicles, we have a similar mission. Get them ready and send them out to find some other colonies. Those need to be lifted and then assembled in space, but we need cargo shuttles to do that.

"First order of business then is to get all those non-lift vehicles into orbit and assembled. We have three lift platforms available for that, the large space-capable cargo shuttle and the two hyperspace ships.

"Only once that's done do we get the hyperspace ships on the way to Amber and Earthsea. And after that, we get the deployment vehicles on their way.

"Things will get real quiet here for a while after that, until we start getting results back, so we're going to start working on figuring out what we need to service whatever kind of hyperspace vessel the downtown desk jockeys come up with.

"We need to work up a terminal plan for here, plan what kind of passenger and cargo shuttles we need to get everything up there to where those ships will live, all that stuff. There'll be plenty to do, and we need to have that ready for when the first hyperspace vessel comes on line.

"When results do come in, we're going to have to turn vehicles and get them ready for more of the same.

"That's what we're going to be about. Plenty of work, and we have all the playtoys.

"Sounds like fun to me."

In a live speech on Monday night, Prime Minister Rob Milbank announced the finding of Amber and Earthsea.

"My fellow Arcadians.

"You all know that we have been pursuing the dream of space travel for a number of years and have had our minor successes. We have transferred a spacecraft into hyperspace and back, and have even had that spacecraft travel to Beacon and back.

"More recently, we have had our two intrepid explorers, Justin Moore and Gavin McKay, travel to Beacon and back. We believe these are the first humans anywhere to travel through hyperspace.

"Tonight I want to announce one more success. Unmanned reconnaissance craft have traveled through hyperspace to far distant locations and used radio detection to find two other human colonies that were planted, like us, a hundred and twenty-two years ago.

"We now know where Amber and Earthsea are. Soon, we will send hyperspace craft to those colony planets to determine what sort of people they are, if they have the sort of culture and government that would make them good trading partners and friends.

"I'm sure we have things we can sell or trade to them, things we can teach them, benefits they can accrue from such a friendship. And the same goes for us. What do they have that we don't? What can they teach us? What benefits can we gain from such a friendship?

"We will also soon be sending out other reconnaissance craft to look for the other twenty-one human colonies we know exist. We have the capability now, thanks to our years of effort.

"We are on the verge of an exciting era, an era of human interstellar civilization. I will keep you informed of our progress as we carry on into this bright future.

"Good evening, my fellow Arcadians."

There had been some grousing about the design work on the hyperspace vessel being split off, but that quieted down after Gannet's kickoff talk. They had all the vehicles, and all the action would be here. The people still at the hyperspace facility were not, by and large, office types.

Both groups bent to their tasks. Both groups made good progress on their portion of the project, freed from the concerns of the other portion.

ChaoLi kept a close eye on both groups as they kicked off. It looked like her splitting the project was going well.

# All The Playtoys

The hyperspace operations facility at the Arcadia City Spaceport was a maelstrom of activity for the next several weeks. It took ten shuttle flights to orbit to get all eighteen additional RDF satellites, six deployment vehicles, and twenty-four large JATO bottles to space.

Dragging the payloads out of the assembly rooms. Latching them together on the shuttle pads. Landing the shuttles on them and latching them for transit. Preparing the shuttles for orbital operations. There was always something going on.

Attaching the deployment vehicles and their RDF parasites together into their deployment configurations in orbit took more days of work, with mission control supervising some of the work from the ground. They simply did not yet have enough space-capable pilots.

Justin Moore and Gavin McKay spent more time in orbit than they did on the ground during this period.

Finally, the RDF missions were assembled and the hyperspace ships were back down on the ground being prepped for their missions to Amber and Earthsea.

All they needed now was their mission profiles.

JieMin had been spending much of his time playing with his bubble model, and following his vision in selecting deployment locations for the RDF satellites. He took to using another set of bubbles one hundred and twenty-two light-years in diameter, to ensure his RDF locations were within detection range of potential colonies. He placed those bubbles to encompass as many of the possible colony locations as he could, to increase the overall rather dismal odds as much as he could.

JieMin finalized his location selections and transmitted them to John Gannet.

ChaoLi was working on the flyby approach. The original idea was to fly through the system collecting networking data. The issue was that they didn't know where in the system the planet was in its orbit. They could fly through the system on the other side of the sun from the planet, transit a hundred million or more miles away, and not pick up any data at all, even though they might have given away their existence.

The other problem was the inverse, though at lower odds. They could fly through the system closer to the planet than they intended, and be within pickup or shoot-down range of the planet and any orbital facilities it had.

They decided to play it safe, and, despite additional complication, stop a few hundred million miles out to reconnoiter the system and locate the colony planet.

The hyperspace ships would then make their high-speed flybys of the colony planets by going back into hyperspace to get closer and build their exit speed. They would only be going two million miles an hour in normal space, but that was probably enough as the hyperspace ships would be several million miles from their target planets for their flyby.

ChaoLi had her staff finalize those mission profiles and send them to John Gannet.

Monday four weeks in, Gannet pinned down Bellamy.

"So how are we doing?" John Gannet asked.

"We're pretty close actually," Chris Bellamy said. "We had to convert the mission profiles we were sent into actual instructions, and then design all the fallback responses for various scenarios, then simulate all of those to test our instruction files. We're not done, but we're close."

"When can we launch?"

Bellamy took a deep breath. Gannet knew she hated to commit – all project managers hated to commit – but time was moving on. It had been four weeks now since the groups had separated.

"Next week. I feel really good about early next week."

"Call it, Chris. I want a day."

Bellamy considered before answering.

"OK. Tuesday for the RDF deployment, Wednesday for the hyperspace ships."

"All right. You're on."

Fixing the date wasn't done without a certain amount of grumbling from the people on the project. Any time a hard date got set, it put pressure on people to move things along. And as critical events approached, the anxiety ratcheted up.

"Launch thirty-two spacecraft within two days. Sure, why not? We got anything else we can shoot up while we're at it?" one simulation tester groused over lunch.

"Well, there's really only three kinds," another said, "and all of the one are parasites to another. So, really, it's only two different kinds."

"Yeah, but they all have to be checked. All the telemetry has to be gone over. All the flight profiles checked. Memory. Computer. Checksums. The whole thing, on thirty spacecraft."

"I can't argue with that. But we'll get it done. We're close as it is."

"I hope they just do them one at a time, so if something goes south, we can pause while we check the others."

"Oh, I think they'll do that."

"These are all leaving from low Arcadia orbit, aren't they?" ChaoLi asked at her weekly meeting Friday morning with the Operations Group management.

"Yes," John Gannet said. "A hundred miles or so."

"Can we launch when they will be most visible in Arcadia City? Like just after dawn or so?"

Gannet looked to Bellamy, who consulted the orbit schedule.

"It's a ninety-minute orbit, and they should be overhead at seven-thirty and again at nine. Which is best for you?"

"With the sun on them against the dark sky, seven-thirty is probably best. Will we be able to see the JATO bottles fire off?"

"Oh, I would think so, ChaoLi," Gannet said. "When we test fired several of them, they produced a lot of smoke and steam. They should be very visible."

"Excellent. Let's do that, then. So everybody can see. We can announce it in advance, and get some great publicity."

"If everything goes according to plan, that is," Bellamy said.

"Oh, publicity is publicity," ChaoLi said. "If everything is successful, we are making great use of the public's money. If things are unsuccessful, it's because we don't have enough money. It's all in how you spin it."

Bellamy laughed.

"Well, that's your department, ChaoLi. Mine is making sure it's the former and not the latter."

On Tuesday morning, ChaoLi, JieMin, and the boys had an early breakfast and went up on the roof of the Chen apartment building to watch the launch of the deployment vehicles and their RDF satellite parasites. Rob Milbank's office had announced the launch times the night before, and there were a number of other people up on the roof and the other roofs nearby.

Also on the roof were Chen Zufu and Chen Zumu, seated on pillows on the roof. Attending them were their heirs apparent, David Bolton and Chen YongLin, who would become Chen Zufu and Chen Zumu when Chen MinChao and Jessica Chen-Jasic retired.

LeiTao and ChaoPing and their husbands DaGang and JuMing were also up on the roof for the launch.

Everyone was looking up, directly above Arcadia City, where a scatter of tiny white dots looked like salt grains spilled on the tablecloth of deep-blue sky.

"Coming up soon," JieMin said, checking the countdown in his heads-up display.

"This is very exciting," ChaoLi said.

They only had a few more minutes to wait before one of the salt grains emitted a plume of smoke and headed away from the others in a white streak. That streak stretched out for a few minutes, then it stopped, and restarted.

"Second JATO bottles ignited," JieMin said.

The streak was moving faster now, and, after a few minutes, it, too, disappeared. They could no longer see the white dot that was the deployment vehicle and its parasites.

"Too far away to see now," JieMin said.

Another salt grain erupted with a plume of smoke and headed away from the others. It, too, had a break in the plume at a few minutes, then disappeared after the second streak.

"Two away," JieMin said.

Four more times, a deployment vehicle and its parasites ignited the JATO bottles and streaked away from Arcadia. They all headed in more or less the same direction. Once they were in hyperspace, they would change course for their destinations.

After all six deployment vehicles had departed, there were only two dots remaining where there had been eight before.

"Those last two are the hyperspace ships," JieMin said. "They won't leave until tomorrow morning."

"And, without the JATO bottles, won't be anywhere near as showy," ChaoLi said.

"No. Their regular rockets are less impressive, at least from here."

Jessica's tea girl came up to them then.

"Chen Zumu requests you both attend her."

"Of course," ChaoLi said.

ChaoPing and her husband led the boys back downstairs while ChaoLi and JieMin walked across the roof to their seated superiors.

"Chen Zumu," ChaoLi said with a small bow of her head.

"Ah. ChaoLi. And JieMin. You know David Bolton and Chen YongLin, of course."

"Yes, Chen Zumu. Good morning, David. YongLin."

She bowed to them both, and they bowed back.

"I called you over to congratulate you both," Jessica said. "We are off to find the other human colonies now. That is an exciting and major accomplishment."

"Thank you, Chen Zumu," ChaoLi said. "There were many people involved in this achievement."

"Yes, of course, though none so much as you two, I think. In any case, congratulations to you both."

ChaoLi and JieMin bowed to her.

"Thank you, Chen Zumu," they both said.

All over Arcadia City, people watched the launches and cheered.

Rob Milbank and his wife Julia Whitcomb watched the

launch from the patio of their home before he headed in to the office.

Karl Huenemann watched the launch with a bunch of project people and their spouses up on the roof of the office building downtown. Huenemann supplied coffee, tea, and donuts for everyone. Wayne Porter and his wife Denise Bonheur were there, with her sister looking after the kids this morning.

At the hyperspace facility at Arcadia City Shuttleport, the sudden release of tension from the successful launches resulted in cheers. Gannet and Bellamy provided donuts, coffee, and tea for everyone, as well as a fruit punch. Many opted for the uncaffeinated fruit punch, as they would be getting to bed early again today in preparation for the launch of the hyperspace ships at dawn the next day.

After their little celebration, most headed home. Mission control would fire up again late this evening, working up to the launch of the missions to Amber and Earthsea in the morning.

Wednesday morning saw ChaoLi and JieMin back up on the roof. This launch would be much less spectacular than yesterday's, and the roof was less crowded. Their own boys were downstairs in their twelfth-floor apartment getting ready for their day. Two early days in a row had been one too many to arrange.

The Chen family management team, too, was thinner. Only Chen Zumu was on the roof this morning. She had two other pillows there and invited ChaoLi and JieMin to sit with her.

"I thought that you two would not miss this morning," she said as they sat.

"No, Chen Zumu," ChaoLi said.

"It will be less spectacular today, though, Chen Zumu,"

JieMin said. "The hyperspace ships' rocket engines are much cleaner burning, without the smoke plume, and they are smaller. They burn for a longer time - seventy-five minutes - and the ship's velocity will actually be greater than that imparted to the deployment vehicles by the JATO bottles, but it will be a much less spectacular launch."

"So I understand," Jessica said.

Waiting for the launch, they could see the last two little dots now, bright against the still-dark sky in the light of the rising sun. JieMin was watching the countdown in his heads-up display.

"Less than a minute now," he said.

When the first hyperspace ship launched, the little dot got a bit brighter, then started, slowly, to move away from its companion. It accelerated, but at nowhere near the rate of the deployment vehicles yesterday. It continued to move off, gaining speed as it went.

Then the second dot grew brighter, and started off after its sibling. It was falling behind the first launch, whose speed had been steadily growing, but it was also on its way.

"And tomorrow they make their hyperspace transition," Jessica said.

"Yes, Chen Zumu," JieMin said. "And then Friday the deployment vehicles will make theirs."

"Remarkable," Jessica said. "I am happy to have lived to see this day."

Jessica lowered her head to look at the two.

"It will be another two years or so before MinChao and I retire. Perhaps on the one-hundred-twenty-fifth anniversary of the colony. In three years. I hope to see a hyperspace vessel completed before I retire."

"That should be about the right timeframe, Chen Zumu,"

Chao Li said.

Jessica nodded.

"The design of this vessel is our new priority," Jessica said. "We need to make sure the mundanities are taken care of as well as the exciting bits."

"In what way, Chen Zumu?" ChaoLi asked.

"Supply of the vessel. Getting passengers to and from the vessel. How we mass-produce such vessels so the first one isn't the only one. We cannot afford to hand-build them all. These are the things you two need to concentrate on now. The exciting bits will be taken care of by others. You two need to make sure the more mundane essentials are covered as well."

"Yes, Chen Zumu," ChaoLi said. "We will take care of it."

Jessica nodded.

"Well, that's as much jiggling of your elbow as I'm going to do today," she said with a smile. "Thank you for sitting with me this morning."

"Of course, Chen Zumu."

On Thursday, mission control noted the loss of carrier on each of the hyperspace ships in turn as they reached the safe transition distance and began their journeys to Amber and Earthsea.

On Friday, mission control noted the loss of carrier on all six of the deployment vehicles in turn as they reached the safe transition distance and began their journeys to their deployment locations for the RDF satellites.

Once those transitions occurred, the operations group was at loose ends for at least three months.

All the playtoys were on deployment.

# Mundanities And Vision

It was another Monday morning kickoff meeting of sorts at the operations group. Gannet was on the floor.

"OK, everybody. That was great work. In six weeks, we got everything buttoned up, all the mission profiles loaded, and everything out the door.

"Now we have at least three months before anything comes back. Meanwhile, the design group is downtown drawing up plans for the big hyperspace vessel.

"What do you think are the chances the blue-sky types are going to design a vessel that can be serviced, loaded with cargo and passengers, keep its passengers alive, and actually be operated at a profit?"

Gannet waited for the laughter and the shouts of 'zero chance' to die down before continuing.

"Right. Well, it turns out I agree with you.

"So what we are going to be doing while we wait for all our wayward children to return, eh?

"I'll tell you what we're going to do. We're going to draw up a set of requirements for the hyperspace vessel to accommodate those needs. How much supplies? How does the crew get at them? How do they get carried aboard? How do the passengers get carried aboard? How do they embark and debark in zero gravity? What are the environmental requirements?

"There are a lot of questions that need to be asked and answered before any ship can be built that will actually prove useful.

"And there's one more question. How do we build a bunch

of these ships, without having to assemble them all in space, by hand? The first one perhaps, but after that?

"So have at it everyone. What questions need to be asked and answered before we can sign off on the design of a large hyperspace vessel?

"Because they may have the design, but we have the signoff."

Karl Huenemann had encouraged Gannet to provide him with the operations group's requirements as they were being assembled, so the design group could start building in such considerations from the start. He got the first list of questions and possible answers two weeks after Gannet's challenge to the operations group, and passed them on to the design group.

Wayne Porter looked at the requirements in dismay. So many things he hadn't thought about!

A couple of them really threw him. The hyperspace drive had to be located on the center of mass – or near it – so the resulting thrust wouldn't just spin the ship in circles. So much for the open tube design.

How did the crew get supplies into the ship? Presumably the supplies came up in containers. Did they transfer supplies into internal holds while in zero gravity? That didn't sound like a lot of fun. If not, how did they get into the containers while under way?

Same question for passengers, really. How did they get into the ship in zero gravity? At least some of them could be assumed to have never been in space before. Worse than herding cats, it was herding floating cats.

He was at something of a loss when he got a meeting request from Professor Chen JieMin, at the university. He had seen Professor Chen at the restaurant two months ago, the day he received his promotion to the design group. Professor Chen requested a meeting in Porter's office, so Porter sent an acknowledgement and waited, not knowing what the famed mathematician could possibly want.

JieMin took the elevator down to the third floor, walked from the Chen Hall of Science through the pedestrian bridge across First Street to the main university building, through that building to a second pedestrian bridge across Quant Boulevard, and on into the original downtown office building.

He took the elevator up to the design group's floor, and walked directly to Wayne Porter's office. Once JieMin had visualized Arcadia City as a three-dimensional grid system, when he first got to the city from the Chen family's tea farms in Chagu, he never got lost or needed directions to anywhere.

Porter's office door was open, and he was in, looking into the three-dimensional display in the far end of the office. JieMin tapped on the doorframe.

Porter spun around and leapt to his feet.

"Professor Chen," Porter said, and made a little bow.

JieMin returned his bow.

"Call me JieMin, please, Mr. Porter. I hope I'm not interrupting."

"No, no, not at all, Prof– JieMin. And please call me Wayne."

Porter seemed at a loss for a moment.

"Uh, have a seat."

"Thank you, Wayne."

They both sat, and JieMin looked curiously at what was in the display. It was another spaceship design, in its early stages. It didn't look promising.

"I'm trying to come up with a design that meets all the requirements coming out of the operations group," Porter said, gesturing at the screen. "It's harder than I thought."

"That's what I wanted to chat with you about," JieMin said. "I rather like the hollow cylinder design. It's a good design, and I think it has great promise."

"But there are a lot of problems with that one, JieMin. The thrust of the hyperspace generator is off-center, there's no way to get at provisions under way – lots of problems."

"Can you bring that cylinder design up for me?"

"Of course."

Porter used his heads-up display to change the view to the design Huenemann had showed everyone weeks ago during the kickoff meeting.

"Yes, that's it," JieMin said. "What I was wondering is whether the cylinder has to be an open tube to get the benefits of the design, or if it could be closed on just one end. The rear, say."

"Close it off? Like this?"

Porter converted the rendering to wireframe, connected several points, and tagged the planes between them. When he switched it back to a rendering, there was now a bulkhead across the rear of the cylinder.

"Yes, but make it a volume, rather than a bulkhead. Perhaps fifteen percent of the ship's length."

"OK."

Back in wireframe, Porter duplicated the new bulkhead, slid the copy forward, and rendered again.

"Yes. Yes, that's it. One more thing if you would. Can you slide that volume forward ten percent of the ship's length?"

In wireframe, Porter slide his two previous additions forward and rendered again. Porter stared at the rendering, spun it around on a vertical axis. JieMin sat and watched him.

"Well, now the hyperspace generator could be located in

that new volume, which gets rid of the off-center thrust problem," Porter said.

"And if you put containers around that small extension in the back?" JieMin asked.

Porter stared into the display, then started.

"Of course! The containers could be up against the bulkhead. Some sort of sealing mechanism, and those containers could be accessed from inside the ship. Same with water containers. Just put the plumbing on one end."

"Environmental, as well," JieMin said.

"Yes. Yes, of course. The environmental filters could be in containers and used where they are. When they need to be changed out, just swap them for fresh and renew them on the ground."

Porter added containers around the back extension of the cylinder.

"We still have the passenger issues," he said.

"I have one thing to show you on that," JieMin said.

JieMin pushed him a rendering of the passenger containers that the original colonists had been moved to Arcadia in. Porter opened it up in his heads-up display, then put it in an inset in the display volume.

"The original colonists to Arcadia were transported in these," JieMin said. "They remained strapped in throughout the zero-gravity of the transit, and only emerged once they were on the planet."

"Transport the passengers the whole way in containers?" Porter asked.

He stared at the display for several seconds, while JieMin said nothing.

"No, of course not! Leave them in the containers until there's enough spin built up to move them safely in artificial gravity.

They can just unbelt from their seats and walk into the ship."

Porter looked to JieMin, who was nodding.

"As I said," JieMin said, "it's a good design, Wayne. Start from there and see where you get."

JieMin got up, and Porter jumped up from his chair.

"Thank you so much, JieMin. Thanks for the help."

JieMin waved a hand in a brushing away gesture.

"You would have gotten there, I think. You have vision, Wayne. Real vision. Don't get bogged down in details. Release your vision, and see where it takes you. Then handle the details."

After JieMin left, Porter set to it with a vengeance. He adjusted the distance of the aft bulkhead from the aft edge of the cylinder to be the optimum length for containers. He adjusted the thickness of the new volume between the bulkheads to accommodate the nuclear power plant and the hyperspace drive. He sketched up passenger containers with the entry/exit doors in the end of the container so they would be in the right place to interface to the aft bulkhead.

Porter then sat back and let his mind run with the design. He imagined shuttles bringing up cargo containers, supply containers, people containers. Usually those containers were brought up in blocks, four across and two rows high.

How would that work with the circular shape of the inside of the cylinder? Then again, why was the inside of the cylinder a circle? Would it not be better to have it be a polygon, with sides at least as long as four containers were wide? Then the containers would lay flat on the surface.

Even better, have the sides be longer than the width of four containers. Cargo was often two rows of containers deep. If the sides of the polygon were wider than four containers, then eight containers could be on each side and just barely touch at their upper edge. With that in place, how would the next rows of containers be mounted?

What about the connections for the supplies containers in what he now thought of as aft storage, as opposed to the cargo storage in the front recess of the cylinder? Those may be brought up in four-wide by two-high blocks as well. Supplies, environmental filters, water, passenger containers.

Porter started adding plumbing connections, environmental connections, and airlocks to the aft bulkhead. He was imagining the processes involved.

Wait! One more. There had to be at least one nuclear power plant. Maybe more than one. Those could be containerized, too, rather than built into the ship. Would it not be better to service those on the planet, rather than do it in space, while the vessel was out of commission? How about two plants? Swap them out one at a time, so the ship retained power, then service them planetside.

Porter worked through lunch without noticing, and was shocked when people started saying good night to him through his open office door as they headed home at the end of the day. He tore himself away from his design at that point and headed home himself.

Porter was somewhat distant that night at dinner, and he apologized to Denise for being distracted.

That evening, he stared out the window of their apartment, watching in his mind's eye as passenger and cargo shuttles serviced the big hyperspace vessel against the night sky.

The next day Porter was back at it. He incorporated some enhancements he had seen in his vision the night before. He added textures and slight color variations.

Porter then imported models of cargo shuttles and containers. He started generating different types of container. A supply container, with an airlock-mating door in one end. A water container with piping connections. A powerplant container with electrical connections. An environmental container, with air-tight connections for air circulation.

Porter also imported the model of the passenger container of a hundred and twenty years before, that had ferried the colonists to Arcadia. He modified it to have the airlock doors in the front of the container, doing all the detail work he had raced past yesterday.

Porter then built an animation of the hyperspace ship being serviced. It was in three dimensions, with cargo shuttles loading up the forward cargo space as well as the aft supplies space. He annotated it with legends below so the viewer could tell what was being done at each point.

It took several days to get all the textures right, all the movements right, all the lighting and shadows right. At the end, though, Porter had an animation of the hyperspace vessel being serviced and the passengers being delivered. He watched it several times through with a critical eye, then sent it on to his boss and project management.

Porter also sent a courtesy copy to Professor Chen JieMin, attached to a short 'Thank you' note.

JieMin received the 'Thank you' note from Porter, then opened the attachment in the display in his office.

It was breathtaking. JieMin felt like he was adrift in space, watching from a distance as shuttles approached the huge vessel and delivered their cargoes. The polygonal cross-section of the cargo volume was new, and puzzled him until he saw shuttles delivering four-across container payloads. That was a nice trick there.

The simulation could be pivoted around. JieMin turned the display to watch the loading of supplies in the aft container space. He noted the dedicated spots for water, electric, and environmental containers, as well as the spots with gasketed air-tight doors for cargo and passenger containers.

Very nice.

JieMin sent a short note back to Porter congratulating him on his work, and encouraging him to keep it up.

"Hey, Mikhail," Huenemann called to Borovsky. "Did you see Porter's latest work?"

"Yes. I think he has most of the issues handled."

"So do I. It's fuckin' great. We should send it out to Gannet and Bellamy, don't you think?"

Borovsky thought for a few seconds.

"Yes, I think we probably should," he said. "I think it's far enough along, I'd like to know from them what they think isn't covered yet."

"All right. Done."

Huenemann clapped his hands.

"Now we gotta engineer it all. All the little bits and details. I love that part."

Borovsky chuckled and shook his head.

Huenemann was just, well, Huenemann.

Gannet and Bellamy both got the mail from Huenemann. They sat together to watch the attachment in the big display in the conference room.

"Well, I guess it's time to see the latest whiz-bang design from downtown that completely ignores our needs."

Bellamy chuckled.

"Well, you never know," she said. "Maybe they have something that does everything we want."

"Yeah, but what are the odds?"

They watched the simulation through three times before they were done.

"I'll be damned," Gannet said. "They got everything in there."

"All our big-ticket items, anyway," Bellamy said. "I think we ought to distribute this to the operations staff and see if they come up with anything they're missing."

"One thing I can come up with is the chillers for the hyperspace generator. Containerize those, too, like the nuclear powerplants, and we can service them on the planet."

"I'll circulate the simulation and start a list. But I think they're pretty close."

"I do, too," Gannet said. "Somebody down there got religion, in a really big way."

He shook his head.

"Surprised the hell out of me," he said.

# Details, Details, Details

Of course, having a basic ship design in hand left thousands upon thousands of details to be decided.

How many crew? How many passengers? How many cabins? How many staterooms? How would they be laid out within the volume of the ship? How would wastewater treatment be handled? Would water be recycled?

It went on and on. Rather than having worked himself out of a job, Wayne Porter had guaranteed his job security. With a workable overall design, there were a near-infinite number of design details to work out.

Months passed as they refined the design. Pushed forward and then fell back in their efforts as some things panned out while others didn't.

It was high-stakes engineering, and Karl Huenemann was in his element, with Wayne Porter hammering out design after design for the interior spaces of the big ship and the engineers working out the stresses and the structure.

ChaoPing, now twenty years old, had her first baby, a boy, named LingTao. Three months later, LeiTao, just turned seventeen, had her first baby, a girl, named XiPing.

ChaoLi and JieMin settled into their role as grandparents with ease. It had not been so long ago, after all, that they had had their own children. Arcadia's large families and early marriage made for young grandparents, as well as young aunts and uncles. Uncle JieJun was only nine years old.

"Congratulations, ChaoLi. Again," Jessica said.

"Thank you, Chen Zumu."

"You may proceed with your progress report."

"Thank you, Chen Zumu."

ChaoLi gathered her thoughts, then jumped in.

"The engineering and design work on the hyperspace vessel is going well. The overall hull design is working out well, and they don't anticipate any changes in that as they go forward."

"So it will look like the simulation we have seen?" MinChao asked.

"Yes, Chen Zufu."

"Excellent."

He waved a hand for her to continue.

"We are anticipating the return of the hyperspace ship from Amber soon. It had the shorter distance to travel. The hyperspace ship from Earthsea should return a few days later."

"And we are prepared to start analyzing their network data?" Jessica asked.

"Yes, Chen Zumu. We do not anticipate any problems there. We started from the same tech base, and encoding methods tend to be sticky."

Jessica nodded.

"The hyperspace ships will then be ready for additional trips. Do you intend to send one to vet Earth in the same manner as Amber and Earthsea?"

"No," MinChao said. "No, not yet, I don't think. We will hold them and await the finding of other colonies. We can also use them to carry messages to Amber and Earthsea if we wish. Set up some preliminary communications."

"I don't understand, Chen Zufu. I would think vetting Earth would be a priority."

Jessica took a deep breath and let it out slowly.

"That was my decision, ChaoLi. Earth and the colonies are not peers. There may be some feelings of ownership toward the colonies there. And Earth has a very checkered history."

ChaoLi looked puzzled. Jessica frowned, trying to put her thoughts into words.

"Consider, ChaoLi. Would young people rather go to the beach with their peers or their parents?"

"With their peers, Chen Zumu. I think I see."

"So we will establish communications with our peers first, ChaoLi. Make friends in the neighborhood, if you will. Then we will deal with Earth. It isn't going anywhere. But approaching it as a group will be a better strategy, I think."

"I understand, Chen Zumu."

Three months after launch, in February 2368, the first hyperspace ship came back, from Amber. It started dumping the recordings it had made of Amber's networks and other radio traffic while it was still en route to Arcadia.

The operations group started analyzing the data while waiting for the hyperspace ship to land. The entire data package wouldn't be available until the ship landed and they could use higher-speed access methods than the ship's radio.

The operations group necessarily had a lot of communications people for contact with their spacecraft, all of whom were at loose ends at the moment. They confirmed the protocols used were unchanged from those they had all set out from Earth with, and decoded the raw signals the flyby had recorded into data streams.

In analyzing the full package once the ship landed, they were quickly in over their heads. John Gannet sent the decoded data streams package to ChaoLi.

ChaoLi called an extraordinary meeting in the conference room of her offices downtown. Attending were Professor Chen JieMin from the university, Chen MinYan from Chen JongJu's accounting team, and Prime Minister Rob Milbank from the Arcadia government.

"Thanks for coming, everybody," ChaoLi said. "We have a very large analysis problem to do, and we need to get it right. It has technical, financial, and governmental aspects involved, so I need to work with all of you to get this done."

"Sure, ChaoLi. What's going on?" Milbank asked.

"We have the data capture back from the Amber colony. The communications people confirmed it was encoded the same way ours is, a legacy of our common tech base, and decoded it into data streams. We now have a capture of a very large chunk of network data from Amber. several hours worth of planetary communications.

"Now this is all routine traffic, right? It's not someone dictating to us all the things we want to know. It's all the unencrypted data of everyday life on Amber. News wire articles. Public forums. People sending each other their favorite recipes. The kids' school schedules.

"What we need to do is try to glean from that slice of everyday routine what their situation is."

ChaoLi gestured to Milbank.

"What their government is like."

She gestured to MinYan.

"What their economy is like."

She gestured to JieMin.

"What their technology is like.

"We don't know anything about them except they started from the same position as us, and with the same resources. Where they took that, where they went with it, we don't know.

"In particular, we need to decide whether these are people we can deal with, in terms of setting up a friendly relationship. Can we trade with them? Can we safely have people go back and forth between here and there? Can we set up diplomatic relations? Or do we say, 'Wow, these people are really messed up,' and have nothing to do with them. Just leave them be.

"We don't know, and we need to know before we initiate contact with them."

ChaoLi looked back and forth at the others. They were all nodding. She turned to Milbank.

"Your part of this may be easiest, Rob. The news wires will surely have information about what the government is up to. The politics channels should give you some good information to work with."

Milbank nodded.

"And I have just the group to look into it," he said. "We've been expecting this sooner or later, and I've collected some good people into that group in anticipation. They have other duties, of course, but nothing of this priority. They're my forward-looking policy group, and they're perfect for figuring this out."

"Excellent. And the financial side shouldn't be too hard," ChaoLi said to MinYan. "The business channels will have lots of data and analysis. Pulling together the big picture from lots of little details makes it involved but straightforward, I think."

"Yes, we shouldn't have trouble with that," MinYan said. "It sounds like fun, actually."

ChaoLi nodded, then turned to JieMin.

"The hardest part of this is yours, I think, JieMin. People don't write about the technology they currently have. It becomes part of the environment, part of the background. I'm not sure how to approach the problem, and that I'll leave up to you."

JieMin nodded. She was right, he knew. Technology writers wrote about not what was happening, or what had happened, but what might happen in the future. Getting a good idea of where they were would not be straightforward. ChaoLi was relying, he knew, on his ability to pull the essential elements out of a large mass of data.

"We'll dig into it and see where we get," he said.

"All right. Good."

ChaoLi looked up and down the group.

"I've just sent you all a pointer to the data stream repository for Amber. We're all working off one big master copy.

"I've also set up an account you and your people can access to post your findings. Be on the lookout for things that would be of help to each other, like some government policy being debated to regulate some new technology, or some financial news about some technology company or government policy under consideration. Things that bleed across your areas.

"And don't forget. Keep records of what works and what doesn't work in your analysis, because once we have a handle on this, we get to do it all over again.

"The data from Earthsea comes in next week."

Rob Milbank had a spring in his step as he crossed the pedestrian bridge over Arcadia Boulevard between the downtown office building and the administrative building.

Some people might consider it strange that the manager of the hyperspace project could call the prime minister of the planet to a meeting and hand out assignments. But it wasn't that way at all.

The hyperspace project was a government project, heavily funded by the government and working to the government's goals. More, it was Rob Milbank's pet project, his big dream for Arcadia. That it was being carried out under contract by the Chen, rather than by the bureaucracy, was a big bonus. It meant it would actually get done.

And finally, Chen ChaoLi, Chen JieMin, Chen MinChao, and Jessica Chen-Jasic were Rob Milbank's friends. He had known the couple who had become Chen Zufu and Chen Zumu for decades by this point, and he had grown close to Chen ChaoLi and Chen JieMin during the years of the project.

So rather than being miffed, Milbank was delighted. His project was paying off now. Delivering real results.

The end goal? Diplomatic and trade relations with at least two more human planets.

And Rob Milbank was in the perfect position to ensure some asshole in the bureaucracy didn't fuck it up.

JieMin went back to his office and considered the data streams repository.

The highest bandwidth input to the human mind was vision. The eyes were actually direct extensions of the brain, and the brain had a whole processing unit – the visual cortex, paradoxically located at the back of the skull – dedicated to interpreting visual input.

JieMin set his display to project just the images from the data stream, one after the other, on two-second intervals.

He sat in his office and stared into the display, watching the images from that other planet, Amber, three thousand light-years away.

Chen MinYan went back to her accounting group and called her team leads Chen JieLing and Chen FangTao into her office.

"We have a new assignment. A short-term, high-priority

one. They have data back from the colony planet Amber. It's whatever they managed to suck up from the airwaves as they did a flyby of the planet.

"We need to analyze those streams and get a picture of what their economy is like.

"I think there's three areas that would give us a good picture of what is going on over there. First, what kinds of companies do they have that we don't? That would tell us where they've exceeded us, or at least have activity we don't. Second, what kinds of companies do we have that they don't? That would tell us where we've exceeded them, or at least have activity they don't.

"The third thing is to compare the companies where we both have activity. What are their relative sizes? We can compare prices of goods and services to get a correction factor for the value of the currency.

"All those differences could be indicators of trade potential, and that's one of the things we're looking for. The other is the overall state of their economy. The per-capita GDP.

"We all good on that?"

"No problem, MinYan," JieLing said.

"Sounds good to me, MinYan," FangTao said.

"All right, then," MinYan said. "Let's get everyone started."

When Rob Milbank got back to the office, he had a couple other things on his schedule, but at his first break he called the head of his forward-looking policy group to his office. Darius Mikenas arrived about five minutes later.

"All right, Darius," Milbank said. "This is the big assignment. The data from Amber is here. I want you and your team to go through it and prepare me a full briefing on the political aspects you can find out from it. Structure of the government, who's in power, what their policies are, how secure they are in their position, bios on all the major players. Everything you can find out from what we have."

"Understood, sir. We can handle that."

"This is front burner. Everything else can wait. And next week we get the data from Earthsea, and I'm going to want the same thing."

"We have it, sir. We won't disappoint."

"Excellent."

# About Amber

When JieMin hit an interesting picture in his scanning, he sometimes stopped to see if it was the illustration for an article. He might read the article – or rather, have the display read it to him – or not. He might follow up on that article, looking to see if there were others related to it, or not. He just sort of followed his nose.

JieMin also occasionally looked in on the shared scratch space to see if the other teams had found anything interesting. One of the major economic areas the accounting team reported for which Arcadia had no analog was medical nanotechnology, with companies with evocative names like MedNano.

JieMin found the name compelling, and searched the data streams for it. Then he searched on nano-technology, and finally on nanites.

When he had run that trail down, JieMin went back to his previous scanning. He had no idea what he was looking for. Was not, in fact, looking for anything in particular, other than to gather enough input to trigger an integration.

Another interesting side investigation was into political affairs. The government team had unearthed an overview of Amber's government's evolution since the colony was founded. They also found some demographic data on the colony.

JieMin reviewed those findings as well, then moved on.

The hyperspace ship that had done the flyby of Earthsea came in eight days after the Amber flyby ship. It also began downloading data as soon as it emerged from hyperspace. This download was curious though, in that the package had a lot more local radio traffic and much less traffic back and forth to communications satellites.

They wouldn't be able to piece that together until the ship landed and the entire package could be downloaded.

The Earthsea flyby ship was still on its way to Arcadia when ChaoLi called a meeting to summarize what they had learned of Amber.

ChaoLi knew JieMin had had an integration the night before. He had spent much of the evening in the big armchair scribbling in his notebook and consulting his heads-up display. With the Earthsea data imminent, it was probably worth seeing what JieMin and the others had come up with on Amber.

The attendees were the same as before, ChaoLi, JieMin, MinYan, and Milbank.

"So what have we found out?" ChaoLi asked. "Who wants to start?"

MinYan, JieMin, and Milbank all looked back and forth at each other, then Milbank shrugged.

"I guess I can start," he said.

He consulted his heads-up display, then launched into a précis of the Amber government.

"The initial colony governor on Amber did not consolidate power as Mark Kendall did here. He began working toward a representative government only ten years' into the colony's development. They had their equivalent to our Charter over thirty years before we did. It is similar, in that it was also derived from proposals in the colony headquarters archives.

"He also spent considerable sums on the hospital and university from the get-go. Where the Kendall governments spent money on aggrandizing themselves and the government itself, Amber's initial colony governor – one Adrian Jansen – spent money on higher education and medical research.

"Their earlier establishment of their current government has had some downsides, too. Their government has grown monotonically since that earlier date, and is now larger than ours by quite a bit. Our big reset under Matt Chen-Jasic has us earlier on the flight path they're following now.

"So their bureaucracy is bigger. Their government exercises some powers over their citizenry that we would consider unacceptable, and their civil rights have been somewhat more curtailed."

"Our big reset, as you call it, taught us a lesson that stuck, then," ChaoLi said.

"Yes, at least to a certain extent. As I say, we're earlier in the same flight path, but we're tending the same way as societal memory of the Kendall regime fades."

ChaoLi nodded.

"And their government's structure?"

Milbank shrugged.

"Similar to ours. As I say, they started from the same core document from the colony headquarters. They have an elected president, though, so their legislature and their executive are more often at loggerheads than we are here. Sometimes people vote in an executive of one party and a legislature of the other. Divided government.

"That doesn't happen here. Which is not to say that I and the House and Chamber agree on everything, but the House and I are usually on the same page on most items, since they elect me. On Amber, that's not so.

"As for the current president, he seems a competent sort, and he currently has his legislature behind him. They're not fighting at the moment – not in any big way – and the government is pretty united on most things.

"The big issue for us, though, is that they are a democratic republic similar to us, and a trade and diplomatic relationship is possible."

"Excellent," ChaoLi said, and turned to MinYan. "What about their economy?"

"They're similar to us, but with some interesting differences. The overall GDP per capita is about the same, once you correct for the valuation difference in the currency, and they have the same amount of workers as a percentage of the population.

"Their average age is a bit higher than ours. Their life expectancy is quite a bit higher, apparently, and people join the workforce at a higher age, so they have the same percentage of workers, but in a higher age range.

"Their population is a bit larger than ours, and again that's due to the increased life expectancy.

"As for differences within the economy, there are some areas where they are more advanced than us, technologically. Medical technology is one big area. This may be due to them getting an earlier start on serious funding for the university and hospital, resulting in a more developed medical research capability.

"They are behind us, obviously, on space flight and especially hyperspace, concentrating their efforts primarily on communications satellites and the like. They don't have anything we found that is an analog to our hyperspace project."

ChaoLi nodded.

"Thank you for that. Sounds like there must be some things we can trade for there. That longer life span is interesting."

She turned to JieMin.

"What about their technology?"

"The medical technology is most interesting, as you say. They have apparently developed a nanite technology for treating certain long-term degradations of the body.

"Primary among these is heart disease and stroke, though they also have cures for some forms of cancer and are working on cures for the others. There has also been progress made in battling various forms of dementia, including Alzheimer's Disease and senile dementia, although the cures are spotty at this point."

"Spotty?" ChaoLi asked.

"They work for some people and not for others. It looks like rather than one disease, there is more of a group of diseases, and the cure works or does not work depending on which one of them you have."

"I see. What else?"

"There are some cultural and economic things that came out of my search.

"There are some aspects of their economy that are larger than ours, because they cater to that older population. There is also some difference in the relative costs of items, due to the lack of relatively more inexpensive young workers. Almost all the workforce is adult, and wages at the bottom reflect that.

"On the cultural front, average age at marriage and at having a first child has trended upward a bit, and is perhaps two years higher than here on Arcadia.

"One other interesting cultural difference is that there is a nudity taboo on Amber that is very different than Arcadia, and is more like Earth was when the colonies left."

"They have laws against nudity?" ChaoLi asked.

"And toplessness for women. But I get the impression it's not so much a matter of law as it is that it's something one simply doesn't do. It's a cultural thing.

"It wasn't that way in the beginning of the colony, for much the same reasons as here on Arcadia. The remoteness of shower and laundry facilities in the early period of the colony, combined with the cost of clothing.

"But their government's emphasis on getting civil society up and running early on – with things like democratic government, higher education, and medical research – also exhibited itself in the speed with which residential plumbing became available. When it did, people reverted to their Earth behaviors."

"Whereas the Kendall government's emphasis on central facilities delayed residential plumbing until acceptance of nudity on Arcadia was culturally frozen?" ChaoLi asked.

"That's just my conclusion, though it's pretty solid, I think. They had residential plumbing much sooner than we did. That much is clear. And Earth-standard norms of behavior reasserted themselves."

"Interesting. And they wear clothes to go swimming?"

"Oh, yes," JieMin said. "There are some pictures of their beaches in the data stream. A news wire article on the completion of some project to build updated cabanas for changing into one's swimsuit. The pictures of the beach were startling for the difference with Arcadia. Everybody on the beach is wearing clothes."

"So the Kendall government is the reason nudity is accepted on Arcadia? More than a little irony there."

"Yes, and that acceptance was solidified by Kevin Kendall's attempt to outlaw nudity and the Chen's rejection of the ban. Due to Kendall's nascent tyranny trying to ban it, public nudity became a symbol of political and personal freedom."

"As the twig is bent, so grows the tree, huh?'

"Always," Milbank said.

"Well, there's something to watch out for in our negotiations, Rob," ChaoLi said. "We don't want to have our negotiating team all show up in lavalavas and nothing else. At least not if there are women involved. What else do you have, JieMin?"

"They do not have a tea culture as we do here. On Arcadia, if you go to a business meeting, people will normally offer you tea. This is mostly the Chens' doing, as the Chen family brought dozens of different varieties of tea with them from Earth.

"On Amber, if you go to a business meeting, they will offer you coffee."

"Ugh. Coffee is terrible," ChaoLi said.

"Yes, the few varieties we have here are. But, much as with the Chen, some enterprising family from South America brought dozens of varieties of coffee with them to Amber, and the skills of knowing how to properly grow, harvest, and roast it. It is the dominant drink. If you go to a business meeting there, you are offered coffee."

"I predict if trade is established, coffee will become a luxury drink here, and tea will become a luxury drink there," MinYan said. "With the additional cost of interstellar shipping, each will become the luxury drink on the other planet."

"And a tremendous source of trade that will be," ChaoLi said. "Together with their nanites. What counters the nanites? What's the corresponding trade item?"

"Interstellar freight itself," Milbank said. "It's our ships plying that route, don't forget."

"Of course," ChaoLi said. "Anything else, JieMin?"

"One other thing so far. They have more usage of autodrive cars and less of buses than we do. I suspect that is part and parcel of the difference in average ages."

ChaoLi nodded.

"That makes sense, too," she said. "Anything else so far?"

ChaoLi scanned the other attendees.

"All right. Good work, everybody. I'll watch for your written reports. And the Earthsea information ought to be available to your groups tomorrow or the next day."

MinChao and Jessica talked about the Amber findings after they had a chance to read the written reports ChaoLi sent on to them.

"Coffee. Can you imagine?" MinChao said in a tone approaching disgust.

"Well, it was the drink of choice in many Earth cultures, if not the eastern ones," Jessica said. "There has to be some attraction to it. I wonder what a good cup of coffee would taste like."

"Not like any we have here, that's for sure. And a nudity taboo, if not an outright statutory ban?"

"There we are the outlier, I think. We may find no other colony planet with our attitudes on that subject. From JieMin's analysis, it may be an outgrowth of the Kendall regime and its overthrow. Most human cultures have had similar taboos."

MinChao snorted.

"It seems primitive to me," he said. "A cultural taboo."

"They will probably consider nudity acceptance primitive. Historically, the human cultures without a nudity taboo, like the Australian aborigines, were decidedly primitive."

MinChao nodded.

"That's all the minor stuff, though," he said. "The medical nanites is something else entirely."

"Agreed. That is definitely a technology – or at least a

product – we want to purchase. There the failure of the Kendall regime hurt us badly. We started out fifty years behind. More, if you consider what we lost and had to regain, such as the education losses due to lack of communicators for our young people."

"Yes, those bastards really hurt us there. Well, hopefully Rob can negotiate a trade deal that works for everybody."

"I hope so. I wonder who he will send."

"Send?"

"He can't go on a months-long expedition to Amber. He's going to have to send someone to negotiate the deal. I hope he has someone up to the task."

In his office downtown, Prime Minister Milbank was considering the same question.

# About Earthsea

The Earthsea data stream package came in the next day, and the three groups all had the same assignments as before.

When JieMin started to analyze the data – looking, as he had before with the Amber data, at all the pictures – he noticed he was getting multiple copies of each picture. As many as a dozen or more copies. Clicking through to the articles, again they were exact copies, and with the same timestamp.

That explained why the Earthsea data stream package was so much bigger than the Amber one. What JieMin could not explain was the reason for multiple transmission of the same data.

On Arcadia, most radio traffic was to and from the big antenna farm on the administration building downtown. Radio contact to the far locations of the colony was line-of-sight, sometimes to a low peak on the horizon. Even in Chagu, they had direct communication to Arcadia City from a low peak whose summit was visible from both locations.

When farther cities were established, the colony was far enough along to send up a communications satellite as a repeater for those distant cities, all of whom were in the same hemisphere.

Amber had apparently taken a similar path.

Why had Earthsea not done the same?

JieMin set the big computer at the university to de-duping the Earthsea data stream, and posted a note on the shared scratch space for Earthsea that the process was under way.

Meanwhile, JieMin went back to scanning pictures. While he

scanned, he was keeping an eye out for one thing in particular: a map of the colony. Maybe there was something specific about Earthsea that encouraged the multiple transmissions.

Darius Mikena was looking at the political aspects of Earthsea. What was their government like? He noted the multiple copies of most things in the data stream package, but found it no more than a curiosity.

Earthsea had a wildly different government than Amber or Arcadia. The planetary government ruling body was a council with a rotating chairmanship. This was not the council that had been established with the founding of the colony, however. Those council members had been the heads of various subject areas of the colony – food, housing, medical, and the like.

On Earthsea, the council was composed of representatives from the various city-states into which the colony was divided. Their votes were multiplied by the number of people in each city-state before being tallied, so it was still a democracy, if a weirdly structured one.

The chairman of the council was not the executive, however. The executive, called the Director, was elected by the council and ruled for ten years, absent the council voting to relieve him. His powers were very limited, as most government powers were retained by the city-states.

It seemed a bizarre arrangement for a colony to Mikena, but it was his job to write a description, not a critique.

MinYan's group was also working through the data on Earthsea. They also noticed the duplicate messages, but thought nothing of it. Some artifact of the data collection.

Their analysis of the business and economic aspects was something else again. Unlike Arcadia, the city-states of

Earthsea all had manufacturing economies. On Arcadia, manufacturing was centered south of Arcadia City, where the metafactories built new factories for manufacturing.

What did they do on Earthsea? Transport metafactories somehow? How?

They also noticed the Earthsea economy had a larger transportation sector than Amber or Arcadia did, though it was focused on shuttles as opposed to trucks and buses. Also barges, which Arcadia used to ship things, especially bulk commodities to cities up and down the coast. But much smaller truck and bus segments.

One final thing they noted. Earthsea had some companies for which Arcadia had no analog. It was a segment of the communications industry. Earthsea had no satellite communications sector. Instead, they had some other sector that manufactured long-distance radios.

JieMin was keeping up with the other groups' findings on the shared scratch space in between scanning millions of images himself. Then he found it in the data stream. A map of the colony.

The map was intended to show the extent of a couple of wildfires in the mountains, but it showed the whole colony on a sort of three-dimensional map. JieMin gasped when he saw it.

The colony was built into niches in a huge mountain range. Here a city, there a city, wherever you could fit one.

As for the capital, imagine Denver surrounded on three side by the Rockies, and bounded on the east by the ocean. The capital had grown until it filled the space it had. Other cities had taken up the growth of the colony in large parks in the mountains, like North Park or South Park in the Rockies. They, too had filled the available space.

Compare this with Arcadia. Arcadia City was bounded by the east-west chain of the Blue Mountains to the north, and by the sea to the east, but rolling hills and plains stretched away from the city on the west and south. The capital's satellite cities dotted those plains and hills for hundreds of miles.

In contrast, all through the mountains on Earthsea, and on coastal plains north and south, there were scattered the cities – city-states, he supposed – of the colony. With all the colonies approaching a hundred twenty-five years since settlement, they were all approaching the twenty-million population mark.

And none of the city-states of Earthsea looked to be more than about half a million people. Of necessity, some of their land area in each city-state had to be given over to growing crops. Cows could be pastured in some pretty rough country, but mechanized farming required flat fields.

The limited land area of any one location had limited the size of any one city, so they had built a lot of them.

JieMin went back over the findings of the other groups, considering them in light of what he now knew of the topography and the layout of Earthsea.

The emphasis on shuttles over trucks and buses made sense. Mountain roads through those jagged mountains would be a trick. Transportation to isolated, mountain-locked cities would be by shuttle. Or barge, in the case of cities up and down the coast, tucked into occasional coastal plains. So that made sense.

Their form of government made some sense, too, once he thought about it. Most of the decisions would be best made close to home, in the individual city-states. A common council for the colony would have limited scope, and the Director would only consider, or have authority over, colony-wide issues.

What about the distributed manufacturing? JieMin recalled

something he had tripped over when scanning Earth's colony project headquarters documents, tracking down what project information had been hidden. Something about portable factories.

JieMin ran a search, refined his search terms, ran the search again. There it was. A design for a small factory that could build a metafactory. A meta-metafactory? In any case, it could build a metafactory like Arcadia had been using for over a century, and it was transportable by shuttle.

The Earthsea colonists must have searched for some solution to their problem, and found it in the colony headquarters archives. For all JieMin knew, maybe Janice Quant had put it there just for them.

That explained how Earthsea could have distributed manufacturing, though. Have the metafactory build one of these small bootstrap factories, then lift it by shuttle to the new location. It could build a metafactory there, and you were in business. Then the bootstrap factory could be moved to another location and do it again.

JieMin would have to make sure Rob understood the implications for Arcadia. It was time and past time to spread out their manufacturing capability. They just hadn't known how to do it, and, unlike the Earthsea colonists, had not been so motivated as to find the solution in the colony headquarters archives.

JieMin went home for the weekend with one open issue. Why no satellite communications? With those jagged mountains separating the cities of Earthsea, land-based repeating stations would have been a nightmare to install and maintain. He would have thought comm satellites would be the ultimate solution to the communications problem Earthsea's mountains presented.

But they saw no evidence of that. Just duplicate upon duplicate of the message streams, and all with identical timestamps.

It was a quiet Sunday afternoon at home. Both ChaoPing and LeiTao, their husbands JuMing and DaGang, and their children LingTao and XiPing had been over for a big Sunday dinner about two. It was a happy, noisy crowd of eleven around the big table in the dining room.

That was over now, though, and it was the quiet after the storm. JieMin was relaxing in the big armchair in the living room when it hit him.

"Of course! A blind man could see it."

JieMin logged into his university account in his heads-up display and searched on the colonist listing for Earthsea. And there it was.

On a lark, he did the same for Amber.

Oh, Janice Quant, you schemer.

ChaoLi had her next status meeting the next day. She knew that JieMin had had an integration Sunday late in the afternoon. She wanted to hear where everyone else was at, but she really wanted to hear what he had come up with.

Rob Milbank made his presentation of the government structure of Earthsea. As JieMin had posted the map and his conclusions about it to the common scratch space on Friday, Milbank framed his discussion of their government structure in terms of the distributed nature of the colony.

MinYan was next. She, too, framed her discussion in terms of the map, and how that had led to the reliance on shuttles and barges over trucks and buses. She also discussed their distributed manufacturing capability in terms of JieMin's find of the plans for a bootstrap factory in the colony headquarters archives.

Then it was JieMin's turn.

"There are two observed things we have not yet explained," he said. "The multiple copies of all the messages, all with the same timestamps, and the lack of satellite communications. I believe I know the answer to both of those. Earthsea has developed quantum-entanglement radios."

ChaoLi gasped, but Milbank and MinYan looked puzzled.

"Quantum what?" Milbank asked.

"Quantum entanglement radios. We have known for several centuries that if you have entangled particles – entangled on the quantum level – when you wiggle one, the other one wiggles, too, no matter how far away it is. And that interaction goes faster than the speed of light. People have been trying to make that into a zero-time-of-flight radio system since.

"I believe Earthsea has succeeded in making such a system, and uses it to bind its city-states together. The reason we see so many copies of every message is because every city-state rebroadcasts those messages on its local radio system.

"That's why there are no communication satellites. And that's why all the duplicate files have identical timestamps."

"JieMin, are you sure? if so, that's tremendously important."

"It is the only thing that fits all the data."

"Why is it so important, ChaoLi," MinYan asked.

ChaoLi nodded to JieMin, and everyone looked at him.

"As I say, with quantum entangled particles, when you wiggle one, the other one wiggles, too, no matter how far away it is," he said. "That is, it has no distance limit. Quantum entanglement radio could put all the colonies in touch with each other, over interstellar distances, with no transit time."

Milbank and MinYan just stared at him.

That afternoon, JieMin went back to the apartment. He changed into lavalava, then went downstairs to the reception desk. The young man at the desk nodded to him and led him out into the gardens where MinChao and Jessica waited for him on the bamboo mat at the intersection of the gravel paths.

"Please, have a seat, JieMin," MinChao said.

"Thank you, Chen Zufu."

"We've read the reports from this morning's meetings," Jessica said. "Quantum-entanglement radio? Are you sure?"

"I have high confidence I am right, Chen Zumu. There could be another explanation, but the identical timestamps from locations on the planet so far apart is tough to explain any other way."

Jessica nodded.

"And there is one more thing, Chen Zumu," JieMin said. "The reason I asked to see you, actually."

"Go ahead, JieMin," she said.

"When I had the insight that it was quantum-entanglement radio that explained what we were seeing, on a hunch I checked the original colonist listing for Earthsea.

"Three different groups on Earth investigating quantum-entanglement, and who put their names in as colonists, were all assigned to Earthsea, the one planet where it would be most useful to have such radios."

"Really," MinChao said.

"Yes, Chen Zufu. Janice Quant assigned which colonists went to which planets. It was not by accident that all three of those groups ended up on Earthsea, a planet almost designed to defeat standard radio equipment. Janice Quant didn't do anything by accident."

"Remarkable," Jessica said.

"Yes, but there is another data point as well, Chen Zumu.

Four different groups working on medical nanotechnology were all assigned to Amber. It would be remarkable if they had come up empty-handed with that level of expertise and interest concentrated in a single colony."

MinChao and Jessica looked at each other, then back to JieMin.

"So what was our concentration, JieMin?" MinChao asked. "Janice Quant could not have seen you coming along, with your hyperspace vision."

"No, Chen Zufu. And the Chen family and the Jasic group were assigned to Arcadia well before they joined forces. They did not meet until they were at the Texas shuttleport just days prior to departure from Earth."

"Did we have a concentration, JieMin?" Jessica asked.

"I don't know, Chen Zumu. Arcadia under the Kendall governments may not have been fertile ground for what Janice Quant planned here. Or such a plan may not have existed for every colony. Janice Quant may purposefully have left some things to chance."

"How would that make sense, JieMin?" MinChao asked.

JieMin thought about how to explain it.

"I have seen evidence before that Janice Quant planned a lot of things, but in other ways she left some things open to chance. If you plan everything, you may get everything you planned, but anything you forgot to include could be missed."

"So leaving some things open to chance allows an opportunity for the unforeseen," Jessica said. "In particular, the pleasant surprise."

"Yes, Chen Zumu. Like the Chen-Jasic alliance. Like me. Like hyperspace travel. It seems to be Janice Quant's style to sometimes just roll the dice.

"But on Amber and Earthsea, she stacked the deck."

# The Prime Minister

After JieMin had left, MinChao and Jessica remained in the center of the garden where their conversation would not be recorded or overheard.

"If they actually have QE radios, that would be of tremendous benefit," Jessica said.

"Yes, we should probably contact them first," MinChao said.

"Of course. If Rob can negotiate a deal with them, then we can take a QE radio to Amber as well."

"We can start by inviting them to send an ambassador with a QE radio here. Then we can negotiate the deal over their QE radio channel. Rob can do the negotiations rather than a flunky."

"I think that would work out well," Jessica said.

"So how do we structure a deal? We trade technologies?"

"No, I don't think so. We trade in the products. I'm betting the hyperspace generator, the QE radio, and the medical nanites would all be a bugger to reverse engineer. So we can trade in products and services on an ongoing basis rather than a one-time technology swap. Let everybody do what they're best at."

MinChao nodded.

"That bootstrap factory is interesting. I wonder how we missed that," he said.

"We didn't need it. And when my great grandfather did his review of the colony headquarters archives, it would have been a curiosity, no more. Arcadia had no need at the time. We can use it now."

"Yes. Get manufacturing moved out to some of the larger towns. Help them grow. Which also reduces transportation costs, rather than make everything in Arcadia City."

Jessica nodded.

"And again, a nudity taboo," she said. "We may be unique in lacking one."

"All because of the Kendall regime. Funny, that."

"Yes. An irony there, for sure. Kendall metastasized what he wanted to stop."

"Including firearms and the black market."

Jessica nodded and stared out over the gardens.

"I wonder what Rob thinks of all this," she said.

"Well, we can ask him. He's asked for a meeting tomorrow."

"Oh, good. We can plot and plan together."

The young man at the reception desk came around the counter when Milbank entered.

"This way, Mr. Prime Minister."

This morning, the young man led him to what Milbank knew was Jessica's tea room. MinChao and Jessica both awaited him there.

"MinChao. Jessica. It's good to see you both again."

"It's good to see you, as well, Rob," Jessica, as host, said. "Please, have a seat."

Milbank hadn't seen his old friends since LeiTao's wedding, what? Over a year ago now. Working on two. They were looking old. Well, he was getting on as well. Ten years their junior, but still.

MinChao and Jessica had befriended the young member of the House when he took office and asked to be on the science committee. They had helped guide Milbank through the political minefields even as they were being groomed for leading the planet's most well-connected family. That was over thirty years ago. He owed being prime minister to them more than any other factor, and he knew it.

Milbank suspected that, like himself, they were hanging on to see this through. Establish the first human trading network in space. Then they could all retire with satisfaction.

Jessica's tea girl served them all tea and departed. Milbank sipped with satisfaction, followed by MinChao and Jessica. Milbank didn't know which of the many Chen teas they drank when alone, but they always served his favorite when he visited.

Milbank looked between them and saw the statue of Matthew Chen-Jasic on its pedestal in the garden. He nodded to it.

"That's a handsome statue," he said.

"Thank you," Jessica said. "It was a gift."

"That's a great miniature. I see the full-size one every day across the square from my office. Aren't you afraid it will rust outside, though?"

"That metal will not rust," Jessica said, then changed the subject. "But that's not why you have come to see us."

"No, it's not," Milbank said, and turned his attention to her. "Jessica, after all this time, we're finally close. We've actually sent a ship there. To another colony. A ship with a cabin."

"Yes," Jessica said. "Manned is next, I think. But who? And to which planet?"

"Earthsea, of course. Send a ship to bring an ambassador and a QE radio back, then negotiate the deal in real time."

Jessica nodded.

"That was our thought as well, Rob. You could negotiate directly with their Director."

"I could, or you could, Jessica. Their planetary executive is a woman. Valerie Laurent." Milbank shrugged. "We can play it by ear. Their ambassador may have some thoughts on that as well after some preliminaries."

Jessica hadn't thought of that, but it made sense to her. She nodded.

"I'm more concerned about the mechanical aspects," Milbank said. "We have four seats, right? And that's a tiny cabin, with a six-week transit. Two pilots, in case one gets sick or something. So not much room. And they're going to be living in each other's laps."

"There are two jump seats. And there is a small, private bathroom behind the cabin on one side, and a locker for food and water on the other," Jessica said. "Send an ambassador and an aide, and bring back their ambassador and his aide."

"Leave our people there, Jessica?"

"Of course. Even with QE radio, you need an ambassador on-site, if only to tell you when you need to be in touch with them."

Milbank nodded.

"OK, that makes sense. And if they don't agree to the swap, our guys can come back in the ship."

Jessica nodded.

"So how do we get them to agree to the swap?" Milbank asked.

"Send along a video. About us. Arcadia. Explain what we have to offer in a relationship. What we're looking for. Not too specific, but just emphasize things like our government, our civil rights, the things we know are in alignment with their own setup. We can help with that, Rob."

Jessica looked to MinChao, who nodded.

"I think that's right, Rob," MinChao said. "Send a video that shows our progress as a colony. Include the representative government part, which we know they also have. I would stay away from the beach or showing anyone violating their nudity taboo. Their ambassador will just have to deal with that later, when he gets here."

"And we'll have to brief our people as well," Jessica said. "Make sure they have clothing along to local standards and styles."

"How will the ambassador and his aide take along their things?" Milbank asked.

"The hyperspace ship is a cargo shuttle," MinChao said. "It can take one or more containers along. We should probably include a gift of some sort, too. Perhaps a container of assorted teas."

"That's a lot of tea," Milbank said.

"On a planet of twenty million people? Not really."

Milbank nodded.

"OK, that makes sense."

"I'm more worried about the QE radio," Jessica said. "It could be a large item. It's not going to be a tiny communicator-type of thing."

"Larger than the cargo capacity of the shuttle?" MinChao asked.

"I suppose it wouldn't be," Jessica said. "They deployed them to their cities, presumable by shuttle, so that should work. But it may be a couple containers' worth, I think."

"Still not a problem," MinChao said.

"OK, so the mechanicals aren't really an issue, other than the crew and passengers living in close quarters for six weeks each way," Milbank said.

"We'll let them shower when they get here, before they take any meetings," Jessica said with a laugh. "But that brings up the question of who you send."

"Yes. We don't really have a foreign ministry. Never needed to," Milbank said. "I was thinking one of the House members, or perhaps even the Chamber. Someone young enough for the rigors of the trip, but old enough to have some savvy."

"He also has to be willing to go, Rob," MinChao said. "For an assignment that could be several years. And somebody without a wife and family. There's no room for them in the ship."

Milbank nodded.

"Understood. Still, there are some outdoor types who enjoy going up into the mountains. On a planet as mountainous as Earthsea is, they would probably enjoy it quite a bit."

"You have anybody particular in mind, Rob?" Jessica asked.

"Off the top of my head, I thought Tanaka, Ivanov, or Diakos might work out."

Milbank watched Jessica carefully as he mentioned the names. He was very curious about her preferences here.

Jessica considered. All three had excellent people skills, and would be on anyone's short list for a sensitive liaison role. But Tanaka was more politics, Ivanov was a technology guy, and Diakos was pure businessman.

"Diakos, I think, Rob."

"Business, rather than political skills or technology savvy?"

"Yes. What we want most is a business deal. We'll trade you this for that, everybody wins. We don't want technology transfers. I don't care how their QE radios work as long as I can buy or lease them. Same with Amber's medical nanites.

"The colonies are only twenty million people apiece right now. They aren't big enough to support multiple high-tech industries with such levels of complexity. We're going to have all we can do to build the hyperspace ships to make this all work.

"Specialization is why homo sapiens went through such rapid development after hundreds of thousands of years of inch-by-inch development by other hominids. I don't think we want to give up on that now."

Milbank nodded. He had been leaning that way himself.

"Besides," Jessica said, "it makes war less likely."

Milbank tipped his head.

"How so, Jessica?"

"You don't want to bomb some other planet if it means you can no longer buy or lease medical nanites, or QE radios, or hyperspace ships. You're just hurting yourself. But if you make them all yourself, there is no such impediment."

"Inter-dependency, then."

"Of course. Rob, the four-hundred-pound gorilla in the room is Earth. The colonies are perhaps half a billion people, total. Probably a bit less. Earth was four billion when we left. We're strong enough together now – maybe – to hold against Earth trying to assert dominance over us. But that's only if we stick together. We have to avoid squabbling among ourselves."

Milbank nodded. He had noted that the Chens' plans did not include contact with Earth first, but instead with finding all the colonies, and he had surmised why. For that matter, he agreed with them.

"That all makes sense to me. Let me talk to Loukas and see if he would be available for that kind of assignment."

"The other interesting thing that's come up is the bootstrap factory," MinChao said.

"Yes, sitting in the archives all these years, and we didn't know anything about it," Milbank said.

"To be fair," Jessica said, "my great grandfather probably saw it in his review of the colony headquarters archives, but we didn't need it then, so it was uninteresting."

Milbank nodded.

"But the people on Earthsea did need it, much earlier than it would be useful to us," Milbank said.

"Exactly," MinChao said. "But we can use it now, if I'm not mistaken."

"Oh, yes," Milbank said. "JieMin made a point of ensuring I knew about it and knew its implications. I've already contacted the mayors of some of our bigger satellite cities to discuss the possibilities."

"But we don't have any at this point," MinChao said.

"We will soon, MinChao. I've already put a pair of them on the production schedule for our two metafactories. Bumped the existing production queue to get them sooner, for that matter."

"Oh. Good," MinChao said.

The RDF deployment vehicle dropped out of hyperspace and surveyed the system ahead. It was a red dwarf star, but one couldn't deploy an RDF satellite to the middle of nowhere. The deployment vehicle had to be able to find the satellite again to pick it up, and finding something orbiting a known star was hard enough. Finding it in the vastnesses of interstellar space would be next to impossible.

The deployment vehicle re-entered hyperspace for the approach to the star. It adjusted the angle and velocity of its exit from hyperspace with finicky precision. It needed a stable orbit for the RDF satellite, or at least an orbit stable enough to last for six months or so.

Now in orbit about the star, it rechecked the orbit parameters. Good enough. The deployment vehicle cut loose the third of its RDF satellites to deploy, then moved away from the satellite with a small push of its thrusters.

After several hours, it was far enough from the RDF satellite to re-enter hyperspace. It generated the hyperspace bubble and disappeared.

One more deployment to go.

Then it would start picking up the RDF satellites it had deployed, to take them and their scan data back to Arcadia for analysis.

## Construction Plan

JieMin had completed the analysis of the captured Amber and Earthsea data streams and was a bit at loose ends when ChaoLi had her next staff meeting for the design side of the project.

"Your status, Karl?" ChaoLi asked Huenemann.

"We're doing really well, ChaoLi, but one big question keeps coming up. As we move to detailed design, it's becoming an issue."

"What's that, Karl?"

"How are we going to build this thing? I mean, it's not being made for planetary liftoff like the hyperspace ships. It's way too big for that. So we have to build it in space. But we've never done that before.

"Do we make subassemblies here and take them to space? Who's going to assemble them? We don't have any orbital construction experience. Everything we've put into space, we've built groundside and lifted to orbit."

"This sounds like a research project," ChaoLi said, and turned to JieMin.

"I'll look into it," he said.

ChaoLi, Huenemann, and JieMin all knew that the orbital construction problem had already been solved once, by the colony project. The interstellar transporters, the colony buildings, and the warehouses and metafactories of the original Asteroid Belt Project had all been constructed in space.

JieMin's job was to see what, if any, of that prior experience would be useful for building the interstellar hyperspace vessel.

JieMin started with the metafactories of the Asteroid Belt Project. If the hyperspace vessel was not to be a one-off, if they were going to build a commercial hyperspace fleet, they would need orbital construction infrastructure. The metafactories seemed like the best bet for such a continuing capability.

JieMin searched through the colony headquarters archives. He found and tracked down references to the metafactories. The first of these, he found out, had been manually built in space, using the orbital construction experience Earth already had from prior projects.

That was no help.

The subsequent metafactories of the Asteroid Belt project had been built in an automated fashion, by the first, manually constructed metafactories. So they were built with resources already in space.

That was no help, either.

JieMin had just completed the Earthsea data stream investigation, and it was still very much on his mind.

He wondered. Was there something like the bootstrap factory for space-based metafactories? Had Janice Quant put something like that in the archives, all those years ago, like she had the bootstrap factory for groundside deployment?

JieMin searched on several different sets of search terms, but couldn't find any such thing in the colony headquarters archives.

JieMin switched gears, and started reviewing all the materials on the groundside bootstrap factory they used to distribute the manufacturing on Earthsea. It took him two days, but eventually he found it.

An optional configuration for the bootstrap factory.

That optional configuration made it an orbital facility.

JieMin dug into the requirements for such an orbital facility to be operational. It would not be simple.

It was at the next week's status meeting that JieMin could first report his progress.

"What have you got for us, JieMin?" ChaoLi asked.

"Good news and bad news."

"Good news first," Huenemann said.

"Fair enough," JieMin said. "The bootstrap factory they use on Earthsea – and which we now are making two of for use here – has an option for making it a space-based facility."

"Hot damn," Huenemann said, clapping his hands. "Do we have complete plans and programming for a metafactory to make it?"

"Yes. It's all in the archives," JieMin said. "As I say, that's the good news. The bad news is that it needs raw materials – lots of raw materials – and we don't have them close by in space. We don't have an asteroid belt like the Earth does. Nor a sizable moon."

"Hmm. What about the Kuiper Belt? Don't we have a Kuiper Belt like Earth's sun?"

"We should have," JieMin said. "We've never gone out there to look. It wasn't within our reasonable reach until we had hyperspace capability. I suppose we could send a ship out there to look."

"What are the odds we have one of these whatever-you-called-its?" ChaoLi asked.

"Pretty good, actually. Any star that condensed planets is going to have some material left over that never got pulled together. It's going to be a ways out, though."

"Well, if it isn't in close orbit, it's always going to be somewhere we have to get to through hyperspace, and once it is, the travel time is basically the same," ChaoLi said. "The time is going to be dominated by the time it takes to get away from the planet. Then a few seconds in hyperspace. A few seconds more or less doesn't matter."

"Right. That's right," JieMin said. "For that matter, an hour to Beacon wouldn't extend the travel time much, given how long it takes to clear the planet."

"All right, then," Huenemann said. "It sounds like this is a job for the operations group. Go find us some raw materials. They can use the hyperspace ships for that."

"They can use one hyperspace ship for that," ChaoLi said. "The other one is going to be headed for Earthsea."

"Oh, right. Sending a manned visit out to them, I suppose," Huenemann said.

"That's right," ChaoLi said. "So how do we fit this new vessel out, with it being constructed that far away?"

"Oh, once it's bare-bones operational, we fly it back here, send the fitters aboard, and have them finish the job. We'll spin it up to give them gravity, and they can live aboard."

"Will it have environmental by then?" ChaoLi asked.

"Oh, yeah," Huenemann said. "The current design has the environmental – the hard parts, anyway – being made groundside and then taken up as containers. They plug right in."

"OK," ChaoLi said. "Sounds like a plan. I'll talk to operations."

"All right, everybody," John Gannet said. "I just got our marching orders. We need to get both of these birds turned around for new missions.

"The first one, we're gonna send some people over to Earthsea and see if they can't make some friends over there. We may even get some new playtoys out of that trip. But we need to get that bird ready for four passengers and crew on the way there. It'll have four passengers and crew on the way back, too. We can assume they'll help our guys load it up at that end for the return trip, but we need to have a load list for them to work from.

"The second one is our operation front to back. We need to go find some raw materials already in space for building the hyperspace vessel. They got a factory can do a lot of the work, as long as we can find the raw materials. So we're going to be looking around for that.

"That second one is also an opportunity for us to give our new hyperspace pilots some operational experience. Our two seasoned veterans are going on the Earthsea mission. We want that expertise on that mission, since they'll have VIPs aboard.

"For the raw materials mission, it's just our guys aboard, so we'll have a chance to get our newer guys some more stick time in the hyperspace birds.

"All right. You know what you're about. Let's get to it."

Loukas Diakos met with the prime minister in a pricey restaurant in downtown Arcadia City. Michael's was known as much for its security as its food, and its food was legendary. But the entire premises was swept for electronic eavesdropping devices daily, and all the dining booths were subtly soundproofed from each other.

It was the place movers and shakers went to discuss, well, moving and shaking.

"This way, sir," the head waiter said when he arrived.

He led Diakos around to one of the super-private rooms in the back, opened the door, and waved him in.

"Loukas," Milbank said. "Good to see you."

"And you, Rob. How's Julia?"

"Good, good. Have a seat."

The headwaiter took their drink order and disappeared.

Both men considered the menu. When their waiter returned with their drinks, he did not enter, but knocked on the door. Milbank pushed a button on the wall above the table to release the door lock.

The waiter came in, served their drinks, and took their food orders. Then the two men got down to business.

"Loukas, I have an assignment for you if you're willing to do it. You're my first choice. I haven't asked anybody else."

"Sure, Rob. What is it?"

"Ambassador to Earthsea."

"Ambassador to who?"

"Earthsea. Another colony government. We know where they are. We sent a hyperspace ship past the planet to collect radio data, and analyzed it. They have a democratic government, and we want to establish trade relations with them."

Diakos nodded.

"What's the trade deal look like?"

"Well, we're building hyperspace ships, big ones, which we can sell or lease or sell transport on, both passengers and cargo. We have a lot of fine teas, which they apparently don't have. For their part, they have some good cheeses and some other things, but what we really want are quantum-entanglement radios."

"Quantum-entanglement radios? They have zero-time-of-flight radio?"

"Yes. And we want them. To buy or lease or whatever they want. You see why, of course."

"Of course. We can talk to anybody, anywhere, in real time.

We can put one on each ship, for that matter. Space out to a colony, and negotiate a deal in real time from here."

"Exactly. Loukas, I need someone to put that deal together, at least enough to get them to send an ambassador with a QE radio here so we can negotiate the details. And I thought of you."

Diakos nodded. The deal of the century, maybe the millennium. We have hyperspace ships, you have interstellar radio. That was a hell of a combo.

"What's the planet like, Rob?"

"All the land area is very mountainous. People are scattered around in the valleys and coasts in a lot of smaller cities. Nothing like Arcadia City there, because there's no clear spot big enough.

"So their planetary government is a little different. The city-states are nearly independent, with the central government mostly concerned with the currency and balance of payments among the city-states and such."

Diakos nodded. That made sense.

"Now, all we got right now is the small hyperspace ships. After the two pilots, there's only two other seats. So you and an aide, and it'll be cramped as hell for the six-week transit, *and* in zero gravity. That's it until we get the big ships running in a couple-three years. You can take as much cubic as you want, but for people we only have two seats."

Diakos and his wife had separated after their kids were grown and out of the house. They just didn't have enough in common to hold them together after the kids were gone. It had been an amicable parting of the ways, and they were still friends. Diakos, in his mid forties now and darkly handsome, had not had any problems with companionship in the meantime. When he wanted it.

"That's not a problem, Rob. And the mountains sound interesting. You know I'm a climber."

"They may be a challenge to you. They're pretty rugged."

"Even better."

"All right. I have a briefing package I can send you."

Diakos nodded.

"Sounds good."

"All right. And, Loukas? Keep this confidential. We want to announce successes after the fact, not pre-announce attempts that might fall through."

"I understand, Rob. But we'll get a deal. It's too important to both of us."

The waiter showed up with their dinners and Milbank buzzed him in.

The food, as always, was excellent.

## Mission To Earthsea

When Loukas Diakos stepped down from his seat in the House, it fell to the leader of his party to name his replacement to serve out his term. As he was in the majority party, that was up to Rob Milbank.

Most of Diakos's staff stayed in the office, serving as the staff for the new guy, Leslie Carpenter. Les had campaigned for a seat in the last elections, but their district had voted in two of the majority party and one of the minority party. He had been edged out.

As a result, though, the staff all knew him and he knew them, so it worked out to keep the same staff in place.

The one exception was Diakos's chief of staff. Peter Dunhill had hooked on to Diakos's rising star fifteen years before, and knew that Diakos was where the action was. If Diakos was stepping down from the House to take this position, that's where Dunhill wanted to be.

"So what are these guys Diakos and Dunhill like, anyway?" Justin Moore asked. "We're gonna be livin' with these guys for six weeks of zero-g in a thousand cubic feet."

"They're OK, by all accounts," Gavin McKay said. "Diakos is an outdoorsy type, rock climber, and a ladies' man. Dunhill is an ambitious sort, and has decided Diakos is on the way up. Anywhere Diakos goes is OK with him."

"Huh. Well, I'll guess we'll see."

They would be making the trip with two containers latched

below the hyperspace ship. One container held all Diakos's and Dunhill's private cubic for the trip, including all Diakos's climbing gear. That container also held almost everything they needed for the trip back other than rocket fuel and liquid oxygen, both of which they knew were available on Earthsea. Food, water, and other essentials, though, were packed in that container for the trip home.

The other container was full of tea, a gift from the prime minister of Arcadia to the director of Earthsea. Milbank hoped it would help prime the market for Arcadia's products on its new trading partner.

Passengers and crew would all be wearing comfortable fleece lounging outfits and booties for the duration of the trip. They would also have plenty of weightless-sickness pills for the trip, in case any of them grew ill from the prolonged zero-gravity conditions.

The food packed aboard was all low-residue meals ready-to-eat, designed and packaged for consumption in zero-gravity. There was plenty of water, as the big water tank in the first container was piped into the cabin.

It would be a long, uncomfortable trip, but it wouldn't be any more uncomfortable than it had to be.

Passengers and crew had a get-together the week before the trip. The four ate lunch together in the conference room at the hyperspace facility next to the Arcadia City Shuttleport.

"I want to request one thing for the trip," Diakos said.

Here it comes, Justin Moore thought. What special treatment will his lordship want for six weeks?

"Sure," Gavin McKay said. "What do you need?"

"For the six weeks' trip, we're just four guys on a camping trip. Other than Mr. Moore's status as ship's captain with regard to the ship itself, we should all just act like four guys out on a lark. No special status, no titles, none of that nonsense."

"Of course, Mr. Ambassador," Peter Dunhill said.

Diakos chuckled at that, but he was watching Moore and McKay. He saw Moore relax.

"That sounds best to me," Moore said. "It'll be plenty uncomfortable enough as it is without trying to maintain all that hoo-hah."

"Exactly," Diakos said. "I'm an outdoorsman, and have been in more than my share of uncomfortable situations. The group has to pull together and be a group of equals to have the easiest go of it. That's what's always worked best for me."

Diakos shrugged.

"At least we won't be cold."

"Nah," McKay said. "We're sitting on a nuclear reactor that's powering the hyperspace drive all the way there. Cold won't be an issue."

"Well, that's good," Diakos said. "Cold was always the hardest."

"The other thing I would recommend is bringing plenty of entertainment," Moore said. "We'll be out of touch with the colony computer network the whole way, but we have plenty of storage capacity aboard, so bring along whatever books or videos you want. If you have plenty to do, it won't seem so long."

"A good suggestion," Diakos said. "How do we get it on the ship?"

"I'll push you the access pointer and give you privileges," Moore said. "Load it up with whatever you want. Both of you."

"Thank you, Mr. Moore," Diakos said. "That should work out well."

When departure day came, it was very low-key. There was no send-off party or cheering crowds. Diakos had met with Milbank to get his final instructions over dinner the night before. They had all said their goodbyes to friends and familiars earlier.

The departure itself was something of an anticlimax. They all four climbed the portable stairs to the cabin door, got into their seats, and strapped in. Moore and McKay took the shuttle off as they had hundreds of times before. The shuttle maintained thrust – and gravity – until it had the velocity away from the planet that it needed to reach the hyperspace limit in less than a day.

It was only after they had killed the rocket engines and gone to zero gravity that it was really much different than a normal shuttle ride on the planet.

"OK, that's it," Moore told his passengers. "It's all zero-g from here until we make re-entry on Earthsea."

Diakos shrugged.

"Doesn't bother me," he said.

Dunhill, though, looked a little green.

"Don't concentrate on it, Peter," Moore said to him. "Just think of it like a long fall off a big building, but without the nasty splat at the bottom. Or like swimming. That's nearly the same thing."

Dunhill nodded and seemed to get his mental feet under him.

"Anyway, we're about twenty-two hours from hyperspace transition, and that's the next big thing. Until then, it's going to be pretty boring."

As it was, the hyperspace transition was very nearly a non-event. There was no internal change, no sensation of the transition. The windows went to being blanked out, so they lost the view of the stars, and a bit of gravity returned while the ship made its turn for the vector to Earthsea. the ship had been rotated so the outside of the turn was the down direction in the cabin, and about a tenth of a gravity returned while the ship turned.

The turn complete, zero gravity returned, and passengers and crew of the first manned interstellar flight to another human planet settled in for the long ride.

"All, right," Moore told his passengers. "We're about to come out of hyperspace. This is a reconnoiter stop, to see where we are with regard to the planet. Then we'll make another short hop or two to get there."

The ship dropped out of hyperspace, and the computer took its bearings. The windows unblanked during the stop, and they could all see a star blazing bright nearby. They could not see the planet with the unaided eye, but the computer could with its RDF sensors.

After just a couple of minutes, the windows blanked again and they were back in hyperspace.

"The good news is, the computer figured out where we are and we made it," Moore said. "That's Earthsea's sun we saw there."

It was mere seconds before they dropped out of hyperspace again. Then back into hyperspace once more, very briefly. An Earth-type planet, blue against the eternal dark, lay in front of them.

"Earthsea, gentlemen," Moore said. "I guess I ought to call them and let them know we're here."

Moore had the frequency of Earthsea air traffic control from the radio capture the flyby mission had made. He had the radio on the speakers and they all heard the conversation in the cabin.

"Earthsea air traffic control, this is shuttle Hyper-1, inbound from colony planet Arcadia. Estimating arrival in twenty-two hours. Over."

Earthsea air traffic control was one of the planetary government's services, it being a centralized service to all the city-states of the planet.

Earthsea's air traffic controllers had never received an inbound message from an interstellar shuttle before, but the flat, professional delivery of air traffic controllers was unshakeable.

"Roger that, Hyper-1. Maintain profile. Call in when two hours out for airspace and landing clearance. Earthsea over."

"Roger that, Earthsea. Call in for airspace and landing clearance when two hours out. Hyper-1 out."

Having given his instructions, Roger Clement just stared at his display for a few seconds.

Clement could not see Hyper-1 on his display, as he had no sensors to pick up any ship incoming from outer space. And a quick database check in an inset window confirmed Arcadia was the name of one of the twenty-four colony planets established over a century ago.

"Wait," Dieter Kurtz said from the next console. "Did he just say what I think he said?"

"Yeah. Arcadia's not a city. It's another colony planet."

"No shit."

"Yeah," Clement said. "Somebody apparently figured out how to fly here from there."

"I'll be damned. Now what do we do?"

"I'll advise higher. Give them the problem and let them

figure it out."

The message got passed up through channels and eventually reached the office of Director Laurent.

"Repeat that," Valerie Laurent said to her aide, Salvatore Romano.

"Earthsea Air Traffic Control just received an arrival message from a ship claiming to be from Arcadia, a colony planet. Their call-sign is Hyper-1. They'll arrive tomorrow about noon."

"That's what I thought you said."

"It can't be true," Romano said.

"Why not? We got here somehow. Who says someone else can't figure it out?"

"Yes, but– After all this time?"

"No time like the present," Laurent said. "Hyper-1. They must have discovered some sort of hyperspace to travel in. The science types have been talking about that for ages."

"So it's a different form of interstellar travel than the one that brought the colony here?"

"It must be. They didn't just appear on the planet, which is how the colony was transported. They're still almost a day away."

Romano nodded.

"But if they have discovered hyperspace travel, they represent a huge threat."

"And a tremendous opportunity," Laurent said. "If we can deal with them. What are they like, I wonder."

"I guess we'll find out tomorrow."

"Nonsense. If you were going to send someone to another planet – to another *planet,* mind – who would you send?"

"An ambassador of some sort, I suppose," Romano said.

"Someone who could speak for me. Who had instructions of what to say, what to do."

"Exactly. And what would he bring with him, do you think?"

"Information about their planet. A backgrounder for us. I see where you're going."

"Yes," Laurent said. "Let's re-establish contact with them and see if they have any advance information for us."

"Earthsea Air Traffic Control to Arcadia shuttle Hyper-1. Over."

"Hyper-1 here, Earthsea. Over."

"Hyper-1, we have a request from higher to inquire if you have any advance materials for your visit. Earthsea over."

Moore turned to look at Diakos, who nodded his head.

"Roger that, Earthsea. We have an advance package. Advise frequency for transmission. Hyper-1 over."

"We've received an advance package from them, Madam Director. It's addressed to you, actually. By name."

"Push it to me," Laurent said.

"Madam Director Laurent:

"My name is Rob Milbank. I am the current prime minister of the democratically elected government of Arcadia. In this short video, I hope to tell you something about us, an introduction that will lead, I hope, to friendship and trade between our planets.

"First, I should tell you that we already have some information about Earthsea. We previously sent a robot hyperspace ship through your system to collect radio data. We were concerned about what sort of people we were considering contacting. Our analysis of that data was reassuring. You are a democratic republic like ourselves, with limited government powers, strong civil rights guarantees, and a vibrant capitalist economy."

As Milbank continued his talk, his image was replaced by various stills and clips, beginning with a clip of the House in session.

"We based our own government on a prototype charter we found in the colony project headquarters archives. We have an elected bicameral legislature, which selects a prime minister, who selects his cabinet. That charter also guarantees civil rights to Arcadian citizens as a free people.

"With large rolling hills and plains to the south and west of our initial landing, the capital of Arcadia City has grown to be a large modern metropolis. We also have many smaller cities, which hold the bulk of our population. Farms both large and small provide for our food needs.

"Without the mountains of Earthsea, we have concentrated our transportation network on trucks and buses running on highways between our cities, with shuttle flights typically being used only to our farthest-flung locations.

"In addition to growing and manufacturing common staple goods, we have developed some more advanced proficiency in specific areas. In particular, we have a wide variety of teas grown in the mountains north of Arcadia City. I have sent a container of our teas to you as a gift from the people of Arcadia to the people of Earthsea.

"I have taken the liberty of sending my accredited ambassador to Earthsea, Mr. Loukas Diakos. He hopes to engage in discussions with your government about trade possibilities with Earthsea. I am hoping you will accept our ambassador, and send your own ambassador to Arcadia back on our hyperspace shuttle.

"We have discovered hyperspace, Madam Director, and learned to use it to travel interstellar distances. We are building a fleet of large hyperspace vessels to carry passengers and cargo in revenue service. We hope to find all the other colony planets and set up a trade network among them.

"We invite you to be the first colony planet to join us in this trade network, Madam Director. My ambassador can discuss this goal more completely with you.

"Thank you, Madam Director."

"Did you watch the Arcadia video as I asked?" Laurent asked.

"Yes, Madam Director," Romano said

"What do you think?"

"Clearly, they have discovered hyperspace. That does make them a threat. They could drop some large robot ship out of hyperspace inside the planet, and Earthsea would probably break up."

"Yes, of course, Sal. But one lesson of history is that democratically elected governments don't typically start wars. It makes the next election campaign difficult."

"I understand, Madam Director."

"What the hyperspace drive does is make them incredibly valuable as partners."

"But what do we have to offer in return?" Romano asked.

"They said we're the first colony planet they've approached."

"They may not know where the rest of them are."

"I looked them up," Laurent said. "They were third on the transport schedule, after us and Amber. So they found us and they must know roughly where Amber is, too, from a passenger compartment viewscreen analysis. Our viewscreen recordings only show us Earthsea, but theirs must show the first two drop-offs."

"Yet they approached us first. I wonder why."

"I think I know why. They want QE radio."

"You don't think they have it already?" Romano asked.

"Of course not. If they did, they could have put one on this shuttle of theirs, and Prime Minister Milbank could have spoken to me in real time."

"Ah. Right. So they have the hyperspace drive, granted, but we have the QE radios."

"Which are incredibly useful if used together. We have the makings of a deal there, Sal."

# Construction Zone

The rest of the project did not stop while Hyper-1 was on the way to Earthsea. Ambassador Diakos and his party were only halfway there in hyperspace when ChaoLi had a decision to make. She called a rare joint meeting with the operations team and the design team.

"So where are we at on scouting out the possible locations for the construction site?" ChaoLi asked.

"We've had Hyper-2 out to the Kuiper Belt," John Gannet said. "Turns out our sun has one, just like Earth's does. All suns probably do. We've also had Hyper-2 go out to Beacon and scan the system more thoroughly. There's an asteroid belt between Beacon-3 and Beacon-4."

"Any other possibilities we know about?" ChaoLi asked.

"Not at this time," Gannett said. "There are dozens of systems within twenty, thirty light-years, though. We just haven't surveyed them."

"I don't want to take the time to do that if we don't need to," ChaoLi said. "We can switch our base of operations later if it makes sense. Are either of the two current alternatives workable?"

"They probably both are, actually."

"What are the trade-offs?"

"Asteroids are farther apart in the Kuiper Belt. By quite a bit, actually. Perhaps a hundred times. There's much more material overall, but when you're that far out, everything is pretty far apart. We only spectrally analyzed a half a dozen or so rocks, because they're so isolated.

"In the asteroid belt around Beacon, by contrast, we were able to spectrally analyze a couple dozen rocks with less effort."

"So those distances are already complicating things."

"Yes, ma'am."

ChaoLi nodded.

"What about composition?" she asked. "Do they have what we need?"

"They both do. Most of what we need is steel, and lots of it. We have plenty of iron to work with at either site, and both sites have enough heavy metal elements to get the alloys we need."

"And the distances?"

"The Kuiper Belt is centered about six light-hours out, while Beacon is three light-years away," Gannet said. "In hyperspace, the center of the Kuiper Belt is eight seconds away, while Beacon is an hour."

"Neither of which matters, because it's a day to get far enough away from Arcadia to make the transit."

"That's correct."

"All right. I'm open to comments everyone," ChaoLi said.

"It's a wash to me," Chris Bellamy said.

"What about the additional time for moving factories the larger distances in the Kuiper Belt?" ChaoLi asked.

"If we put hyperspace drives on the factories, it doesn't matter. We should probably do that in either location."

"That's something I hadn't thought of," ChaoLi said.

"The Kuiper Belt is closer," Karl Huenemann said. "And it's in-system. No doubt whose it is, and we can keep an eye on it."

"We could always site a monitor there, and have it run for help if something untoward happened," Gannet said.

"True enough," Huenemann said. "That would handle that

objection."

"Actually," JieMin said, "there's an advantage to having it somewhere else. If we don't tell people where it is, a bad actor wanting to hurt us would be hard-pressed to find it."

"We don't tell anyone where we put it?" ChaoLi asked. "But we have to tell them something about where it is, don't we?"

"Sure," JieMin said. "Tell them it's in the Kuiper Belt. The only people who know different are on the project. And there's no way to know it isn't there unless you go look for it."

Huenemann laughed.

"I like it," he said. "We tell them it's in the obvious place. If anybody figures out it isn't, they have a lot of alternatives to sort through. You said dozens of systems within twenty, thirty light-years, right, John?"

"That's right."

"So if someone tries to knock out our construction capability, they go to the Kuiper Belt. And it's not there. Now it's go fish, with dozens of possibilities. Nice one, JieMin."

ChaoLi nodded.

"I like it," she said. "All right. It's Beacon. And it's a closely held secret."

She looked back and forth among them, and all seemed satisfied with that.

"What's the status of the bootstrap factory?"

"Almost complete," Bellamy said. "We should be able to launch with it next week."

"And our pilots? Are they up to it?"

"Yes, ma'am. Those flights to the Kuiper Belt and the Beacon asteroid belt were manned flights."

"And practice runs with such a heavy payload?" ChaoLi asked.

"They have one in already, and they'll do another this

week."

"Two successful practice runs, in a row, before we take the factory up."

"Yes, ma'am," Bellamy said. "We'd planned on that."

"All the way to the hyperspace limit. With the JATO bottles."

"Yes, ma'am. That's the plan."

One of the colony's metafactories had built the space-based bootstrap factory, so it was located in the industrial park. They would take off from there, as the only way to move the bootstrap factory to the shuttleport was with a shuttle anyway.

They came slanting in from the low-altitude flight from the shuttleport.

"Damn, that's a big bastard," said co-pilot Igor Belsky.

"Same-same," said pilot Jeong Minho. "Four wide, two high. We've done this twice already, so we just do it the same."

"Yeah, I know, Manny. Still and all."

Jeong settled the shuttle down on the bootstrap factory with finicky precision.

"You got it," Belsky said.

"Latch it up," Jeong said.

"Done."

A fuel truck from the shuttleport pulled up. They had taken off once already, from the shuttleport, and then been in a fuel-burning low-velocity hover across the city. There was no sense taking off without full tanks. They didn't use oxygen this deep into the atmosphere, so it was only the fuel that need to be topped up. The truck had a boom to reach the fuel receptacle, which was thirty feet off the ground with the shuttle parked on the factory.

"All right, Hyper-2. You're good to go," the voice came over the cabin speakers.

"Roger that," Belsky said into his mike. "Thanks for the juice."

The fuel technician on the ground waved and then got into his truck and moved away from the shuttle.

"Hyper-2 to Arcadia Traffic Control."

"Go ahead, Hyper-2."

"Requesting take-off clearance from location T-17 on the grid, direct to space."

"Roger that, Hyper-2. You are cleared for take-off from T-17 direct to space on vector zero-niner."

"Roger, Arcadia. Cleared to space from T-17 on vector zero-niner. Hyper-2 out."

Jeong had heard the full conversation, but Belsky gave him the go anyway.

"We're cleared to go. Zero-niner to space."

"Due east. My favorite."

The shuttle shuddered as Belsky throttled up the engines to full power. Heavy-lift cargo shuttles didn't need full power on take-off when flying light, but that wasn't the case here. The engines were approaching full thrust before the factory lifted off the ground.

Jeong lifted the nose and rotated the engines partway back as they climbed, until they were pointed straight up with the engines rotated directly aft. When they cleared thirty thousand feet, the computer started bleeding oxygen into the engines to maintain thrust.

When they reached sixty miles above Arcadia, it was time to engage the JATO bottles.

"Coming up on JATO ignition," Jeong said.

"I hate this part," Belsky said.

"You hate every part. You're a born pessimist."

"Nah. I'm Russian."

"Same thing."

Belsky laughed.

"JATO ignition in three, ... two, ... one."

They were shoved back in their seats as the JATO bottles ignited and came up to full thrust.

The JATO bottles were being used because, without them, it would take the shuttle with the heavy factory four days to get to the hyperspace limit. There was only so fast the shuttle's engines could accelerate the heavy payload. The JATO bottles would increase their velocity by a lot, early on, shortening the trip to one day, though not without some pilot discomfort.

"Ah, shit," Belsky said through clenched teeth.

Jeong was satisfied to be miserable in silence.

The minutes stretched out, then the JATO bottles flamed out.

"Thank God that's over," Belsky said.

"We have another seventy minutes or so on the engines before we shut them down. Then it's zero gravity."

"Zero gravity doesn't bother me. Less gravity is good. More, especially a lot more, I can do without."

Jeong chuckled and shook his head.

Hyper-2 dropped out of hyperspace, the on-board computer got its bearings, and then it popped through hyperspace for a fraction of a second. They emerged within a dozen miles or so of an asteroid several miles on a side.

"OK, the computer says we're here," Belsky said.

"Unlatch cargo," Jeong said.

"Done. Cargo floating free."

They watched as the bootstrap factory moved slowly away from the shuttle on its thrusters, headed for its new home.

"Advise when the cargo is clear," Jeong said.

"Roger that. It's gonna be a while, though. It's taking it easy."

"Understood."

They settled back to wait for the factory to get clear enough of the shuttle to head home. It was taking its time because, in space, doing things faster meant more fuel. As you often had more time than fuel, some things just took a while. They could have moved the shuttle away from the payload, but that took fuel, too, and running out of fuel on final approach to landing on Arcadia was a thrill to be avoided.

It was over an hour before the factory was far enough clear of the shuttle for the shuttle to engage the hyperspace field.

"Payload clear," Belsky said.

"OK," Jeong said. "Let's head for home."

"What's our status?" ChaoLi asked at the next meeting with her operations staff.

"The bootstrap factory was delivered last week," John Gannet said. "We don't know how it's doing yet."

"One disadvantage of the Beacon location."

"Yes, ma'am, but we're preparing a couple of hyperspace comm drones. They're basically the RDF deployment vehicles."

"You're preparing two of them?"

"Yes, ma'am. One and a spare."

ChaoLi nodded.

"We'll deliver one the same way as the RDF deployment vehicles. Hyper-2 takes it to orbit, JATO bottles to the hyperspace limit, then it'll run in hyperspace on nuclear. No rocket engines."

"So then we run it back and forth to maintain contact?"

"Yes, ma'am. Couple of times a day ought to be plenty."

ChaoLi nodded. She was curious as to how the bootstrap

factory was doing, but space was space, and there were certain things you couldn't hurry.

"All right," she said. "Let me know when you get your first report.

"Yes, ma'am."

ChaoLi passed on the news at her design group meeting later in the day.

"Operations is preparing a comm drone to cycle between here and the construction site, so if you have any last-minute changes to the hull design, we'll be able to send those before the metafactories get started."

"That's good to know, ChaoLi, but I think we're good with what we sent along with the bootstrap factory. At least, I haven't heard of any oopsies yet."

"All right. Well, keep it in mind, Karl. If there are changes we can accommodate them."

Three light-years away, the bootstrap factory had set up shop, and the first of the metafactories for the Arcadian hyperspace shipyard started to take shape.

## Arrival On Earthsea

Bergheim was a much smaller city than Arcadia City, with only half a million residents, but, as the hub of Earthsea's hub-and-spokes freight system, their shuttleport was just as large and even busier than Arcadia City's.

"The approach instructions are to come in south of the city, then make a short final turn to the north," Gavin McKay said.

"And you can see why," Moore said. "Just look at those mountains."

McKay looked up from his instruments and out Moore's side window.

"Yikes," he said.

"Bergheim is German. It means 'Mountain Home,'" Diakos said.

"Well, they aren't kidding," Moore said. "They must have special approaches for all their cities."

"Listening in on ATC, it sounds like some of their stuff goes suborbital, and then comes in hot," McKay said.

Moore nodded.

"That makes sense," he said. "It also makes sense that this is the hub of their system. There's a clean approach over the water."

"We have our shuttlepad clearance," McKay said. "The computer has picked up the transponder on the pad. Looks like compatible systems."

"Sure," Moore said. "We're both using the systems we shipped out with. Protocols are slow to change. Too much infrastructure to change all at once."

"Gavin, I had a request," Diakos said.

"Sure, Loukas. Whatcha need?"

"Can you ask them if they have a pilot's lounge or something where we can get a shower before meeting with their high mucky-mucks? We're inured to it by now, but it has been six weeks after all."

"Oh, yeah. That'd be good. I'll ask them next time on the air."

"Thanks."

"Gavin," Moore said. "In that same vein, I'm thinking about letting the computer do this one."

"The landing? Are you sure?"

"Yeah. Same transponder. Let the computer bring us in. If it screws up, it wasn't us."

"Yeah, there's that," McKay said. "All right. Go for it."

Moore engaged the auto-landing sequence.

"Computer engaged," the voice came from the cabin speakers. "Shuttlepad transponder locked. Approach nominal."

"Well, it sounds happy," McKay said.

"Just stand by in case it doesn't stay happy."

But the computer stayed happy and brought the shuttle down in a pinpoint landing on shuttlepad 14, per their clearance from Earthsea traffic control. A stairway was brought up to reach the cockpit door of the shuttle high up on the containers latched side-by-side to its belly.

Salvatore Romano, as one of the people already in on the story of where this particular shuttle had come from, was waiting on the top of the stair when the cockpit door opened. The first blast of air from the cockpit smelled like a locker room that the janitor had skipped over for the last month, but he had no reaction to that.

The four men who emerged, each with a little travel bag, though, he addressed directly.

"Gentlemen, I am Salvatore Romano, Director Laurent's personal aide. If you would come with me, we can get you to a facility where you can touch up a bit before meeting with the director."

"That would be very welcome, Mr. Romano," Diakos said.

Romano nodded.

They walked down the portable stairs to where an electric cart waited.

The shuttleport terminal did indeed have a pilot's lounge, a misnomer for a collection of rooms that could better be called pilot services. One of those services was a washroom with showers for cleaning up before heading home from work.

After a shower and a shave, Diakos and his aide dressed in business attire deemed appropriate for Earthsea. Moore and McKay dressed in pilot's flight suits, which they had not worn on the trip. All the fleece lounging sets and booties were put in a laundry bag for servicing later.

"That feels much better, Peter," Diakos said.

"Yes, sir. I agree wholeheartedly."

"Are we all set, then?" Moore asked.

The pilots had been done sooner, but had waited to exit the room, to keep the group together.

"Yes, I think so, Mr. Moore."

"If you would then, please, Ambassador Diakos, lead us on out."

Diakos nodded and led the group out of the washroom to where Romano waited.

Romano led them to a conference room in the pilot's lounge

area of the shuttleport.

"All right, gentlemen," Romano said. "If you could have seats there. We have placeholders for your party."

Diakos nodded, and everyone sat down at their place. Romano scanned the setup.

"Very good," he said. "I will let the director know we're all here."

Romano left then, returning in several minutes.

"The Director of Earthsea, gentlemen."

Diakos immediately rose, followed by the rest of his party. Valerie Laurent strode in, followed by a man in a business suit. Laurent walked up to Diakos.

"Ambassador Diakos, I'm pleased to meet you," she said.

"The pleasure is mine, Madam Director."

"This is Amit Patel, Vice Director of Earthsea."

"Mr. Patel, a pleasure."

"Pleased to meet you, Mr. Ambassador."

"And let me introduce my companions. Mr. Peter Dunhill, my aide. And Mr. Justin Moore and Mr. Gavin McKay, our pilots."

There were handshakes all around and then Laurent's party went around to their side of the table and sat down. Laurent sat opposite Diakos, Patel opposite Dunhill, and Romano opposite the pilots. As Laurent sat down, Diakos slid a parchment document across the table.

"My credentials as Ambassador to Earthsea, Madam Director," he said.

Laurent glanced at the calligraphy at the top of the page. 'By nomination of the Prime Minister of Arcadia, and confirmation by the Chamber, be it known that the Honorable Loukas Diakos is hereby named Ambassador to Earthsea....'

"Very good, Mr. Ambassador," she said. "This is truly

remarkable. You've come from Arcadia?"

"Yes, Madam Director."

"How far is that, Mr. Ambassador?"

"Thirty-one hundred light-years, Madam Director."

"And how long did that take, Mr. Ambassador?"

"Six weeks, Madam Director. In a cabin a fraction the size of this room."

"Remarkable. Thirty-one hundred light-years in six weeks."

"Yes, Madam Director. About three light-years per hour in hyperspace. Perhaps a bit more."

"Prime Minister Milbank says you are building a fleet of large hyperspace vessels, Mr. Ambassador."

"Yes, Madam Director. The design is complete, and the construction was about to begin when we left Arcadia."

"And how large are those vessels, Mr. Ambassador?"

"They will hold a thousand passengers, five hundred crew, and a couple thousand cargo containers, Madam Director."

"And they will be capable of the same speeds, Mr. Ambassador?"

"Yes, Madam Director. As I understand it, that is more a property of hyperspace than of the ship itself."

Laurent nodded. She was also picking up signs of the fatigue of her visitors.

"Well, enough of that for now, Mr. Ambassador. We will have plenty of time to talk later. What I propose right now is that we give you a chance to rest from your remarkable journey.

"We have reserved the penthouse floor in one of our downtown hotels for you on the short term. How about dinner from room service and a good night's sleep in a real bed before we speak again?"

"That would be very welcome, Madam Director."

"Very well, Mr. Ambassador. We will talk to you again tomorrow."

"Of course, Madam Director."

With that, Laurent and Patel got up from the table and walked out of the room. Diakos and his party stood to see them off, then Romano addressed them.

"This way, gentlemen. I have a car waiting to take you downtown."

Diakos started awake at the knock on the door. He was in an armchair in a strange room. He had gravity. Awareness gradually crept back. The hotel in Bergheim. On Earthsea.

The knock again.

Room service.

Diakos got up and went to the door. He opened it and the room service waiter brought in his dinner on a tray. He set the covered dishes out on the small table.

Diakos acknowledged the tab in his heads-up display, which he was surprised worked here on Earthsea. Protocols were sticky, and the interface was the same. Romano had told them he had set up accounts for them in the local system. They would worry about squaring things up later.

The waiter left, and Diakos sat down to eat his first real meal in six weeks. He had kept it simple – bread, eggs, a bit of fruit and cheese – until his digestion recovered a bit from weeks of bland, low-residue meals.

Once finished eating, he stripped down and climbed into bed. He was sound asleep within minutes.

Diakos woke the next day in bed, the early morning sun slanting across the room.

Had all that really happened?

Diakos looked around the room. He was definitely not on Arcadia. Furniture styles were not sticky. They changed at a whim, much less in a century, and this room would be outré on Arcadia.

Diakos went to the windows and pulled back the sheers. Mountains towered to the north and crashed down into the sea to the east, the direction his windows faced. The rising sun had just cleared the shoulder of the last of the hills and was rising over the ocean.

Beautiful planet. His climbing skills would certainly be challenged.

But for right now, his negotiating skills were facing the big challenge. Could he put a deal together? At least an interim deal?

Would they even want a deal?

Diakos checked for mail in his new local account. He had a message from Romano not to be in a hurry, but to get in touch when he had awoken and had breakfast.

Diakos checked the time. He had slept nearly eleven hours. For all that, he was up at daybreak because they had gotten into Bergheim in the early afternoon. He had been in bed by eight o'clock.

Diakos ordered room service. He was famished, and starting off the day with a breakfast steak and eggs never hurt anybody.

Hmm. Better add pancakes.

As he began breakfast, Diakos sent a mail to his three fellow Arcadians, asking them to get in touch once they'd had breakfast. Each got him a message back while he ate, and he set a meeting in the living room of his suite for nine o'clock.

"One thing we need to take care of is to get Peter's and my cubic unpacked so we have our full wardrobes and our other things," Diakos said. "I also want to get the container of tea mobile, so I can give it to the director early on."

"I can take care of that, Mr. Ambassador," Dunhill offered.

"No, I need you with me, Peter."

"We've got it, Mr. Diakos," Moore said. "The accounts Romano set up for us are actually under an Arcadia planetary account, guaranteed by the Earthsea government."

"Really. I guess they know how to do inter-governmental accounts, given their city-state setup."

"Yes, sir. So we can get all the stuff out at the shuttleport done. It's the same setup as the Arcadia shuttleport. There's a parking pad next to the landing pad. We just take the shuttle up off the containers and park it there, then they can move the containers around."

"Excellent. Then we need to get the shuttle serviced and ready for the trip back."

Moore nodded.

"We can do that. I was looking through the freight services this morning, and they have all the things we need. Cabin cleaning, refueling, oxygen, water, local delivery – everything."

"All right. I will leave that to you and Mr. McKay then, Mr. Moore. We need our cubic delivered here, we need the container of tea ready to go, and we need the shuttle turned for the trip home."

"Do you know who's going back with us, sir?" Moore asked.

"Not yet. It could be their ambassador and his aide. It could be Peter and myself. It depends on how things go over the next couple of days. Keep your fingers crossed."

# The Deal

"Thank you for joining me for lunch, Mr. Ambassador."

"Of course, Madam Director."

There were five of them seated around the table, the same five as yesterday, minus the pilots: Diakos, Laurent, Dunhill, Romano, and Patel.

"Your pilots are busy elsewhere, Mr. Ambassador?"

"Yes, Madam Director. Unloading the shuttle and preparing for the return trip. Part of its cargo is a container of tea, a gift from the people of Arcadia to the people of Earthsea. I have brought a small sample for you today."

Diakos produced from the pocket of his suit coat a small elegant hardwood box. Prominently carved into the lid of the box was the Chinese character 'Chen.' He handed the box across the table to Laurent.

Laurent slid open the top of the box. Inside were several ounces of loose-leaf tea. To one side, separated by a wooden divider, was a tea ball of the correct size for a pot of tea.

"Thank you, Mr. Ambassador. I'm afraid I'm not much of a tea drinker, however."

"You may be after this, Madam Director."

"Indeed?"

"Oh, yes. The Chen family brought cuttings and seeds for a large number of Earth teas and spices in their personal cubic when the colony was transported. The teas provided with the colony supplies were, um, seriously lacking, from an epicurean point of view."

"Indeed?"

Laurent turned to the head waiter of the Directorate, the director's residence, standing by.

"Patrick, can we have tea with lunch as well?"

"Of course, Madam Director."

"A pot, I think. Enough for everyone."

"Yes, ma'am."

Laurent handed him the tea box and turned her attention back to Diakos.

"I propose we hold our serious discussion for after lunch, Mr. Ambassador, if that is all right with you."

"Of course, Madam Director."

The head waiter returned with the waiters, who served the salad course.

"I am curious about your trip, however. What is hyperspace like, Mr. Ambassador?"

"We actually have no different sensations during the trip than in normal space, Madam Director. There was no sense of the transition into or out of hyperspace. One could not tell anything happened without looking out the windows."

"Really. That's fascinating, Mr. Ambassador. And what did hyperspace look like?"

"The pilots normally blacken the windows when in hyperspace, Madam Director. They unblackened them at one point, so I could take a look. It's very unsettling."

"In what way, Mr. Ambassador?"

Diakos shuddered with the memory.

"There is nothing to focus on, Madam Director. Nothing that draws the eye. One has the sense of something happening in one's peripheral vision, but when you look there, there is nothing. Just more of the same– formlessness, I would call it. Very disturbing. I was glad when they re-blackened the windows."

They spoke in the breaks in their eating, and the waiters soon brought out the main course, a small brisket of beef with potato wedges with cheese sauce and a pan-fried vegetable medley.

"This cheese is superb, Madam Director."

"Thank you, Mr. Ambassador. Like your teas, I suspect our cheeses will be a major export item. We have quite a variety."

"It's wonderful, Madam Director. You will have no problem finding an export market for cheeses like this."

"Back to your trip, Mr. Ambassador. I find it remarkable that you can perform a thirty-one hundred light-year trip and exit hyperspace so precisely to be within hours of the planet."

"We actually came out of hyperspace outside your system for the computer to get its bearings, then closed in with two more small hops through hyperspace, Madam Director. We are still refining how one might navigate in hyperspace."

"Interesting. And you now have no way to communicate back to Arcadia, Mr. Ambassador?"

"Not without sending a message back the same way, Madam Director. We have no interstellar radio. The fastest we can manage is a hyperspace message drone."

"I see, Mr. Ambassador."

Dessert was a custard that again put point to Earthsea's expertise with its dairy products. They had tea over dessert.

"This custard is wonderful, Madam Director."

"Thank you, Mr. Ambassador."

Laurent took a first sip of her tea, pulled the cup away from her mouth and stared at it.

"This is tea, Mr. Ambassador?"

Diakos chuckled.

"Yes, Madam Director. Not much like the colony supplies, is it?"

"I should say not. I may become a serious tea drinker, Mr. Ambassador. This is wonderful. You will not have any problem selling this tea on Earthsea, either."

When the dishes had been cleared away, they settled down to serious business.

"It is your mission to Earthsea, Mr. Ambassador. You may proceed."

"Thank you, Madam Director."

One reason Diakos had been selected for this assignment is because he was pretty good at reading people with very little input. He thought he had Director Laurent's number. She would be unimpressed with subtlety, and more likely to respond well to a direct approach. So Diakos jumped in with both feet.

"We have discovered hyperspace and how to navigate in it, Madam Director. The first question that comes up then is, Where does one go?

"Not Earth, we don't think. We are, like you, a mere twenty million people, and Earth was stable at four billion people when we left. That, we felt, was best left for later. So going to the other colonies was a natural choice.

"But where are they? We were not told. In fact, the colony project headquarters archives contain no clue. We were able to determine roughly the location of Earthsea and Amber, the colonies transported before Arcadia, from analysis of the viewscreen recordings from the passenger compartments the colonists were transported in.

"We sent hyperspace ships out to where we thought those colonies were and scanned for them. We found both Amber and Earthsea."

"Excuse me, Mr. Ambassador. How did you scan for them?"

"In very low frequency RF, Madam Director. Under one hundred hertz. We were looking for the radiation from your power grid, and that is a frequency band in which stars have very low radiation."

"Ah, of course. Thank you, Mr. Ambassador. Carry on."

"Thank you, Madam Director.

"Having found Amber and Earthsea, of course we wanted to know what sort of planets these were. Would they be friendly? Would they be representative democracies, have civil rights? In short, would they be like us? The history of the human race makes that not something one can assume, however the colonies started out."

Laurent nodded and Diakos carried on.

"So we sent a ship past each planet, capturing what radio emissions we could. We analyzed those radio transmissions to determine what Amber and Earthsea might be like.

"Amber, we now know, is a parliamentary democracy like our own. They are a little further down the path of encysted bureaucracy than we are, because we went through a period of one-man rule under successive council chairmen before that regime was overthrown and our own parliamentary democracy established.

"Interestingly, Amber has medical nanites that treat diseases like heart disease, stroke, and dementia, and they are well along the way to beating cancer."

"Really, Mr. Ambassador?"

"Oh, yes. They will be a fantastic trading partner with those nanites to sell, Madam Director."

"And yet you approached us first, Mr. Ambassador? At least, that's what Prime Minister Milbank said."

"Yes, Madam Director. Our analysis of the data we received from our ship's flyby of Earthsea informed us of your government, which is a loose confederation of more or less independent city-states.

"We also surmised that you have quantum-entanglement radio."

"How did you come to that conclusion, Mr. Ambassador?"

"Two things, Madam Director. First, the colonist rolls for Amber indicated that the colony project headquarters concentrated on Amber those colonists who were most active in medical nanotechnology on Earth. It was almost inevitable they would make major breakthroughs in medical nanotechnology with those resources concentrated in such a small population.

"A similar analysis of Earthsea indicated that the colony project headquarters did a similar thing here, concentrating in one colony the colonists who were most involved with investigating quantum entanglement.

"Second, in analyzing your message data, we discovered multiple copies of identical messages, with identical timestamps. We also learned of your unique topology. It was apparent to us that you had solved the QE radio problem. You were using it to communicate over your mountains without expensive and difficult radio repeaters on mountaintops, then repeating the signals over radio in your city-states.

"Together, hyperspace transportation and QE radios are a powerful combination, Madam Director. QE radios can give instantaneous communications over interstellar distances, but one end of the radio link has to be physically transported.

"Similarly, hyperspace transportation can make interstellar trade in delicacies and technology – like Arcadian teas, Earthsea cheeses, and Amber nanites – possible, but the communications to make such a trade work would be much enhanced by a communications network.

"So we approached Earthsea first."

"And you came to Earthsea to put together such a trade deal, Mr. Diakos?"

"No, Madam Director. I came to Earthsea to propose you send your ambassador to Arcadia with a QE radio. Then you, Prime Minister Milbank, your planetary council members and our parliamentary leaders can all negotiate the larger deal in real time."

Laurent sat back in her chair and considered. Putting together such a large deal was a matter that took some time. It would necessarily be done in stages, and refined with time and experience. That usually involved messages back and forth between key players, all aggravated by the time of travel and the lack of face-to-face discussions.

This was a much more workable plan than trying to put a large deal together right off. She had been afraid Diakos was here to try to cobble something together on the spot. He was ambitious enough – he had all the signs – but he was also smart enough to have attainable goals. She was happy to see she was working with people on Arcadia who knew better than to go for a short-term deal. Who were in it for the long haul.

But he was wrong on one thing.

"But surely you mean send an ambassador to Arcadia with four QE radios, Mr. Ambassador."

"Four, Madam Director?"

"Of course, Mr. Ambassador. One at Arcadia that links to here, the second at Arcadia that links to a third for Amber, and the fourth for Amber that links back to here. Six in total to link the three planets, with two remaining here. You can take Amber's units to them when you first approach them."

It was Diakos's turn to consider. What the director proposed would certainly make the Amber deal go better. The ability to open face-to-face meetings between heads of state on the first visit. She had also as much as admitted the existence of the QE radios in her reply. She had certainly not couched her response in conditionals. 'Were such radios to exist' sort of thing.

But there was one more thing that had occurred to Diakos, just since this morning, and Laurent had missed it. Too close to see it, no doubt.

"That would certainly make a lot of things easier going forward, Madam Director. Your insight there is on target.

"There is one more thing I think you should be considering as we proceed, however.

"Earthsea's century of experience in handling the balance of payments between your city-states is unique. We certainly have no such experience in Arcadia. It gives you a leg up in another area.

"Together with the QE radios, that experience means the Bank of Earthsea would most likely be the best clearing house for planetary payments among colonies."

Laurent's eyes grew wide.

## Return To Arcadia

Later that day, Laurent and Romano were sitting in Laurent's office.

"Sal, I think you're my best option for ambassador to Arcadia. I need someone I can absolutely trust, who isn't going to go off on his own agenda. What do you think of a probably three-year assignment?"

Romano was stunned. Ambassador to another planet? That was a huge assignment. But he understood why trust was such an issue. The last thing Laurent needed was some political operator working his own agenda.

As for being off Earthsea for three years, his personal life was in such a shambles right now, it would probably be an improvement on that score. His marriage had fallen apart earlier in the year, and he had buried himself in his work to avoid the inevitable self-recrimination.

"I'm honored by your confidence in me, Madam Director. I would be pleased to take the assignment."

"It will be a lot easier than Mr. Diakos's assignment, because we'll be in touch as soon as the QE radio is powered up. You won't be on your own."

"Understood, Madam Director. I'll have to think of who I take as an aide."

"You can pull anybody in the government you want, Sal. This is more important than anything else going on."

"Thank you, Madam Director."

"So this Romano guy is going back with us?" Moore asked.

"Yeah," McKay said. "He's OK. Just a little stuffy, but that's because we've only seen him when he's on-stage. You know."

"OK. What about his aide?"

"That guy I don't know."

"Well, I guess we'll see what he's like on the way."

Romano met with Diakos before he departed for Arcadia. They had moved to a first-name basis when Romano was named ambassador to Arcadia.

"What's Prime Minister Milbank like, Loukas? To the extent you can tell me. You know."

"Straightforward guy. He can be subtle when he wants to, but the best approach to him is straight at him. I don't think you'll have any problem with him, Sal."

"That's good news."

"I'll give you one piece of advice. Meet with the Chen."

"The who?"

"The Chen. Chen Zufu and Chen Zumu, the heads of clan for the Chen-Jasic family, the wealthiest and most politically connected family on Arcadia. Pay a courtesy visit. Open up a channel of communication there."

"Will they meet with me?"

"Yes. They'll be curious. But they're behind the scenes of a lot of what goes on. You definitely want a channel there. Just trust me."

Moore and McKay looked over to the stack of containers, three wide and two deep, they were taking back to Arcadia.

"Geez," McKay said. "How much shit we taking back, anyway?"

"Four of them are those fancy radios. Whole container for a radio, believe it or not. Then we got the supplies one with the water, plus the personal cubic for Sal and the other guy. And there's one more that's a gift to Milbank. Cheese, I think."

"We got a whole container of cheese?"

"Yeah."

"Well, at least we won't starve."

"Yeah, if you wanna hold your breath while you go get it."

"There is that."

"Let's get her up on the stack."

The shuttle barely lifted off the parking pad, a mere thirty feet in the air. Moore sidled it over to the stack of containers, then lined it up with finicky precision on the stack.

The shuttle lowered, adjusted, lowered again, and settled on the stack.

"Bull's eye," McKay said.

Moore shut down the engines.

"Latch 'em up."

The next day was departure. The four Arcadians had been on Earthsea almost two weeks. Diakos and Laurent were on a first-name basis in private now. They watched the preparations on the pad from a viewing window in the freight terminal.

"I'm surprised you had three multi-channel QE radio links ready to go, Valerie."

"Those are our big units, Loukas, for connecting our bigger cities. We stock spares."

"And if you have a failure now?"

"We'll manage. We can use multiple smaller units in the meantime if we have to. We're working our spares stock back up now."

Diakos nodded.

"Well, this is a tremendous day. QE radios on a hyperspace

shuttle. It's a major game-changer, Valerie."

"Yes, and thank you for your part in that, Loukas. You painted a compelling picture, and represented Arcadia well."

"Thank you. It's been fun. And I think both planets will do well by the deal."

"No argument there."

Diakos, Dunhill, and Laurent said goodbye to the pilots and the newly minted ambassador and his aide before they boarded. They were already dressed in comfy loungers for the long, boring trip.

"Well, thanks for the lift, fellas. Have a good trip back," Diakos said.

"OK, Loukas," Moore said. "You take care."

When Diakos shook hands with Romano, he had a reminder.

"The Chen. Don't forget, Sal."

"I won't, Loukas. We'll be in touch in six weeks or so."

When all the handshakes were done, the four – Justin Moore, Gavin McKay, Salvatore Romano, and Romano's aide, Paolo Costa – climbed up the boarding stairs to the cockpit door, now twenty-eight feet off the tarmac.

Diakos, Dunhill, and Laurent took the electric cart back to the freight terminal and watched the take-off from behind the viewing window.

"It's strange to see them taking off straight up like that, Loukas, without heading off to one of our cities," Laurent said.

"Yup. Straight to space. It'll be a day before they're far enough away to go into hyperspace, though, Valerie."

"And then in six weeks, we'll get a call from your boss. Mr. Milbank."

"Won't that be something?"

They had made the transition to hyperspace, and given Romano and Costa the obligatory look at hyperspace. Both men were happy to have the windows re-blanked, and the four were settling in for the long trip.

At one point, Moore and McKay turned their pilot seats around to face their passengers.

"Uh, there's one thing we need to talk to you guys about," McKay said.

"Yeah, we didn't make a big deal of it back on Earthsea, but you sorta need to know if you're going to Arcadia," Moore said.

They looked very serious. Romano didn't know what it could be.

"Uh, what's that?" Romano asked with a half smile.

"Well, there's no nudity taboo on Arcadia," Moore said.

"No nudity taboo?"

"Nope," McKay said. "Arcadians don't wear clothes to go swimming. People at the beach are all just naked."

"Well, that sort of makes sense," Romano said.

"And on the bus going to the beach," Moore added.

"Or on the bus going just about anywhere else."

"Or in the stores. Maybe they're buying stuff on the way to the beach."

"Or not," McKay said.

"Kids playing in the parks. People working in their gardens. People out in their lawns taking a shower."

"They're all naked?" Romano asked.

"Yup. Pretty much anywhere," McKay said.

"Now, most of the time, most people wear a lavalava."

"What's a lavalava?" Costa asked.

"A wrap-around. Like a sarong or something."

"Men, too?"

"Oh, yes. Men and women. Of course, women don't usually wear anything else," Moore said.

"Which means most of the women you'll meet will be topless," McKay said. "Everywhere you go."

"Really?" Costa asked.

"Oh, yeah," Moore said. "But it has nothing to do with you , and it's not a come-on. You could be riding on the bus and the first runner-up for Miss Arcadia City gets on the bus, completely nude, and sits down next to you. All in a day, on Arcadia."

"Now, if someone really is interested in you in that way, they'll let you know," McKay said. "Women on Arcadia are not shy about that. But having some completely naked gal come sit next to you on the bus is just a ride on the bus. Nothing else implied or intended."

"We just thought you should know," Moore said.

"So you don't misinterpret things and get into trouble," McKay said.

"Well, I appreciate the heads up," Romano said.

"Me, too," Costa said. "Thanks."

"No problem," McKay said, and shrugged. "You get so used to it, it's not a big thing. But after Earthsea, it's liable to be a bit of a shock."

"Oh, and one other thing," Moore said. "Most people on Arcadia start working at thirteen or fourteen. So you might go into a restaurant and have a fourteen-year-old waitress. Or stop by a store and be waited on by a thirteen-year-old counter clerk–"

"Who's topless," McKay said.

"– but that's just how things are. The population is young, and we have a chronic labor shortage. So people start working young."

McKay nodded.

"I see," Romano said. "Again, thank you for the heads up. Anything else unusual we should know about?"

"No, not really," Moore said.

"Except everybody drinks tea, because our teas are so good."

"Yes, I can attest to that," Romano said. "The tea Mr. Diakos brought to Earthsea was extraordinary."

"Oh, and we like parades, so we may get a parade when we get there," McKay said.

"Yep," Moore said. "Nothing like a good parade."

"Mr. Prime Minister, we've heard from Hyper-1. They've called in to Arcadia Traffic Control. They're about twenty-two hours out."

It had been fourteen weeks since they left, about the time when he expected the hyperspace shuttle to return from Earthsea. Now, what was it? Success or failure? He had a lot of confidence in Loukas Diakos, but he was walking into a completely unknown situation there.

"Can you get me a radio connection to them?"

"I think so, sir. Let me check."

Milbank's secretary returned minutes later.

"Yes, sir. We have a radio connection for you. It's private to the pilot, so you won't be overheard."

"Excellent."

"I've pushed you the link."

Milbank activated the link in his display. It was sound only.

"Milbank here."

"Justin Moore here, sir."

"Am I correct in thinking I can't be overheard by your passengers, Mr. Moore?"

"Yes, sir, but that's not true of me."

"I understand, Mr. Moore. I just want to ask you a few questions."

"Of course, sir."

"Was the mission a success or a failure, Mr. Moore?"

"The former, sir."

"Does that mean you have their ambassador aboard?"

"Yes, sir."

"Excellent. And did he bring a QE radio with him?"

"Four, sir."

"Four, Mr. Moore?"

"Something about another planet, sir."

"Ah, yes. Of course. Connections to Amber as well."

"Yes, sir."

"All right, Mr. Moore. And would your passengers be amenable to a parade?"

"We've already warned them of the possibility, sir."

"Excellent. Well, we'll see you tomorrow, Mr. Moore. Milbank out."

Milbank checked the time. Three in the afternoon. They would need to shower and clean up. He had no doubt what they would look like after six weeks traveling in that cramped cabin.

Five o'clock was always a good time for a parade.

"Was that your prime minister?" Romano asked.

"Yes, Sal. He wanted to know if we would be up to a parade. So I said, Sure."

"I hope we have time to clean up first."

"Oh, that was on the schedule for our return from the start. Gavin and I knew we would need it."

"Oh, good. So what does a parade involve on Arcadia?"

"You ride into town in an open groundcar. You wave a lot.

And when we get to downtown, the prime minister shakes your hand, the mayor gives you the keys to the city, and Miss Arcadia City kisses you on the cheek–"

"And she's topless," McKay said.

"– and you say, Thank you. Then we get to go eat real food and sleep in a real bed for a change."

"Sounds like fun," Romano said.

The shuttle's computer put the ship down on the dot on the transponder for pad twenty-seven, one of the pads in front of the hyperspace facility at the Arcadia City Shuttleport.

The crew assisting them off of the shuttle were all old friends of Moore and McKay by now. They led the four into the hyperspace facility to the washroom, where they all took showers and shaved. They dropped the fleece loungers and booties in a pile and put on street clothes for the parade.

Moore and McKay wore normal flight suits, which were basic coveralls with unit patches for 'Hyper-1' applied. Romano and Costa put on business suits. They had picked items out of their wardrobes that looked most similar to suits they had seen in Prime Minister Milbank's video to Director Laurent.

Then it was into the open car for the trip into downtown. Romano noted how much larger Arcadia City was than any of the cities on Earthsea. There must be a million or two million people living in the capital city.

As their car got closer to downtown, it joined the parade proper, with another couple of open cars, one with the prime minister, and one with the mayor of Arcadia City and Miss Arcadia City. They all proceeded the rest of the way behind a band and a float with a model of the hyperspace shuttle on it. It was quite a production for short notice.

When they got into the downtown proper, it was clear a good number of the residents had turned out to watch the parade. As the car with them and their pilots passed, a cheer went up from the crowds they passed. Many of them were waving their lavalavas over their heads as they cheered.

For someone born and raised on Earthsea, seeing tens of thousands of naked people cheering and waving what scanty clothing they had over their heads was extraordinary.

Romano was glad they had been warned.

At the end of the parade route, they all ascended the stairs to the raised stage. There must have been a hundred thousand people in the square and side streets that Romano could see.

Prime Minister Milbank, aware of their fatigue, simply announced the return of the first manned interstellar trip to another human planet, and introduced Ambassador Romano and his aide.

The mayor then gave Romano the keys to the city, and Miss Arcadia City – every bit as beautiful and underdressed as Moore and McKay had promised – gave them each a kiss on the cheek. Costa, just twenty-eight years old, blushed all the way to his toes, but the crowd loved it and, nude, cheered and waved their lavalavas over their heads.

Salvatore Romano had never seen anything like it.

# First Meeting

Salvatore Romano woke up in the hotel room in downtown Arcadia City. Unlike Loukas Diakos two months before, he knew exactly where he was when he woke up. He lay back in bed and luxuriated in the feeling of gravity once again. Zero-gravity sleep for him had been full of nightmares of falling.

Like Diakos when he arrived on Earthsea, Romano had gone to bed early the night before, and had slept ten hours before waking up at dawn.

Romano went over to the windows and pulled back the sheers. He had a view out to the east, over several miles of city, a couple of miles of green parkland, and the ocean. It was a beautiful day.

Romano ordered breakfast from room service. It was delivered by a young woman, perhaps fifteen, wearing a lavalava and flip-flops and nothing else. He acknowledged the tab with his communicator and she left.

That was interesting. His communicator worked. Well, they seemed to be on top of things here.

Milbank sent a message to Ambassador Romano, telling him to get in touch when he was up and about and had breakfast.

Yesterday, after their initial conversation, Milbank had had a text exchange with Justin Moore. Moore had told him about the arrangements on Earthsea, in which they had found they had accounts on the local computer system, including a planetary account to bill expenses to.

Milbank decided that was a good idea and had his secretary

arrange the same for Salvatore and Costa.

Moore also confirmed that Romano had brought four QE radios, each one being the size of a twelve-foot by twelve-foot by eighty-foot shipping container.

Romano checked his mail. He acknowledged the mail from Milbank and accepted the prime minister's invitation to lunch. With time to spare, he went down to street level and walked around the downtown. He made sure, as the prime minister had, that Paolo Costa was copied on his reply.

Romano walked down the broad boulevard to the next block. Here the street became a pedestrian zone, among the steel-and-glass buildings that had been delivered with the colony.

Romano walked into Charter Square. There was a statue of a woman on one side, holding up a document labeled 'Charter'. Diagonally opposite her was a statue of a seated bald figure. The label on this closer one said 'The Chen,' which reminded him to arrange to meet the current Chen.

Everywhere he went, there were people in the most outrageous variety of dress he had ever seen. Here in the downtown, there were people wearing business suits, of course, but also the lavalavas, with most of the women wearing those being topless. A few percent of the people he saw, male and female, were completely nude, and no one batted an eye. They just were, that's all. So what?

Remarkable.

At ten to noon, Romano went into the administration building behind the statue of the woman holding the charter, and presented himself to the young woman at the front desk for his appointment with the prime minister.

She was topless.

"Ambassador Romano. Good to see you," Milbank said, getting up and extending his hand.

"It's good to see you again as well, Mr. Prime Minister," Romano said, shaking his hand.

"And Mr. Costa. Good to see you."

"Thank you, Mr. Prime Minister."

"Let me introduce my companions here. Haruki Tanaka is a senior member of my party in the Chamber."

"Mr. Tanaka."

"Mr. Ambassador."

"And David Bolton, who is a senior member of the Chen-Jasic family."

Despite his name, Bolton was at least part Asian. Chinese, Romano guessed.

"Mr. Bolton."

"Mr. Ambassador."

"So let's all have seats. Our custom is to leave serious business until after food. Is that all right with you, Mr. Ambassador?"

"Of course, Mr. Prime Minister."

They were all seated, and the wait staff brought in the salad course. They were in the Prime Minister's private dining room, so there was no one else present.

"Although I do have a small gift for you that is perhaps best presented now, Mr. Prime Minister."

Romano reached across the table to put a small cylindrical container, perhaps five inches in diameter and two inches high, in front of Milbank.

Milbank took the lid off the container to find a small cheese wheel. Ever the gourmand, Milbank sniffed at the cheese appreciatively.

"What an outstanding bouquet. Martin, can we serve this as

well?"

"Of course, sir," the head waiter said.

Romano took a bite of his salad. The salad dressing was a vinaigrette with a number of spices in it. He knew all the spices available on Earthsea, and some of the spices in the salad dressing were not available at home.

"What a remarkable dressing, Mr. Prime Minister."

"Yes, Mr. Ambassador. Mr. Bolton's family brought seed stock and cuttings of many of the Earth's exotic spices with them from Earth in their personal cubic. We have all benefitted since from their foresight."

Romano inclined his head to Bolton, who bowed in return.

"I was advised that I should meet with the Chen at some point, Mr. Bolton."

"I can arrange a meeting with Chen Zufu and Chen Zumu for you, Mr. Ambassador. The heads of our family, and my superiors. Just mail me when a time is available for you."

"Thank you, Mr. Bolton."

Bolton just bowed his acknowledgement.

"I detect Mr. Diakos's involvement there," Milbank said. "It's a smart move. The Chen-Jasic family is likely to be our biggest exporter. They also are driving the hyperspace project."

"Not the government, Mr. Prime Minister?"

"No. We tried that, and it didn't work out. All the decisions on the project are technical decisions, while any decision made by government is by definition a political decision. So the government contracted the project to the Chen-Jasic family, and the quality of the decision-making improved dramatically."

Romano nodded.

The main course was next, and with it was served tea. Romano sipped his. It was a different tea than he had had in the first meeting on Earthsea, but it was just as delicious.

"This is a different tea than was presented to Director Laurent on Earthsea, I believe, Mr. Prime Minister."

"Yes, Mr. Ambassador. This is Oak, a personal favorite. I believe that one was Walnut."

At Romano's quizzical look, Milbank chuckled. It seemed Milbank was never far from a chuckle.

"Oh, they both have Chinese names, Mr. Ambassador, but I can't pronounce them. Most people refer to the Chen's pricier varieties by the wood of the box they come in."

"I see, Mr. Prime Minister. Yes, I believe that one was Walnut."

The main course itself was a stir-fried pork dish, with vegetables and a delectable sauce, and with a seasoned rice on the side. The pork was wonderful, very tender, and the rice was delicious. The seasoning in the rice was something Romano couldn't identify.

"What is the seasoning in the rice, Mr. Prime Minister?"

"Two, actually, Mr. Ambassador. Ginger and sesame."

"Well, it's wonderful, Mr. Prime Minister. As is the pork. Very tender."

"Both also from the Chen-Jasic family, Mr. Ambassador. I'm afraid we're trying to impress you with the things we have to export to Earthsea."

"Then you've accomplished your mission, Mr. Prime Minister."

"Excellent. And this cheese is wonderful as well, Mr. Ambassador. I don't think I've ever had this variety before. Not something we have on Arcadia."

"That's a favorite of mine as well, Mr. Prime Minister."

Dessert was a chocolate cake that was spicy. Romano took a taste and raised an eyebrow to Milbank.

"Five-spice cake, Mr. Ambassador. Clove, fennel, cinnamon,

star anise, and pepper."

"Of those, I think we only have cinnamon and pepper, Mr. Prime Minister."

"We will rectify that, Mr. Ambassador. We will rectify that."

Romano nodded and dug into his cake with gusto.

Once the dishes were cleared away, and everyone's tea refreshed, the serious business began.

"So what do you think of Arcadia, Mr. Ambassador?" Milbank asked.

Romano couldn't help it. He mentioned the first thing off the top of his head.

"The dress code will take some getting used to, Mr. Prime Minister."

Milbank chuckled, and Romano tried to backpedal.

"I guess I'm surprised no one objects," he said.

"To what, Mr. Ambassador? To how someone else does or does not dress? How is it anyone else's business?"

"There are no laws on this, Mr. Prime Minister?"

"No, Mr. Ambassador. Nor is there any law against red shoes, paisley shirts, or anything else someone might object to."

"Well, I understand those things, Mr. Prime Minister. But completely nude?"

Milbank shrugged.

"There are only two kinds, Mr. Ambassador. Seen one, seen 'em all."

"I suppose," Romano said, but he didn't sound so sure.

Milbank's chuckle was back.

"What else about Arcadia, Mr. Ambassador?"

"The size of the city surprised me, Mr. Prime Minister. There is no city of this size in Earthsea. We simply don't have a space this big."

Milbank nodded, and Romano continued.

"I'm surprised city services – water, sewer, electricity – are able to be provided effectively to such a large, crowded area."

"It's not without its challenges, Mr. Ambassador. But all those problems were solved on Earth long ago, and we have all their records."

"Of course, Mr. Prime Minister."

Romano shifted in his seat, and the bulky document in his pocket reminded him of its existence.

"Oh, and we should take care of this little detail, Mr. Prime Minister."

Romano extracted the document and handed it across to Milbank. The prime minister opened it and saw the header, 'By nomination of the Director of Earthsea, and confirmation by the Council, be it known that the Honorable Salvatore Romano is hereby named Ambassador to Arcadia....'

"Excellent, Mr. Ambassador. Thank you."

Romano nodded.

"And now, Mr. Ambassador, since this is your mission, what is next on our agenda?"

"I have brought two things of interest with me, Mr. Prime Minister. The first is a container of our cheeses, a gift from the people of Earthsea to the people of Arcadia."

"Thank you, Mr. Ambassador, on behalf of the people of Arcadia."

"The second thing I brought with me is four quantum-entanglement radios. QE radios exist in pairs, Mr. Prime Minister. Two of these are paired to each other, one for here and one for Amber, so one will stay here and the other you can take to Amber when you contact them. The third is also for Amber, paired to one on Earthsea, and should also go to Amber on your mission. The fourth stays here and is paired to one on Earthsea, to establish communications from Arcadia to

Earthsea."

"And that fourth one is the one we should hook up immediately, Mr. Ambassador? To be able to talk to Earthsea?"

"Yes, Mr. Prime Minister. Now, Mr. Costa here is not a diplomat. He is instead a QE radio technician and installer. He will be able to tell you the requirements, and to bring the link up."

"Excellent, Mr. Ambassador."

"These units will be controlled out of the network operations center on Earthsea, Mr. Prime Minister. Whether they stay up and operational, and are ultimately turned over to broader traffic, depends on how your negotiations with Director Laurent turn out."

"No more than I would expect, Mr. Ambassador."

That was a relief to Romano. He had worried about that last bit. These radios were not gifts, they were loaners, so they could put the final deal together.

"What are the requirements, Mr. Ambassador?"

Romano turned to Costa and nodded.

"A forty-kilowatt power supply and a chiller loop, Mr. Prime Minister," Costa said.

Milbank looked to Bolton, whose background was in engineering. Bolton nodded to Milbank and turned to Costa.

"How much heat transfer in the chiller, Mr. Costa?"

"Twelve tons, Mr. Bolton. A hundred and fifty thousand BTU per hour. Thereabouts."

Bolton nodded.

"Are there any siting requirements, Mr. Costa? View of the sky, that sort of thing?"

"No, Mr. Bolton," Costa answered. "They could be in a deep cave. Nothing can block the signal."

Bolton nodded and turned to Milbank.

"At the powerplant, I think, Mr. Prime Minister. We can easily meet both of the requirements there, and it already has site security."

Milbank nodded and turned to Costa.

"That will work, Mr. Prime Minister. As long as the radiation levels aren't elevated."

"Very well then," Milbank said.

He turned to Romano.

"I think we have a plan, Mr. Ambassador. Mr. Costa will get the unit to Earthsea operational, and then I will speak with Director Laurent."

## Cheese And QE Radio

Rob Milbank had the idea of having a cheese-tasting in downtown Arcadia City, hosted by the Earthsea ambassador, but he worried about how much cheese there was, and if there would be enough.

With the shuttle moved off the containers to the parking pad, he directed the containers be unstacked and the weight of the cheese container be determined. They had container lifts out at the shuttleport that could move up to a million pounds.

More to the point, they could weigh it.

"Sir, the cheese container weighs almost half a million pounds."

"How can that be?" Milbank asked his secretary.

"If the container were full, sir, it would be more like seven hundred thousand pounds. But some of the volume is taken up by packaging. Wood crates, cardboard boxes, voids between cheese wheels. Cheese is almost as heavy as water."

"My word. So even if two hundred thousand people showed up, there would be over two pounds of cheese per person?"

"Yes, sir. Even allowing for the weight of the container."

"That's a lot of cheese."

"Yes, sir."

"All right. Thank you."

Milbank knew a party like that in Arcadia City would draw a hundred or a hundred and fifty thousand people. Arcadians liked to party. But even at that, he would not run out of cheese. Not by a lot.

He started making plans.

Out at the Arcadia City Shuttleport, the Arcadia end of the Earthsea-Arcadia QE radio link was being set onto a truck. This would be a wide load, from the shuttleport to the nuclear power plant. The nice thing is it didn't have to go through downtown. There was a direct route, along T Street, two miles south of the downtown, that cut all the way from the southwest side to the southeast side.

There was a storage building at the nuclear power plant site that had been built as part of another project. With that project complete, the building sat empty. It had four-hundred-amp service of 480 VAC, though, so it had plenty of power. Enough for two QE radio links and two chillers both.

Paolo Costa and some engineers from the hyperspace facility supervised the move and installation of the QE radio and the chiller.

By the end of the day, Costa was beat. He would try to start up the link tomorrow morning, when he was fresh.

"A cheese-tasting party, Mr. Prime Minister?" Romano asked.

"Sure. It'll be a great party, Mr. Ambassador. You can be the official host. We'll give away free slices of cheese to people. You know. Snack-sized chunks. And if they want to buy some of their favorite, we'll sell them a pound and put that toward financing the Amber trip.

"It'll be great fun, and great PR for you, for Earthsea, and for your cheese products. It will also help me keep funding the construction of the big hyperspace ships, because if there are no freighters, then there's no more of that great cheese. We all win."

"Well, you know your people, Mr. Ambassador. But a hundred thousand people or more, wandering around the downtown naked, eating cheese?"

"You're a little stuck on the whole nudity thing, aren't you, Mr. Ambassador? Trust me. It will be great fun, people will enjoy it a lot, and it will all be because you're such a great guy. 'You know, those Earthsea people are all right. And they make great cheese.' You see?"

"Yes. Yes, I get it. All right, Mr. Prime Minister. Let's do it."

"There you go. You know, Mr. Ambassador, you might suggest Director Laurent do the same things on Earthsea. Have a big tea party with Ambassador Diakos as the official host. You can do separate ones in your various cities, and link them all by display or something."

"Yes, she might be able to do that. Although it takes a lot more coordination than here, Mr. Prime Minister. All the mayors have to get on board."

"Oh, I'm sure if she gets a few mayors in the biggest cities on board, the smaller cities will jump on, Mr. Ambassador. They'll want to show they're just as good as the big boys."

Romano nodded.

"That's very often exactly the way it works, Mr. Prime Minister. I'll bring it up to her."

"Excellent, Mr. Ambassador. Excellent. My understanding is they were going to install the QE radio today?"

"Yes, and test the chiller loop. Mr. Costa will attempt to bring up the link tomorrow morning. If that goes well, Mr. Prime Minister, we will have communications sometime around mid-day."

"My proposal, Mr. Ambassador, is that we use the link to catch up with our own people at the other end. So you can talk to Director Laurent and I can talk to Ambassador Diakos. We get all caught up, and then Director Laurent and I have our first virtual meeting, perhaps in a couple of days."

"That sounds good to me, Mr. Prime Minister. We should do some catching up and not jump into things blind."

"All right, then, Mr. Ambassador. It's a plan."

Paolo Costa nodded to the plant engineer at the power center for the building. The engineer turned on the breaker for the chiller unit, then walked over to the chiller and turned on its master switch. He watched his panel there for a few minutes.

"We're OK on the chiller, Mr. Costa. We've got circulation."

Costa nodded and turned toward the QE radio link. Of course, he didn't have to be looking at it for what he was going to do, but it seemed more right somehow.

"OK," Costa called back. "Turn on the power to the QE radio."

The engineer walked back over to the breaker panel and turned on the breaker for the QE radio.

When power was applied to the QE radio, the only thing that should come up is the local maintenance interface. He logged into that with his communicator, and a control panel came up in his heads-up display, superimposed over his real vision of the container.

It was as if the container had sprouted a control panel. So far, so good.

Costa had the start-up software for the QE radio link in his communicator. He initiated the transfer of the start-up software to the QE radio. The machine loaded the software, checked version compatibility, and went to yellow stand-by status.

"All right," Costa said under his breath. "Here goes."

Costa pushed the 'Initiate Link' button and hoped for the

best. He'd had two fail before, but those were both with earlier versions of the hardware. Hopefully....

The 'Link Established' light came on, and Costa breathed a sigh of relief. He initiated a download of the full software package from the Earthsea end. Even though it was the software package for the QE radio itself and the software package for the Arcadia network that would handle seamless communications over the link, the big multi-channel unit had an insane amount of bandwidth and the downloads were nearly instantaneous.

Costa installed the QE radio link package first. It walked him through configuration details, like the name of the link, the name of the node, its ID in the local system, the current permissions, and alternate routes.

When Costa had all that configured, he connected to the Arcadia system and logged into the QE radio through its local ID. He had asked Milbanks's people to configure that for him. It came up, so that had worked out. Now he uploaded the connection routing software from the QE radio into the Arcadia communications network.

Milbanks's people should also have configured his permissions to install this code package, so he went ahead and initiated the install. He didn't get a permission violation, and the package started the installation process. This piece was self-configuring with the data it got from both ends, the QE radio and the Arcadia network.

When the software had installed, Costa activated it. While logged into the Arcadia system, he placed a call to the Earthsea Network Operations Center. A face popped up on his heads-up display.

"Earthsea NOC. Planck here."

"Hi, Jeff. Paolo, on Arcadia."

"No shit?"

"Yeah. First interstellar call. Thirty-one hundred light-years. Ain't that somethin'?"

"I'll say. Paolo, you're as clear as if you were down the block. No difference."

"That's great. I wasn't sure this shit would work."

"Yeah, me neither. Not at that kind of distance. So how's it going over there?"

"It's great. The food's good. Spicy. The people are nice. And, Jeff, get this. All the women here run around topless all the time."

"C'mon."

"No, it's true. When they aren't completely naked, that is."

"Now I know you're pulling my leg."

"Oh, yeah? You should have Arcadia news wire access now. Look at the coverage of our arrival parade a couple days back."

Planck turned slightly to look at another area of his display.

"Holy shit. Hey, Paolo, we're gonna have to censor this stuff. I don't think we can just open this up to people here, can we?"

"Not our decision, Jeff. For right now, we're locked down to a very few people with permissions. Let them figure it out. That's way above my pay grade."

Planck kept glancing off to the side.

"Yeah. OK. I'm with you there– Geez, would you look at that! That naked gal just kissed you."

"Half-naked. Yup. She kissed me on the cheek. 'Welcome to Arcadia,' she said."

"That's some welcome."

Planck looked aside at his other display window again.

"My God, she's beautiful."

"Yeah. Miss Arcadia City or something like that. Hey, I gotta go report we're up. Talk to you later, Jeff."

"OK, Paolo. Try not to get in any trouble over there."

Planck looked back at the other side of his display.

"Criminy."

Once Costa told him the link was up, Salvatore Romano put in a call to Valerie Laurent. The two capitals were not in sync at the moment, it being early afternoon in Arcadia City on Arcadia and the beginning of the day in Bergheim on Earthsea, but it was close enough.

"Valerie Laurent."

"Good morning, Madam Director."

"Sal! You got the link up."

"Yes, ma'am."

"So how are things going?" Laurent asked.

"Generally speaking, very well, Madam Director. The people here are very friendly, the prime minister and I have hit it off, and they seem to earnestly want a deal. I detect no hidden agenda at all."

"That's excellent, Sal."

"Yes, ma'am. Overall, very positive. There is one thing that concerns me, however...."

Laurent talked about Romano's concern with Loukas Diakos before Diakos got in touch with Rob Milbank. When Diakos and Milbank talked, Diakos filled him in.

"You've got to be kidding me, Loukas," Milbank said. "They're upset because we don't dress to their standards?"

"It's more than that, Rob. They have freedom of the press here, and they think that means if they open up the link to Arcadia, people will log into our news wires and see pictures of naked people."

"Well, of course, they will. Pictures of naked people

somewhere else where the rules are different. And that's a problem how?"

"They brought it up, Rob, not me. They really have their lavalavas in a bunch about it.

"Now, that aside, they really want a deal. This whole balance of payments thing between their cities? They have a century of experience with it, and they're good at it. We had accounts under a planetary account for Arcadia when we got here.

"With all that experience, I think they have a leg up on becoming the clearinghouse for all the planetary payment streams. I pointed out that possibility to the director, and she got even more excited about a deal."

Milbank had a moment's pang of greed for that banking business, but Diakos was right. If they were really that good at it, they would win that business eventually anyway. In the meantime, he could use it as a bargaining chip.

"All right. Thanks, Loukas. Let me think about it."

"There's one other thing you need to be thinking about," Diakos said.

"What's that?"

"What's the date, Rob?"

"July second, 2368."

"That's on Arcadia. On Earthsea it's April seventh, 2376."

"What? How can that be? We haven't had time dilation or something like that, have we?"

"No, Rob. It's much simpler than that. On Arcadia, we have a twenty-five hour day. So we just kept using the same calendar, but we logged four percent or so fewer days than Earth.

"On Earthsea, the day is twenty-three and a half hours long or so. Like us, they make up the difference in the middle of the night with extra minutes or something. But, just counting day cycles, they logged two percent or so more days than Earth.

"So we're six percent or more off from each other, and over a hundred and twenty-two years or so, it adds up."

"I'll be damned."

"Yeah, so I can see another sticking point coming up. Whose calendar do we use?"

"Oh, shit."

## The Chen Step In

Milbank decided to consult MinChao and Jessica on this one. He asked for a meeting, and met with them mid-morning the next day. Once he was seated and tea was poured, he told them what was going on.

"We have a little problem with the Earthsea deal," Milbank said.

"They don't want a deal?" MinChao asked.

"No, they really want a deal. But they have an issue with our lack of a nudity ban."

MinChao and Jessica looked at each other and back to Milbank.

"They have a problem with how someone dresses somewhere else?" MinChao asked.

"Perhaps the nineteenth-century playwright was correct," Jessica said. "'He is a barbarian, and thinks that the customs of his tribe and island are the laws of nature.'"

"I think it's more subtle than that, Jessica. They have freedom of speech and of the press, just as we do here. But if we open the QE radio link between the planets, our news wires would be accessible from Earthsea. The government can't block them."

"Ah," MinChao said. "But if they look up the footage from your little parade earlier this week, as an example, people are going to get screenfuls of naked people running around."

Milbank nodded.

"That's it exactly. They can't block them, but they think maybe they should, because if they don't people will get upset, so couldn't we please put some clothes on or censor our news wires for them?"

"Neither of those will fly here either, Rob, as you well know," MinChao said. "Nudity acceptance on Arcadia was burned in by the Kendall regime. When Kevin Kendall's regime sought to ban nudity as just one facet of its tyranny, being able to dress – or not – however one wanted became an enduring symbol of freedom. Any kind of nudity ban would be seen as an attempt at tyranny. The government would fall."

"I know, MinChao," Milbank said. "And we have freedom of the press and freedom of speech, too. And those don't permit censoring in the way they want, either."

Milbank sighed.

"I'm not sure what to do with this one."

They sat and sipped their tea for several minutes. Finally Jessica stirred.

"There may be a solution to this that doesn't violate either planet's sensibilities," she said.

"I'm all ears, Jessica, because this stupid thing could kill a deal that's good for everybody."

"Consider, Rob. Freedom of speech and of the press mean you can say or print whatever you want. They do not mean you can force someone else to listen to you or read what you publish.

"What about a warning label on interplanetary connections that warns people that the customs and practices of other planets are not the same, and they can choose not to read text or see imagery from the other planet."

"Put a warning label on Arcadia content?" Milbank asked.

"No," Jessica said with some force. "Put a warning label on the interstellar link – all interstellar links – in both directions."

"But what would an Arcadian find offensive about their

culture?"

"How about people being legally required to wear clothes when swimming? That sounds like tyranny to most of Arcadia."

Milbank's eyes got wide, then he nodded.

"And if the links have warning labels and opt-ins in both directions," he said, "it keeps it from being some sort of implied indictment of one planet by the other."

"Exactly," Jessica said.

Milbank nodded.

"That may work. I'll try that on them and see how it goes. We potentially also have a calendar issue. They have a shorter day than Earth, and we have a longer one, but we just kept counting along every day. We've slipped almost eight years. For them, it's 2376."

"I don't see a problem there, Rob," Jessica said. "We have a similar issue with time zones now. Everybody understands you can't call someone two time zones away at nine in the morning because it's too early over there. So we don't have to pick one calendar or another."

MinChao nodded.

"As far as business is concerned, it just needs to be specified in the contract," he said. "If you lease something for a year, whose year are you using? As long as it's specified, it's not a problem. From that point of view, we should probably use Earth's calendar for business, because it's neutral."

"Again, not favoring one planet over the other," Milbank said. "I like it."

Milbank thought about it, then nodded.

"Thank you so much for your help," he said. "I was spinning my wheels on these, and wasn't getting any good ideas from staff."

"No problem, Rob," MinChao said. "That's what friends are for."

After Milbank had left, MinChao and Jessica planned for their afternoon meeting with the Earthsea ambassador.

"Busy day today," MinChao said.

"Yes. Well, if we can help out getting this deal done, we should do that."

MinChao nodded.

"By the way, I think we should meet the ambassador in my tea room rather than yours."

"Why?"

"Because I have the display installed already."

MinChao nodded. They had decided to put a display in each of their tea rooms. It had been a tough decision, because those rooms were normally used for contemplation as well as receiving guests. They each had offices for more mundane tasks.

But the availability of a display in meetings with guests, as the hyperspace project had geared up, had become more pressing. Jessica's had been installed first, and hers was now operational.

"Going to show him the simulation?"

"I'm going to show him the reality."

The liaison from the Prime Minister's office had a short briefing for Ambassador Romano before his meeting with the Chen.

"The Chen-Jasic family is the wealthiest and most politically connected family on Arcadia, and they are personal friends with the prime minister. As well as pretty much anyone else of influence on Arcadia, for that matter.

"They are called simply the Chen, but he, Chen MinChao, is called Chen Zufu and she, Jessica Chen-Jasic, is called Chen Zumu. Zufu and Zumu mean honored grandfather and honored grandmother. They are the senior couple of the family and make all the big decisions, and are consulted on most minor ones as well.

"The meeting will likely be in a tea room, overlooking their downtown gardens. This is where their truly priceless seed stock and hybrids are grown now. Large-scale production is elsewhere, mostly in the mountains to the north.

"You will sit on pillows, a low tea table between you. A tea girl will serve you all tea. You, as their guest, must sip your tea first. The conversation will be friendly and low-key, but make no mistake about the impact of it. These people are major players in Arcadia business and politics.

"Both of them are in their seventies now, and have been running the family business for close to twenty years. The inside skinny is that David Bolton, who you've met, and his wife are their successors, and will likely take up the reins of the family within the next five years.

"They will call you Mr. Ambassador. You should call them Chen Zufu for him and Chen Zumu for her. You can remember because it's 'f' like in father and 'm' like in mother.

"The conversation may have long periods of silence for contemplation. That's perfectly OK. You should let them break the silences. And you should request and receive their leave to depart before getting up to go.

"Do not make the mistake of underestimating them. He has an education in business and finance, she in engineering. Both are very accomplished – in fact, the most accomplished people in an accomplished family.

"Oh, and do not record the conversation with them. That

would be seriously unwise. An unforgiveable indiscretion.

"Do you have any questions, Mr. Ambassador?"

"No," Romano said. "You've been most thorough. Thank you."

The liaison left. Romano had, of course, recorded the meeting, and listened to it twice more before leaving for the Chen-Jasic family compound.

Mindful of the liaison's last admonition, before he left Romano turned off the recording function of his communicator, lest he forget later.

Prime Minister Milbank had dispatched his car, with driver and shotgun, to take Romano to his meeting with the Chen. They pulled up in front of a large apartment building. The driver opened the door and Romano got out of the car.

Across the street was a large building, down this whole side of the block, UPTOWN MARKET in tall letters running down this side. It was busy, with people in and out constantly. Part of the facade on the first floor was a restaurant, on the corner across from him, with a sign that displayed a single Chinese letter, one Romano could recognize already. It had been on the tea gift box presented to Director Laurent on Earthsea by Ambassador Diakos.

Just one Chinese character on the sign: Chen.

"Through those doors, Mr. Ambassador," the driver said. "The counter clerk will take you to Chen Zufu."

"Thank you."

Romano walked through the doors to the lobby. Behind a counter to one side, a young woman, perhaps sixteen years old, was studying in her heads-up display. She looked up when he walked in.

"Good afternoon, Mr. Ambassador. This way, please."

She came out from behind the counter and motioned him to follow her. She was wearing a floral-print lavalava and flip-flops. She was topless.

She led him down a short side hallway, through a locking security door that unlatched as she approached, presumably unlocked by her in her heads-up display, around a corner and down another hall. She stopped at a doorway with a wood and rice paper sliding door.

She knocked once on the door frame and slid the door open.

"Ambassador Romano, Chen Zumu."

"Show him in, JiGang," Romano heard a woman's voice say.

JiGang waved him through the door and slid it shut behind him.

"Mr. Ambassador, welcome," Jessica said. "Please be seated."

She waved to a pillow across a low tea table from her and a man Romano guessed to be Chen Zufu.

Romano took in the scene. The couple before him were, as the liaison had said, in their seventies. He wore a lavalava, and was bald. He was at least half Asian, likely Chinese, but there were other strains there, too, including a large dose of European and perhaps a little African.

She was also half Asian, a large part European, and perhaps a little Indian. She wore her long, white hair straight, pulled together at the nape of her neck, and was dressed in a robe of royal blue, with multi-colored dragons rampant among trees, flowers, and clouds. The stitchwork was incredible. That robe had been a labor of love.

Romano's field before going into government was history, and it was still his hobby. He recognized with a shock that her robe was silk, and too new to have been brought from Earth over a century ago. He couldn't begin to guess its value. But the larger point was not lost on him: They had successfully transplanted silkworms to Arcadia!

The Arcadians had not even mentioned silk as a trade good, but the trade route across Asia to Europe in antiquity had been called The Silk Road, after all. Romano thought again that he had to make this deal work. Had to. He just didn't know how.

Behind the couple, a large teak-beamed doorway framed the view into a beautiful garden, a slice of paradise transplanted into the heart of the city. Young men and women in lavalavas worked in the garden.

Between his guests he saw a statuette, an exact miniature of the statue he had seen in the downtown square, set upon a carved jade pillar on a carved stone base. The statue itself was a yellow-tinged white metal he didn't recognize, but it showed no signs of rust or wear from being out in the weather.

As he looked out the doorway, a young woman – child really – of perhaps thirteen entered carrying a teapot. She wore a lavalava and flip-flops, and was, like all the rest, topless.

She poured tea for each of them in turn, beginning with him. She set the teapot down on the table, bowed to a spot between them, and left without saying a word.

Mindful of his briefing earlier, Romano picked up the tea cup and sipped. MinChao sipped next, then Jessica sipped. The tea was yet a third variety and was, like the others, incredible.

After a pause to enjoy their tea, Jessica broke the silence.

"So, Mr. Ambassador, what do you think of Arcadia?"

"I like it a great deal, Chen Zumu. The people have been very friendly, your food is wonderful, and your teas are amazing."

"You hope to be able to put a trade deal together then, Mr. Ambassador?"

"I hope to, Chen Zumu, but I am wrestling with a couple of

issues that I don't know how to address."

Jessica nodded.

"Yes, we spoke to Prime Minister Milbank about them this morning. These are not without solutions, Mr. Ambassador."

"I hope you can help then, Chen Zumu, because I am somewhat at a loss."

"First, the calendar issue we have no concern about whatsoever. This was all solved with respect to time zones both on Earth as well as on Earthsea and Arcadia long ago."

"It was?"

Jessica looked to MinChao, and he stirred.

"Of course, Mr. Ambassador," he said. "When one specifies a contract, for instance, one specifies it in terms of the time zone. It is from midnight to midnight in this time zone. Bergheim Time, say, or Arcadia City time, for example. It is not from midnight two time zones east to midnight two time zones west, or vice versa. One would be four hours longer, and the other four hours shorter.

"So contracts need to use dates with a specification of whose calendar one is using, nothing more. For simplicity, we should probably just use Earth's calendar. Then neither planet 'wins' or 'loses' in the selection of a universal calendar."

"That is a splendid solution, Chen Zufu," Romano said. "And, as you say, it builds on our experience with time zones. The other problem, though, is likely to be more intractable."

Jessica nodded.

"The issue of our lack of a dress code for our citizens," she said.

"Yes, Chen Zumu," Romano said. "We have freedom of the press, but if we open the interstellar links to the news wires, many people on Earthsea will be offended."

"As will many people on Arcadia, Mr. Ambassador. Being

forced to wear clothes while swimming, for example, will look to the people of Arcadia like tyranny."

Romano started at that. It was a viewpoint he hadn't considered.

"Yes, Mr. Ambassador. Both populations are likely to be a little nonplussed by the other, at least at first."

"Then what do we do, Chen Zumu?"

"Consider, Mr. Ambassador. Do you not have friends who have their little quirks? Something that other people might find offensive, but, in the context of your friendship, you consider innocuous, or even charming in a way?"

Romano thought about it and nodded.

"Then why not between friends like Earthsea and Arcadia, Mr. Ambassador?" Jessica asked. "'Oh, you know those Arcadians. Running around half-naked all the time. Tsk, tsk.' Or 'That's Earthsea for you. Nice place if you don't mind getting all dressed up to go swimming, believe it or not.'"

"A mutual tolerance of our disparate quirks, Chen Zumu?"

"Of course, Mr. Ambassador."

Romano nodded.

"I can see that happening over time, Chen Zumu. But how do we get from here to there? Without violating freedom of the press?"

"One's right to free speech does not put a duty on others to listen, Mr. Ambassador. Nor does freedom of the press include a compulsion on others to read.

"We can put a notice on interstellar feeds that the culture of one planet is not identical to the culture of another. Make people opt in to receiving the news wires and other materials from the other planet. In both directions. If they are offended, they can opt out just as easily."

"That may work, Chen Zumu."

"Of course it will work, Mr. Ambassador. But I thought I would up the ante a bit for you. You've no doubt noted my robe and wondered. So, yes, it is real silk, and yes, that silk was made here. Tea and spices and silk, the staples of the Far East trade on Earth for centuries.

"Most of that trade was well before there was radio communication on Earth. The caravans and tea clippers did not have instantaneous communications. They carried messages back and forth. That system worked quite well without other, faster, methods of communication.

"If Earthsea decides not to join a trade consortium of the colonies, that is up to them. We will carry on without them. The QE radios would be very nice to have, but interstellar trade does not depend on them, Mr. Ambassador."

The threat was clear, and Romano nodded.

"I understand, Chen Zumu."

"And now I will show you something no one else has seen, Mr. Ambassador. But first, where we are headed."

Jessica gestured to the side wall, and it came alive with the largest three-dimensional display Romano had ever seen in a private home. It encompassed the whole wall. In the center of the display floated a large cylindrical ship, against a star field, being serviced by a number of shuttles delivering containers. It was a three-dimensional simulation, but it was a good one.

Romano picked up on size cues. Windows, containers, shuttles. The ship was huge.

"Very compelling, Chen Zumu."

"Ah, but that is more than a dream. Mr. Ambassador. This is where we are now."

The display changed. This was no simulation, but three-dimensional camera imagery, and it was so real Romano almost clutched at the table to keep from being sucked out into space through the open wall.

In the center of the display, three metafactories worked at producing the hull of the ship he had seen in the simulation. It was perhaps a quarter complete, growing out of the asteroid as the factories pushed the completed portion away from them. Lights blazed on the asteroid face so the computers could camera-guide their tools. The flares of welding arcs were continuous in dozens of locations.

And it was real.

"With fitting out and stocking ahead of us, we are perhaps two years away from beginning the tea, spice, and silk trade all over again, Mr. Ambassador.

"It is up to you to make sure Director Laurent understands. We are going to do this. Earthsea can be a part of it, or not."

## Intermezzo

As it turned out, Valerie Laurent was as desperate to get to an agreement as Salvatore Romano was. Laurent was a student of history as well, and nobody needed to tell her that Arcadia could go it alone if they wanted to. QE radios or not, there would be a trade consortium. Arcadia would be fielding the modern equivalent of clipper ships, running tea, spices, and silk to the other colony planets.

Aside and apart from the QE radios and its magnificent cheeses, Earthsea stood to dominate the interplanetary banking transfers that went along with such a trade. A small percentage fee on very large transactions still added up to a great deal of money.

Laurent wanted that business, and when the Chen's solutions were presented for the two potential problems that had cropped up, she seized them and ran with the ball.

As in most high-level negotiations, by the time the principals met, the details had been ironed out.

What Director Laurent did do in her private conversations with Prime Minister Milbank is give him permission to transport the two QE radios destined for Amber. It was decided Paolo Costa would be one of the passengers to Amber, to get the QE radios up and operating on the Amber end.

Before he left, Costa oversaw the installation of the second QE radio staying on Arcadia – the one paired with one of the Amber units. This unit, though, was installed at the hyperspace facility at the Arcadia City Shuttleport. There was no point in placing both units in the same building, or connected to the same power, when they were redundant nodes in a multi-point self-patching network.

Costa used a radio link to the other QE radio to download the software from Earthsea into that unit, and brought it up. He left it in 'Configured – Waiting For Connection' status. When he brought the second Amber unit up, they ought to connect easily.

The other person going on the trip to Amber was Sasha Ivanov. Another political ally of Milbank, Ivanov was a scientist and engineer with a broadly based understanding of technology. Milbank brought him in at the tail end of discussions with Laurent so he would be up to speed on the negotiations for a multi-planet consortium.

Ivanov would attempt to extend the Arcadia-Earthsea agreement to Amber.

The broad shape of the Arcadia-Earthsea agreement was simple. Each planetary government would allow entry to the other planet's products without any import tax or duties other than the common sales tax that applied to their own domestic products.

There would be no attempt at price setting. The prices of goods and services would instead be allowed to float. And the exchange rate between their currencies would be determined by market forces as well, with the Bank of Earthsea maintaining a market in currencies.

They also opened up the Arcadia-Earthsea QE radio link to public access. There were two levels of opt-in, one for text-only content and the other for imagery, both still and video.

There was some grumbling on both sides about the other side's cultural differences – described as backwardness from both ends – but it was hard for someone to legitimately claim offense at something they had opted in to read or see.

Going along in the containers to Amber were the two QE radio units, one for the link from Amber to Arcadia and one for the link from Amber to Earthsea; a container of water and other supplies for the trip back, which also contained Ambassador Ivanov's personal cubic; and a container half of cheese and half of tea.

Milbank had asked Laurent's permission to ship half of Earthsea's gift of cheese to Arcadia as Earthsea's gift to Amber.

"As it was our gift to you, that is a generous offer, Mr. Prime Minister," Laurent had said.

"Madam Director, we are either in this together or we are not. Let us always work toward being in it together. Over the long haul, everyone will be better off."

"As you say, Mr. Prime Minister. And thank you."

From Milbank's point of view, it was better optics if the cheese-tasting party sold out than if there was cheese left over.

With one deal in the bag, Milbank decided to herald the departure for Amber. News crews were invited to video the intrepid hyperspace travelers boarding Hyper-1 at the Arcadia City Shuttleport. They broadcast the launch live on the news wires.

It all went off without a hitch, and then it was time to settle down for the fourteen-week wait again.

Wait! No, that was wrong. With the QE radios along, it would only be a six- or seven-week wait.

During this time, Hyper-2 continued to deliver raw materials to the shipyard in the Beacon asteroid belt. Ball bearings, copper, and water were, for the time being, easier to ship from Arcadia. It meant there were no delays in the progress of the hull of the new ship.

Ever the promoter, Milbank had run a contest for naming the new ship, with the people of Arcadia selecting the winner via the news wires. *Star Runner* was the clear favorite.

In Beacon, the bootstrap factory had moved on. It had built the first metafactory, and then it and the new unit had each built one more, putting three metafactories on *Star Runner*. It was these three metafactories that Jessica had shown Romano during their meeting.

The bootstrap factory now had moved to a new asteroid and built a new metafactory. The two of them were each building one more, so there would be three metafactories to begin work on the hyperspace ship *Star Tripper*, the second runner-up in Milbank's ship-naming contest.

*Star Runner* would not be the only ship in her class.

Not by a long shot.

"Have a seat, ChaoLi," Jessica said.

"Thank you, Chen Zumu."

"You asked for this meeting, ChaoLi. You may proceed."

"Thank you, Chen Zumu."

ChaoLi gathered her thoughts while Jessica was content to sip her tea.

"We are perhaps six months away from moving *Star Runner* to Arcadia for fitting out, Chen Zumu. That will take the better part of a year."

"So long?"

"There is a lot of work to do, and one can only have so many people working on it before they get in each other's way. There is also the issue of feeding them and dealing with human waste before the systems to deal with those issues are in place."

"An interesting problem."

"Yes, and we have some innovative solutions. One is to take self-contained units from here up to the ship for mess and lavatories, and plug them into the unused passenger container locations. These can be swapped out as they need servicing. Once the on-board facilities are built out, we can dispense with those, and use the self-contained ones on the *Star Tripper*."

"That's clever. So your staffing is limited until the on-board facilities are built out."

"Yes, Chen Zumu. Then it's limited by the need for people to have room to work. Not be in each other's way."

Jessica nodded, then waved a hand for ChaoLi to continue.

"My point today, Chen Zumu, is that it may be time to begin organizing both the fitting-out process and the spacing process as new companies, and begin hiring and training their employees."

"Pursue these activities as new companies, ChaoLi?"

"I think so, Chen Zumu. They are different skill sets than we currently have in the design and operations groups, right up through the management levels. Our current activities are all technical, and these are not.

"The fitting-out phase is going to be dominated by the need to create a pleasing passenger environment while maintaining reasonable budgets. The spacing phase is going to be all about operations numbers. You know, margins and costs and demurrage, the timing of receipts, cash flows. All that sort of thing.

"We likely need different people on those activities, who can fine-tune their focus on those issues over time. Not try to be shifting gears back and forth in their thinking. The shipping company, in particular, is going to have to be very hardheaded about their numbers to make it work."

Jessica nodded. It made tremendous sense to her. The new activities required a different view of things, and would require dedicated staff and management.

"Very well, ChaoLi. Let us consider this. I will have a decision for you soon."

"Thank you, Chen Zumu."

Jessica talked to MinChao about ChaoLi's proposal later that day.

"I think ChaoLi is right," MinChao said. "The emphasis is completely different, and requires different thinking."

"And they're also different from each other, so two companies," Jessica said.

MinChao nodded.

"There's another benefit, of course," he said. "If one of the companies goes bankrupt, we don't lose both. It also keeps management from hiding bad numbers in one activity with good numbers in the other. Both have to be managed properly."

"I think the shipping activity is likely to be the most difficult to manage," Jessica said. "Shipping companies were always difficult on Earth."

"Oh, yes. There are some notorious examples."

"What do we call them?"

MinChao thought for a moment before replying.

"The company to do the fitting out is all based here, and on Arcadia I think the family name is best."

"So Chen Shipfitting?"

"That works. What about for the shipping company? On other planets, the Chen name gives us no benefit."

"How about Jixing Trading Company?" Jessica asked.

"Lucky Star? That works for me."

ChaoLi was called to a meeting with Chen Zumu later that day. She left her downtown location early and went straight to Jessica's office. When ChaoLi showed up, Jessica was seated behind her desk doing paperwork. She was not asked to sit.

"Yes, Chen Zumu."

"You have a competent second to manage the design group, ChaoLi?" Jessica asked.

"Of course, Chen Zumu."

Jessica nodded.

"ChaoLi, you are relieved of responsibility for the design group effective immediately. You will turn this responsibility over to your second.

"You will incorporate a new company, the Jixing Trading Company. The current operations group will be your ground operations arm on Arcadia. Work out a transfer price for that operation.

"You are to begin hiring and training crews for the hyperspace ships, and organizing the company to conduct interstellar freight and passenger operations.

"You will be the chief executive officer of the company.

"That is all for now, ChaoLi."

"Yes, Chen Zumu."

JieMin had also been busy. Janice Quant's concentration of quantum entanglement researchers on Earthsea and medical nanotechnology researchers on Amber got him to wonder what other concentrations of specialties Quant might have arranged, on other colony planets.

JieMin found the colonist rosters for all the colony planets in the colony project headquarters archives. He set up a matching algorithm across the colonists' occupations and specialties, and let it run. It was a difficult problem, but the computer wasn't the final say-so. JieMin would just use the computer to point out the possibles, then he would look at them individually.

When he looked at the possibles, JieMin found that some colonies, like Arcadia, did not have out of the ordinary concentrations of any one specialty, but more than half of colonies did.

Looking deeper, of those concentrations, some of them were caused by the colonists themselves. That is, researchers had put a group together for the colony lottery that included their friends at other research locations. They thus ensured that, if they were selected, they would end up at the same colony.

But others of the research concentrations looked to have been engineered by Janice Quant. The AI had put them in the same colony, JieMin assumed, on purpose. Given that Quant knew more about which research paths would likely pan out, these specialties were grouped together to facilitate their discoveries.

Quantum entanglement research on Earthsea and medical nanotechnology research on Amber, sure. But there were other colonies with concentrations. Direct virtual reality research, materials science research, in metals, plastics, and ceramics, anti-aging research. Over a dozen areas where Quant had manipulated a colony's makeup to encourage advancement by grouping specialists together.

JieMin wondered how far some of them had gotten.

If they found the other colonies, they would find out.

That night – the night ChaoLi was made CEO of Jixing Trading Company – was their weekly night out. YanMing and YanJing were at home with JieJun, who at ten was still a bit too young to be left at home alone.

They ate at Chen's, of course, and sat at their favorite table in a quiet corner.

"Big news from work today," ChaoLi said.

"Me, too," JieMin said.

"Oh, you go first."

"All right. Earthsea and Amber weren't the only colonies to have concentrations in specific specialties. In fact, three-fourths of them did. Arcadia is in a minority in terms of having no concentrations in a specific specialty that I could find."

"Oh, now that's exciting," ChaoLi said.

JieMin told her of the findings of his research, completed just that afternoon.

"So we now have a list of the colonies and what specializations they had, if any?" ChaoLi asked.

"That's right. So if we find a bunch of colonies at once, we can visit them in whatever order seems most logical to us."

"That's really something. We'll have to take a look at your list and see what makes the most sense."

"OK, now your big news," JieMin said.

"I was relieved of the design group today. Denise Peterson will be taking over the design group."

"And what will you be doing?"

"Chen Zumu made me the CEO of a new company. Jixing Trading Company. We will be the hyperspace shipping company."

"What about the operations group at the shuttleport?"

"They will be the Arcadia ground operations group. In support of the big hyperspace ships."

"And that is still under you?"

"Yes. That's part of Jixing Trading now."

"And you're CEO. Wow. That's a huge vote of confidence."

"And a huge job. I hope I can do it."

"You'll be fine. Make sure you get a really good financial officer, though. That's a numbers business."

JieMin, originally caught flat-footed by her announcement, thought about it.

"You know, there's a lot of Earth history about how to run such a company."

"A lot about how not to run one, too."

JieMin nodded.

"So there's a lot of source material for you there."

"Yes, and I'll be studying all of it."

"There is one other good part of all this," JieMin said.

"What's that"

"You're not my boss anymore."

"Not at work, anyway," ChaoLi said with a twinkle in her eye.

# Mission To Amber

"Amber Control to Hyper-1. Repeat your last transmission."

"Hyper-1 to Amber Control. Inbound from colony planet Arcadia. Arriving from space in twenty-two hours. Request instructions."

"Roger that, Hyper-1. Maintain profile. Contact Amber Control when two hours out for landing clearance."

"Roger, Amber Control. Maintain profile. Contact Amber Control for clearance when two hours out. Hyper-1 out."

McKay laughed.

"That got him flustered enough to ask for retransmission," he said.

"Gave himself time to think," Moore said. "Traffic control guys hate to act like anything unusual's going on."

"Looks like a nice planet," Ivanov said, looking out the side window.

Costa by this time was getting jaded. He shrugged.

"From space, they all look about the same. I'll just be glad to be down on the ground again and have a shower."

"Mr. President, we have a situation," Vaclav Brabec said.

"God, how I hate that word. What is Ms. Sellick up to now?"

Amber President Jean Dufort had had problems recently keeping the leader of his party in the Assembly happy. He had the majority, but it seemed they were even harder to please than the minority party. Maybe that was because, with the presidency and solid majorities in both houses, his party expected more.

Whatever the reason, the Honorable Josephine Sellick was a major pain in the ass.

"No, sir. This is weirder than that. We've just been contacted by a shuttle that claims it is inbound from Arcadia, one of the other colony planets."

"I'm sorry. What was that?"

"Amber Traffic Control says they've just been contacted by a shuttle that claims it is inbound from Arcadia, one of the other colony planets."

Dufort sat back in his desk chair. That was a stunning piece of news. How would it play into his political situation?

For Amber was in a weird period right now. Everything was political. The two parties were at each other's throats, and both sides of the aisle seemed to be trying to score points with the public by seeing who could do the best job of roasting him.

It was worse than that, he realized suddenly. Sellick had been a big proponent of space exploration, and making a massive effort to come up with some sort of interstellar drive. He had fought to keep the funds and effort on more mundane – literally earthly – things.

And now here comes someone on an interstellar ship to Amber. He groaned.

"Sir?" Brabec asked.

"Sellick has been pushing me to work on an interstellar drive. I fought it as daydreaming. And now here comes someone with such a drive. She'll go completely loony over this."

"But, sir, doesn't this prove you were right all along?"

Dufort eyed his chief of staff narrowly.

"How so, Vaclav?"

"Her argument has been that having an interstellar drive meant we would be able to market our medical technology products to other planets. We ended up with a lot of medical nanotech types here, and we must be ahead of planets without that head start."

"Right, and I said No."

"Yes, sir. But it turns out we didn't need to spend the money and effort to come up with an interstellar drive. Someone else did. So you saved all that money and effort, but we still get to market our technology to other planets. You were right, sir."

"Hmm. That might work if we handle this properly."

Dufort nodded.

"Yes, that might work. All right, Vaclav, can we get whoever is on that shuttle here quietly? And maybe put the shuttle in a hangar, or cover it, or cover its markings or something, so it isn't obvious it came from somewhere else?"

"I think so, sir. They have those big hangars out there at the shuttleport."

"OK. Get it in a hangar and then shut it down. Guards and such. Nobody gets in. Then bring the pilots and whoever else there is here so I can figure out what's going on before we go public with anything. And do it quietly."

"Understood, sir. We can do that. They won't be here until tomorrow morning. They said they were twenty-plus hours out."

Dufort nodded.

"Understood. Oh, and Vaclav?"

"Yes, sir."

"Get traffic control to ask them if they have a briefing book or something for me."

"Sir?"

"You don't send a mission to another planet without materials, Vaclav. See what they have for me."

"Yes, Sir."

"There it is, right on cue," Moore said. "They want any materials we have for fearless leader."

"Geez, you'd think these guys do this every day," McKay said. "Like they all have the same playbook or something."

"Mr. Ambassador, are we OK to transmit the video?" Moore asked Ivanov."

"Back to Mr. Ambassador, is it?" Ivanov said with a chuckle.

They had all been on a first-name basis the whole trip.

"Well, we're sorta back to business, sir."

"Understood, Mr. Moore. Yes, let's go ahead and transmit the video to them."

"Very well, sir."

Dufort watched the video through twice before meeting with Brabec.

"Did you watch the video, Vaclav?"

"Yes, sir."

"So those two planets have already been in contact with each other. Arcadia and Earthsea."

"Yes, sir," Brabec said. "Arcadia was the third drop, so they would know where we and Earthsea both are. As the second drop, we've known where Earthsea was for a long time."

"Yes, we just didn't know how to get there. As Ms. Sellick has been wont to remind me these last ten years."

"So Arcadia solved the interstellar travel problem and approached us."

"They approached Earthsea first," Dufort noted.

"They apparently knew that Earthsea had solved the quantum entanglement radio problem, sir. That would make sense, to contact them first."

"Yes, and now Prime Minister Milbank and Director Laurent say they have QE radios on this shuttle for us to use to set up a three-sided communication network with them."

"That's exciting, sir," Brabec said. "You'll be able to talk with them directly, in real time. Negotiate some sort of agreement or treaty with them."

"Yes."

Dufort drummed his fingers on the table.

"I wonder what sort of agreement they'll want, Vaclav."

"They said so, though, sir. Didn't they?"

"A completely bilateral, open-borders, free-trade agreement. Yes, of course. That's what everybody always says they want, Vaclav. The devil is in the details."

"Yes, sir."

Dufort was lost in thought a few minutes. Brabec waited, not having been dismissed.

"All right, Vaclav. Nothing else to do about that until they get here. What else do we have today?"

"Amber Control to Hyper-1."

"Hyper-1 here. Go ahead, Amber."

"Hyper-1, what is your stack?"

"We're two wide, two high, Amber."

"Roger, Hyper-1. You are cleared to land on shuttlepad twenty-one. Then dismount. We are moving you under cover."

"Roger, Amber Control. Cleared to land on shuttlepad twenty-one and dismount. Hyper-1 out."

McKay turned to Moore. Moore had heard the whole thing, but repeating instructions was ingrained.

"Cleared to land on pad twenty-one and dismount," McKay said.

"Maybe they don't have any taller stairs."

"They said they were getting us undercover."

"Undercover, huh?" Moore asked. "What about those

containers? Earthsea makings on both of the radios, and it would be hard to miss the big red Chinese character on the other two."

"Maybe 'Chen' means something different here."

McKay shrugged and Moore laughed.

"Well, when in doubt, follow instructions," Moore said.

Once they had confirmed transponder compatibility, Moore let the computer do the work. It put the shuttle down pinpoint center on the pad. McKay unlatched the payload, then Moore let the computer move the shuttle to the parking pad next door.

A shuttle tug came out of the hangar next to the pads and pulled the shuttle into the hangar. Once stopped, a portable stair drove up to the shuttle.

They all gathered up their small bags with their toiletries and a change of clothes. Moore opened the shuttle hatch and waved Ivanov ahead.

Ivanov was met at the top of the stairs by a young man who looked very nervous. Ivanov put on his most calming and reassuring demeanor.

"Hello, I am Sasha Ivanov, Arcadia's ambassador to Amber. Pleased to meet you."

The mundanity of introductions seemed to calm the young man.

"Pleased to meet you, Mr. Ambassador. I am Michael Grant. I am an aide for Vaclav Brabec, President Dufort's chief of staff. I'm to take you all directly to the president, sir."

"Yes, yes, of course. Just as soon as we've had a chance to freshen up," Ivanov said, stroking his six weeks' beard.

"They said directly, Mr. Ambassador."

"Of course."

Ivanov looked around the hangar. There were offices and

supplies rooms to one side. Moore need not have worried about the containers. There was already a container lift moving them into the hangar.

"I'm sure there's a bathroom here we can use. Over there, isn't it?"

"Uh, Mr. Ambassador–"

"Mr. Grant, have you ever seen anyone shown in to meet with your president in our current, er, state of hygiene?"

Ivanov moved closer to Grant. Ivanov was a big man, and six weeks without a shower was more than casually evident.

"Oh. Oh, no, Mr. Ambassador."

"You see, then? You don't want to be the person to set that sort of precedent, Mr. Grant. Just show us to the bathroom, and we'll be along presently."

"Uh, yes, sir. If you're sure it's all right, sir."

"Absolutely. And my fault, after all, Mr. Grant. I insisted, and I outrank you."

"Yes, sir. Thank you, sir. Right this way."

Ivanov turned around and winked at his companions. Moore and McKay were trying hard not to laugh, while Costa just wanted to get into that shower.

The hangar did in fact have bathrooms with showers. They took over both of them, and emerged twenty minutes later showered, shaved, and changed.

"Excellent, Mr. Grant. We are now at your disposal. Lead on, please."

"Yes, Mr. Ambassador. Thank you. This way, sir."

Grant led them out to the front of the building where a large groundcar waited. It was unmarked, and looked like it might be someone's personal vehicle.

"Not exactly a parade," Costa noted under his breath.

Ivanov caught it.

"Not like Arcadia, eh, Mr. Costa?"

"No, and probably no kiss from a pretty girl, either."

Costa didn't notice that he hadn't included what had been a nearly obligatory 'half-naked' to describe Miss Arcadia City. A month on Arcadia had changed his reality.

Ivanov chuckled.

Grant drove the car himself. They gazed curiously around as they headed into the city of Amber, which shared the name of the planet. Much more like Arcadia City than Bergheim, it was a big sprawling metropolis, unimpeded by circling mountains.

Grant took to the side streets as they approached the city center, and approached the original colony administrative building from the back side. He stopped at a rear service door. A guard there opened the door for them.

Grant gave the keys to the car to the guard.

"Thanks, Frank."

"No problem, Mr. Grant."

"This way, gentlemen," Grant said to Ivanov and his companions.

Grant led them into the building to the rear elevator bay and up to a high floor. They got out and walked down a hallway to a small conference room. There were place holders on the table at their seats.

"Please take your seats, gentlemen. It will be just a moment."

Grant himself took a seat and waited with them. Ivanov looked around.

"I think I've actually been in this room before. On Arcadia."

Grant started, and Ivanov explained.

"There were a couple different styles of administrative building in the original colonies, Mr. Grant, but Arcadia has the same one."

"Ah. I see, Mr. Ambassador."

Two men walked into the room, one obviously in charge, whom Ivanov recognized from his briefing as President Dufort. They all stood, and the two men came to their side of the table.

"Mr. Ambassador?"

"Yes, Mr. President. Sasha Ivanov. My companions are Paolo Costa, who is a QE radio installation and service technician from Earthsea, and Mr. Justin Moore and Mr. Gavin McKay, our pilots from Arcadia to here."

"My chief of staff, Mr. Ambassador. Vaclav Brabec. And you've already met his aide, Michael Grant."

"Indeed. Mr. President."

There were greetings and handshakes all around, and then Dufort and Brabec moved to the other side of the table with Grant. Dufort took the seat opposite Ivanov.

"Well, this is a big surprise, Mr. Ambassador, as I imagine you appreciate."

"Indeed I do, Mr. President. But we could not let you know in advance we were coming. The big disadvantage of QE radios is that they are paired when manufactured, and one can only set up a link by dragging one of the pair to where you intend to set it up."

"So I understand. And now here you are."

Ivanov pulled a folded document out of the pocket of his suit coat.

"My credentials, Mr. President."

Ivanov handed the document across the table to Dufort, who glanced at it and handed it to Brabec.

"And your mission, Mr. Ambassador?"

"To begin a conversation toward a trade deal among our three planets, Mr. President. Arcadia and Earthsea have executed such an agreement already, which we invite you to join."

"And the terms of this agreement, Mr. Ambassador?"

"If you will configure computer accounts for us on your planetary system, Mr. President, I would be happy to push you a copy of it. But in broad terms, it is free and open trade, unhampered by, er, protectionist impediments."

"And both planets have agreed to this, Mr. Ambassador? Both Arcadia and Earthsea?"

"Yes, Mr. President. It is expected that the cost of interstellar shipping will be impediment enough to importing products which are already available locally."

"I see."

"But as our first step, Mr. President, I would recommend installing the QE radios here, and then you can discuss the potential agreement directly with your fellow heads of state."

Dufort nodded. That made sense.

"Very well, Mr. Ambassador. And I am hoping you might brief me a bit on the personalities involved. To make things go more smoothly."

"Of course, Mr. President. But I think right now what is most in order is dinner and a good night's sleep for me. Zero gravity makes for disturbing dreams."

"Yes, of course, Mr. Ambassador. We will put you up close by here downtown. I will ask all you gentlemen to keep your, er, provenance a secret for the time being. The political situation here could make things more difficult than they need otherwise be were you not to do so."

"I understand, Mr. President. We will be happy to do so."

# Pushback

Sasha Ivanov luxuriated in the feeling of a bed with gravity again. He had had a wonderful night's sleep, and lay back now just enjoying the bed in the hotel suite in downtown Amber.

The room-service dinner last night had been good, if a little bland for Arcadian tastes. Their culinary efforts would also benefit from the availability of Arcadia's spices.

Ivanov's computer account had gone live while he was eating, and he had pushed President Dufort a copy of the Arcadia-Earthsea agreement before collapsing into bed.

Now to check mail and see what was on the schedule.

"Did you look at the Arcadia-Earthsea agreement, Vaclav?" Dufort asked.

"Yes, sir. It is remarkably straightforward."

"I agree. Surprising, really. I expected preferences and set-asides, requirements and concessions."

"I didn't see any, sir."

"I didn't either."

"Unlike Prime Minister Milbank and Director Laurent, though, you can't sign it on your own authority, sir."

"Yes, I know. Sooner or later I have to run it past the Assembly, and that means dealing with the Honorable Ms. Sellick."

"Yes, sir."

Dufort sighed.

The founders of Amber's government had assumed that there would eventually be contact between colony planets.

They had built into Amber's constitution a ban on the president signing any interstellar treaty without the advance approval of the Assembly. Not just advice and consent after the fact, but advance approval.

Which meant – despite how clean the agreement was, how little nonsense there was in it – he would have to bring Josephine Sellick into the conversation sooner rather than later.

It was not a prospect he looked forward to.

"When are we next scheduled to meet?"

"Not until next week, sir."

The way he said it told Dufort what Brabec was thinking. He could instead have said, 'Soon, sir. Next week.'

"You're probably right. We're going to have to bring her in sooner than that. Let's meet with the Arcadian ambassador today, and get this Costa fellow installing those radios. We can plan on talking to Ms. Sellick tomorrow or the next day. Look for a spot in my schedule."

"Yes, sir."

"Mr. Ambassador. Thank you for agreeing to have lunch with me today," Dufort said.

"And thank you very much for the invitation, Mr. President," Ivanov said.

Dufort waved Ivanov to the seat opposite himself at a table for four in the small dining room next to the president's office. Brabec was also there.

Salvatore Romano, the Earthsea Ambassador to Arcadia, had assisted Ivanov in selecting a present for the president of Amber. Ivanov had selected Arcadia's present himself. Ivanov withdrew both from his suit coat pockets now and set them on the table.

"While the discussion is on food, Mr. President, allow me to present gifts from Prime Minister Rob Milbank of Arcadia and Director Valerie Laurent of Earthsea."

The gift box for the Arcadian tea was crafted from solid maple. The Chen's Maple tea was a favorite of Ivanov. The Earthsea cheese gift, packaged the same as the one to Milbank from Laurent, was also one of their premium varieties.

"Why, thank you, Mr. Ambassador."

Dufort signaled to the head waiter standing nearby.

"Can we serve these with lunch, Cindy?"

"I'm sure we can, sir. I'll take care of it."

The wait staff brought in the salad course.

"I think serious discussions should wait until after lunch, Mr. Ambassador."

"Always a wise choice, Mr. President."

"So what do you think of Amber, Mr. Ambassador?"

"I quite like it, Mr. President. It is much like Arcadia. Oh, there are differences, of course. But people have been very friendly, and the city is big and vibrant. It has–" He struggled for the word, waving his hand in the air. "– It has juice, Mr. President. An essence. Substance."

"And Arcadia City is like that, Mr. Ambassador?"

"Oh, yes, Mr. President. There is a vibrancy, with perhaps a slightly more youthful edge."

Dufort nodded.

"We probably have a higher average age, Mr. Ambassador. Our life expectancy has been increasing steadily as a result of our medical advances. We have a life expectancy of close to a hundred now."

"Indeed, Mr. President. I knew something of the kind, of course, from our advance work, but not actual numbers. That's most impressive."

"The end result is that many of our younger people strike

out for opportunity in other cities, giving Amber perhaps a more adult air."

"That is it. That is it exactly, Mr. President. I think you've put your finger on the difference I perceived."

The main course was served, along with a plate of sliced Earthsea cheese and a pot of Arcadian tea. The head waiter served the tea in cups she brought out with the pot.

Dufort sipped his tea and sat stunned. What a wonderful concoction. Ivanov noted his reaction and smiled.

"This specific variety is a particular favorite of mine, Mr. President, though we have many others."

"That is astonishing, Mr. Ambassador. We have nothing of the sort here."

"Yes, the colony project stock teas were, at best, plebeian, Mr. President."

Dufort next tasted the cheese.

"This cheese is from Earthsea, Mr. Ambassador? It's extraordinary."

"Yes, Mr. President. The Earthsea folks have spectacular cheeses. We have nothing like this on Arcadia, I'm afraid. Until now, at least."

Dufort nodded.

"But all is not lost, Mr. President. To tide you over until we can establish regular trade, I have brought an entire container of tea and cheese with me, gifts from the people of Arcadia and Earthsea to the people of Amber."

"Thank you, Mr. Ambassador."

Ivanov simply nodded his head once, like a bow.

Once the dishes were cleared away, they settled down to business.

"I read the Arcadia-Earthsea agreement, Mr. Ambassador. I

was astonished by its clarity and lack of complication."

Ivanov nodded.

"I was present for some of those discussions, Mr. President. The goal was to come up with a model agreement. One which any other colony planet might be invited to sign as an equal partner."

"Such as Amber, Mr. Ambassador?"

"Yes, Mr. President, but the others as well. All twenty-four, we hope."

"You know where the other colonies are, Mr. Ambassador?"

"No, Mr. President. Not yet. But we are looking for them. Our people have discovered a pattern in the way colony planets were located, and are exploiting that to send out RDF satellites to look for them."

"You hope to find them all in this way, Mr. Ambassador? That seems unlikely."

"No, we hope to find the twenty-fourth, Mr. President, and locate the rest with parallax analysis of the viewscreen recordings of the colony passenger compartments."

Of course, Dufort thought. If they found the twenty-fourth colony, they had, in effect, found them all. Even if they found only the twenty-third or twenty-second, they would find most of them in the same way that Amber had known where Earthsea was.

But Arcadia had the means to go to each of them in turn, the agreement in hand, signing them up. And they would sign, too. The agreement was very well done.

He just wasn't sure if he could get the Assembly to vote for it. Especially if Sellick stood opposed.

"I see. That will likely work, Mr. Ambassador, to find most of them at least," Dufort said. "You may not find the exact last one."

"Exactly, Mr. President," Ivanov said.

"Well, as I say, Mr. Ambassador, the agreement is very well done. I think you will have a lot of takers. Whether my own political situation allows us to enter the agreement or not is another question."

"I served in the House and then the Chamber on Arcadia for several terms each, Mr. President. I would be happy to work with you in whatever way I can to make this happen."

Dufort looked at Ivanov, and Ivanov merely shrugged.

"All right, Mr. Ambassador. Let's start with the situation inside my own party."

Dufort laid out the current political chaos on Amber with a frankness that more than once had Brabec raise his eyebrows. When Dufort had finished, Ivanov was thoughtful.

"You know, Mr. President, there is sometimes an alternative to conciliation and compromise, once they have been shown to merely embolden the other."

"And that alternative, Mr. Ambassador?"

"Goad them to rash action, Mr. President. Get them way out on a limb."

"Yes? And then?"

"And then prune the limb from the tree."

After another hour of discussion, Dufort had one observation.

"Mr. Ambassador, I believe politics on Arcadia may be even rougher than politics on Amber."

Ivanov nodded.

"At one time it was, Mr. President. But you never really forget the old tricks."

Brabec simply looked on in astonishment.

The Honorable Josephine Sellick did not get to be the

majority party leader in the Assembly, the lower house of the Legislature, by being a shrinking violet, and she hadn't become one since. She was more than willing to tilt with the president.

Sellick had known this president would need watching. Every president did. They were always trying to expand executive power. That was the game. But this president played that game better than most, so she had remained vigilant.

Sellick's informants had told her something was going on, but individually they couldn't put their finger on it. Considering all their reports in aggregate, though, Sellick thought she knew what was going on. It seemed incredible, but nothing else fit all the facts.

It also meant she had been right, and Dufort had been wrong.

"Good morning, Mr. President," Sellick said as she was shown into the conference room.

"Good morning, Madam Chairwoman. Please, have a seat."

Brabec was there, of course, so she had brought her chief of staff, Bertrand Leland. They took chairs opposite Dufort and Brabec.

Sellick and Dufort were not on a first-name basis. To clear the cumbersomeness of titles, they usually referred to each other with a slightly frosty sir and madam.

"You called me to this meeting, sir," Sellick said, taking the initiative.

"Yes, madam. Something has happened that I feel I should bring you in on."

"Indeed. And what would that be, sir?"

"We have received visitors from another colony planet. Two, actually."

Ha! She had been right. Oh she was going to enjoy this.

"Two visitors or two colony planets, sir?"

"Two colony planets, madam. Four visitors, from Earthsea and Arcadia."

Earthsea, Amber, and Arcadia had been the first three drop-off planets, in that order. Just as Amber had known where Earthsea was, Arcadia would know where both Amber and Earthsea were.

"So Arcadia came up with some sort of interstellar drive, sir?"

Dufort couldn't put it past Sellick. She was quick, if opinionated and mulish.

"Yes, madam. Arcadia has an interstellar drive, while Earthsea has quantum-entanglement radios, which have interstellar reach."

"It's a pity we didn't do it first, sir."

"My understanding is that it has taken them over twenty years to be able to send a manned shuttle through space, from the time of their first theoretical breakthrough. If we had started it ten years ago, or likely twenty, madam, we would still not have such a capability."

Sellick brushed that aside with a wave of her hand.

"So why are they here, sir? Have they told us their goals?"

"Yes, madam. They have signed a trade agreement between them, and hope we will sign up as well, on the same terms."

"Do we have a copy of this trade agreement, sir?"

"Yes, madam. Let me send it to you."

Dufort sent the trade agreement to Sellick in his heads-up display. Sellick scanned it quickly. It was not a long document.

"And what do they have to trade, sir?"

"For Arcadia, in addition to the hyperspace ships, they hope to find a market for their teas, spices, and silks. For Earthsea, in addition to the QE radios, they have a variety of splendid cheeses."

"We're going to trade our medical technology for a better grade of cheese, sir?"

"No transfer of technology is anticipated, madam. The hyperspace ships, the quantum-entanglement radios, and the medical nano-technology products would be traded, but not the technology behind them."

"And reverse engineering, sir?"

"My understanding is that reverse engineering any of these technologies would be extremely difficult to pull off, madam. There is little danger of that, I think."

"Hmpf."

Sellick scanned through the proposed agreement again.

"Well, this agreement may be all well and good between Arcadia and Earthsea, sir, but it will not work for Amber."

"Really, madam?"

"Absolutely, sir. There are no protections for our domestic producers, while the Arcadians would control all the shipping prices. We could be flooded with imports, while our exports are priced out of foreign markets."

"And the guarantees of equal treatment, madam?"

"Are completely inadequate, sir."

"What do you propose we do then, madam?"

"The Assembly will take up the agreement. We will make it something Amber can approve. That is what the Assembly is for, sir."

"Very well, madam, if you are sure...."

"Absolutely, sir.

*I was so hoping you would say that,* Dufort thought.

"That was much easier than I thought, Mr. Ambassador," Dufort said. "How did you know?"

"I have seen the type before, Mr. President. It's as predictable as it is depressing."

Dufort nodded.

"Well, she is off to the Assembly to work on the agreement now. I wonder what they will do, Mr. Ambassador."

"With no one to speak for the other side, Mr. President? They will load it up with preferences for Amber, with no concessions to Arcadia or Earthsea whatsoever. You did tell your bloc not to try to hold her back, didn't you?"

"I sent the word to a couple of trusted people, yes, Mr. Ambassador. The sort of people the others will look to, before they jump one way or the other."

"Excellent, Mr. President. Let them wrangle with it for a while, and then we will have a surprise for them."

Paolo Costa, meanwhile, had been hooking up QE radios. He now had links running from Amber to both Earthsea and Arcadia, and he had tested to check that, on the failure of one link, traffic would re-route.

Per Ivanov's instructions, the only people with access right now were Ambassador Ivanov and himself.

## The *Star Runner*

Rob Milbank was initially surprised by Sasha Ivanov's report.

"It is not that surprising, Rob. Remember who was the whip for your party in the House just a few years back, when the hyperspace project had its first colossal failure?"

"You think Josephine Sellick is a duplicate of Gerard Laporte, Sasha?"

"Not a duplicate, surely, but she could be his sister. She sees this whole thing as a way to increase her power relative to the executive. It has nothing to do with space, or trade, or anything else."

"Then what's our best path forward?" Milbank asked.

"Let her hang herself. Let them go on with their debate, and their amendments. It will take weeks. And, like Laporte, she will be overtaken by events."

"Which events, Sasha?"

"*Star Runner*, as I understand it, is within a month or so of being moved to Arcadia orbit for fitting out. While that takes a long time, an unfitted-out *Star Runner* looks much like a completed one from the outside."

"Yes, that's certainly true."

"And the other events that are rushing at us are the return of the RDF satellites. We will soon have a lot of other planets to trade with. There is no need for an Amber deal at all, much less soon."

Milbank nodded.

"And the tipping point, Sasha?"

"It turns out that, while President Dufort must have the Assembly's advance approval to sign any interstellar treaty, he doesn't need any approval at all to open up public access to the QE radios, which are, for the time being at least, a gift."

Milbank's eyes got wide, and Ivanov nodded.

"Yes, Rob. Dufort can open the channels to Arcadia, and all the news about *Star Runner* and the discovery of the other colonies, to his populace without any additional authority. It will put The Honorable Ms. Sellick on the wrong side of history."

Milbank nodded. Gerard Laporte's fall had been as fast as one might have hoped. At some point, he was just– gone. Still a member of the House, but out of the leadership. Unaccustomed to being a mere member, he had retired from politics and did not stand for the House in the next elections.

"In the meantime, Sasha, President Dufort, you, me, Director Laurent and Ambassadors Romano and Diakos should probably all be in cahoots," Milbank said. "Can you open up the QE radio channel to Dufort on your end? So we can have some discussions about all this?"

"Of course, Rob. I think that's a good idea, but I wouldn't do it without your OK."

"No, we're good. Let's get that done."

"Mr. President, it's good to speak with you," Milbank said.

"And to you, Mr. Prime Minister," Dufort said.

"My friends call me Rob, Mr. President."

"And mine call me Jean, Rob."

"Excellent. Jean, I want to tell you a story."

"Does it have a happy ending?"

"Oh, yes."

"I'm all ears, Rob."

Milbank told Dufort the inside story of the downfall of Gerard Laporte, and how Milbank had engineered it. Dufort listened raptly.

"A very similar situation, Rob."

"Yes, and your situation could have a similar denouement."

"You canceled the project."

"Yes, and then ensured it was carried on anyway."

Dufort nodded.

"I see. I think I see. At some point, after people have gotten all excited about it, I can announce the treaty is dead."

"Yes. Exactly. Arcadia and Earthsea have lost patience with Amber, and gone off to plow more fertile fields among the other colony planets. Too bad, but that's what happened, due to the Assembly's actions under the Honorable Ms. Sellick."

"Oh, I like it. I like it a lot."

Dufort stared off into the distance for several seconds, then focused back on Milbank.

"You know, Rob, I think getting the trade agreement approved may not even be as big a benefit as the removal of Ms. Sellick from a position of power."

"Now that, Jean, is something I understand completely."

While Hyper-1 sat in the hangar on the Amber Shuttleport, Hyper-2, -3, and -4 were busy in Arcadia. ChaoLi had authorized the construction of two more of the hyper-capable shuttles, and new crews were trained up.

Now all three shuttles ferried containers to the Beacon Shipyard. The shipments of copper, water, and ball bearings continued, of course, for the construction work on *Star Tripper* and *Star Gazer*. In addition, computer modules, hyperspace drives, nuclear powerplants, and chillers – all containerized, and all in redundant pairs – were transferred to Beacon and installed in the waiting receptacles of the aft, completed, portion of the *Star Runner*.

When, finally, her bows were complete, the metafactories would shove her loose. With her powerplants, hyperspace drives, and computers aboard, she would be independent.

*Star Runner* would then make the trip to Arcadia under her own power.

As the weeks went by, Ivanov's prediction proved correct. The Assembly on Amber was producing a lengthy and cumbersome document, with set-asides and preferences for Amber and guarantees and requirements on Arcadia and Earthsea.

Dufort's faction of the majority party, under instructions from his lieutenants, sat back and watched, first in horror and then in bemusement, as Sellick's faction and the minority party loaded up the treaty with provisions that no other planet would ever agree to.

To any suggestion that they might be going too far, Sellick responded with a breezy, "They'll sign it. They have to. They want our medical technology. Who cares about cheese and tea if you can have a longer lifespan? We're in the driver's seat here."

The news that visitors had arrived on Amber from Arcadia and Earthsea got out when the Assembly started hashing out their version of the trade agreement. There was no way to have such a debate in the Assembly without it leaking.

The press started to pressure Dufort for information. In response to the repeated questions, about a month into the Assembly debate he – oh, so reluctantly, of course – opened the interstellar links to Earthsea and Arcadia to the general public.

Dufort coordinated the timing with Milbank. They wanted to be sure they had the links open to the public before *Star Runner* appeared in the sky above Arcadia.

Before the Arcadia news wires went wall-to-wall with pictures of the first interstellar cargo and passenger ship.

The original three metafactories finally quieted down. They pushed *Star Runner* out of the way and started on *Star Dreamer*.

*Star Runner* drifted away from the asteroid. It sped its departure a little bit with real-space thrusters that had been charged from the fuel tanks that were the last containers loaded.

Several hours later, far enough away from the asteroid to engage the hyperspace field, *Star Runner* disappeared from normal space-time.

One hour later, it appeared back in space-time a couple of days out from Arcadia orbit. It started using its real-space thrusters to slow the big ship to orbital velocity from its hyperspace exit velocity.

There was no one on board. *Star Runner* had flown itself.

When the ship arrived in Arcadia orbit, there was a huge celebration. Milbank had saved his cheese-tasting party for when the *Star Runner* arrived in Arcadia orbit, and it was a crowded festival. It was made more festive by the ship passing overhead every ninety minutes. The huge vessel was clearly visible to the naked eye, especially lit by the sun against the evening sky.

The ship was now in the hands of Chen Shipfitting. Cargo shuttles had started running supplies up to the ship in earnest before it even arrived, meeting it in orbit. The first container was full of compressed air tanks, to fill the passenger and crew spaces. Other early containers held redundant environmental systems for the big ship, galley and mess for the work crews, and fitting-out supplies, especially paint.

The other thing those first shuttle trips did was beam down cockpit videos of the ship being serviced by multiple shuttles.

The news wires, of course, covered all these events in breathless detail, all of which was being piped to big display screens around Arcadia Square and its side streets, where people cheered and waved their lavalavas over their heads at every new shuttle docking.

These events were also being piped to Amber over the QE radio link President Dufort had opened to public access. The people of Amber were treated to images of the huge starship being serviced by the relatively tiny shuttles, mixed in with views of the *Star Runner* from the ground and scenes from the big party of half-naked – and naked – Arcadians celebrating in the capital city.

Karl Huenemann and the design group, together with their spouses, were celebrating, too, watching everything in the big three-dimensional display in the conference room of their downtown facility. They took turns running down for cheese samples whenever they ran out. Huenemann had also popped for a number of different beverages, including a very nice red wine that went well with the cheeses.

When the shuttle cockpit views came on and the *Star Runner* was shown on the screen against space, being serviced by shuttles, it reminded everyone of the simulation Wayne Porter had done two years before.

Huenemann walked over to where Porter was standing with Denise Bonheur, his wife, and clapped him on the shoulder. Huenemann pointed at the display.

"Nice job, Wayne. Really nice job."

"Thank you, Karl. Lot of other people involved, too."

"Oh, I understand, Wayne. But the vision for that was yours."

Huenemann looked back at the display.

"That's fuckin' great."

"Well, they sure are an enthusiastic bunch, aren't they?" Josephine Sellick asked Bertrand Leland, her chief of staff, as they watched the celebration on Arcadia.

"Yes, ma'am. Does this change our calculations on the trade agreement in any way?"

"No, Bert. If that bunch of naked savages can build a starship, so can we. Actually, I think this undermines the counter-argument that it will take us twenty years to duplicate the feat."

"Ah. I see. We'll have to make sure we make that argument before the Assembly, ma'am."

"Of course, Bert. I wouldn't miss an obvious opportunity like that," Sellick said.

With all the hoopla on Arcadia around *Star Runner*, it brought attention to the other people involved. In particular, it brought attention to ChaoLi, the CEO of Jixing Trading Company, who had run the hyperspace project for the Arcadia government.

ChaoLi was interviewed by one of the news wires at the urging of Rob Milbank. They discussed his goals for the interview, and why it was important to their Amber strategy.

ChaoLi thought she would be nervous for the interview, but she would have some editorial control of it. In particular, she could edit any answer where she really messed up. Compared to meeting with Chen Zufu and Chen Zumu, especially when she was younger, the interview wasn't that big a deal.

Daniel Nordstrom, a reporter for Arcadia's biggest news wire, came to her downtown office and interviewed her in her office. She wore one of her business suits.

"Tonight we are talking with Chen ChaoLi, the CEO of Jixing Trading Company, which will be spacing *Star Runner* and other starships to other colony planets. Hello, ChaoLi."

"Hello, Dan."

"Before you were the CEO of Jixing Trading, you were actually the manager of the hyperspace project, is that right?"

"Yes, that's correct."

"How did you end up running a project like that?"

"I was in the financial group that oversees the Chen-Jasic family's business interests. When the government hyperspace project failed, the Chen-Jasic family bought the land the project was on out at the shuttleport. We looked at the project and thought, Can we finish this and make it work?"

"And clearly you did make it work. One only needs to look up in the sky to know that. But didn't the government ultimately fund that project?"

"In a way, Dan. The government made advance payments for starships. We used those payments to carry forward the project. And the payments got larger every time we got closer to the goal. Every milestone."

"So the income stream of the project was advance payments from the government?"

"That's right, Dan. As a result, the government of Arcadia owns all the starships coming along right now. *Star Runner, Star Tripper, Star Gazer,* and *Star Dreamer*. They all belong to the government."

"Yet Jixing Trading will be running these ships, ChaoLi?"

"Jixing Trading has contracted with the government to lease those ships, Dan. They're still the government's ships. We will be leasing them to run passenger and freight business to the colony planets."

"Will you have a monopoly on interstellar shipping?"

"Perhaps for a few years, we will. My assumption, though, is that the government will continue to build additional ships. I know Denise Peterson's design group is working on the next generation of starships right now. We may lease some of those future ships, but I assume the government will also be leasing them to other companies.

"They will be your competitors, then, ChaoLi?"

"Of course, Dan. My assumption is that Jixing Trading will be operating in a competitive environment against other shipping companies, based here or elsewhere, who will also operate ships leased from the Arcadia government. We will have a head start, and I intend to use that to impress our initial customers with our efficiency and customer service, but medium term we will not have a monopoly on interstellar trade. That would be silly."

"Why would that be silly, ChaoLi?"

"Because monopolies are inefficient and wasteful, Dan. I want to compete, to provide services that please our customers. That's also the easiest way to please your employees. Put them in a position where they can know they are doing a good job."

"Thank you, ChaoLi. That's fascinating. We've been talking today with Chen ChaoLi, CEO of Jixing Trading Company, and the person who managed the hyperspace project that resulted in the *Star Runner*."

After the interview, ChaoLi asked Rob Milbank how she did.

She had sent him a copy of the pre-release video for his review. Mostly she wanted to know if they needed to edit anything.

"How did I do, Rob?"

"You were great, ChaoLi. Truly."

"Really?"

"Oh, yes. Don't change a thing. You got in every one of the points I wanted to make."

"And that will help with Amber?"

"Oh, yes. We are knocking the props out from under Ms. Sellick's position, one at a time. You got a couple of them in there."

ChaoLi sent Daniel Nordstrom permission to air the interview as it was.

"What did you think of the Chen ChaoLi interview, Jean?" Milbank asked.

"It's perfect, Rob. She's beautiful, smart, well-spoken, and credible," Dufort said. "That's going to help a lot here."

"Excellent."

# Return Of The RDF Satellites

The deployment vehicle had completed the pickup of its last RDF satellite. Now with its full complement of four, it energized its hyperspace field, disappeared from normal space-time, and headed for Arcadia.

The six deployment vehicles had been sent out in the six galactic compass directions from the Arcadia, Earthsea, Amber, Earth cluster in JieMin's bubble map: galactic north, up from the plane of the galaxy's disk, determined by the right-hand rule on the galaxy's direction of rotation; galactic south, down from the galaxy's disk; galactic west, inward along the Orion Arm toward the center of the galaxy; galactic east, outward along the Orion Arm toward the edge of the galaxy; spinward, across the Orion Arm in the direction of rotation of the galaxy, toward the Perseus Arm; and anti-spinward, across the Orion Arm against the rotation of the galaxy, toward the Sagittarius Arm.

Some of the deployment vehicles and their satellites had farther to go to reach what JieMin had considered the optimum location for them to pick up electromagnetic emissions from the power generation and distribution systems of the target colony planets. Particularly in the spinward and anti-spinward directions, as there weren't a lot of stars between the arms.

Nevertheless, the first of those deployment vehicles and its RDF satellites was due soon.

Meanwhile, the debate in the Assembly of the Amber Legislature continued. It didn't look like it would be over anytime soon. To observers in the media it looked like Josephine Sellick was trying to kill the potential trade agreement, preferring to hold out for Amber developing its own interstellar drive.

Which was exactly what Sellick was doing, though she denied it.

"I'm just trying to get the best deal we can for Amber. Who could possibly oppose that?" she asked.

But public support for her position was wavering. Why not make a deal now? Arcadia had starships that would soon be ready to start trading among the colonies. Jixing Trading Company would be the big player there initially.

And didn't that pretty CEO for Jixing Trading say they expected competitors on the medium term?

The first deployment vehicle to return to Arcadia sent its results in to the operations headquarters from its location at the hyperspace limit. One of its four satellites had found a colony planet. The other three had been too far away – more than one hundred twenty-two light-years – from any colony planet to detect any power grid emissions.

What they had was the exact location of each of the RDF satellites when they did their scans, and the precise vector from the successful satellite to the colony it had found. They knew nothing else, in particular the name of the colony planet they had found. It could be number four or number twenty-four.

JieMin marked the satellite locations on his bubble map of potential colony positions. He encircled all four with bubbles with diameters of two hundred and forty-four light-years. He blanked out the bubbles of the three unsuccessful satellites. No colonies in those bubbles.

JieMin also marked the vector to the observed colony planet

in the bubble of the successful satellite. So if the colony planet lay along that line, between the satellite and the bubble edge, which star was it orbiting? There was only one G2 star – the same category as the suns of Earth, Arcadia, Earthsea, and Amber – along that line.

JieMin marked it on his map, then marked it with a fixed bubble with diameter of three thousand light-years. He let the other, unfixed, bubbles move around.

Hmm. He had some new potentials in there.

"So now what do we do?" ChaoLi asked at her operations group meeting, which had carried on as before.

"Well, the obvious thing to do is to run one of the hyperspace shuttles out there and do a flyby of the planet, so we can find out which colony it is and gather some intelligence on them," John Gannet said.

"Can we do that?"

"Sure. We have the program and the instrument package and everything."

"Should we wait until other satellites come back?" ChaoLi asked.

"No reason to. We're going to have to do it sooner or later. Might as well do it now, before the others come back."

ChaoLi nodded.

"The only problem I can see, ma'am," Chris Bellamy said, "is that if the satellites keep coming back with colony planets, we're going to run out of shuttles."

"And we also have the activities around fitting out *Star Runner,* which we have to keep doing. Running people up there and back, carrying supplies and materials. All of that."

"Yes, ma'am," Bellamy said. "We can use regular shuttles for that. But we're one hyperspace shuttle short as it is."

"Because it's sitting on the ground in Amber."

"Yes, ma'am."

"All right," ChaoLi said. "Let's get a hyperspace shuttle tricked out for the flyby and get it on its way."

"Yes, ma'am," Gannet said.

On Amber, the Assembly took one of the month-long breaks in their normal calendar. Their version of the trade agreement sat unfinished, with a long list of further amendments to be debated and considered.

The second deployment vehicle returned to Arcadia perhaps a week after the first. None of its RDF satellites had found a colony planet. JieMin added those two hundred and forty-four light-year diameter bubbles to his map as negative spaces for colonies. The unfixed bubbles moved around.

Two weeks later, the third deployment vehicle returned to Arcadia. It had found one more colony planet. JieMin added the negative bubbles to his map, as well as the fixed bubble around the G2 star on the detection vector from the successful satellite. His unfixed bubbles moved around again.

"Now what do we do?" ChaoLi asked.

"You mean, about a flyby of this new colony planet?" John Gannet asked.

"Yes. We can't spare another shuttle for a flyby. Even with people working ten days on, five days off, we're still moving people back and forth to the *Star Runner* continuously. And they're going through a lot of fitting-out supplies up there. Together with meeting their own food and sanitation needs, it's all we can do to keep up now."

"We were talking about that, ma'am. Is there any reason we

can't use the deployment vehicles for flybys?"

"Do they have the comm suite for that?" ChaoLi asked.

"No, not completely. Close, though. And they can use the RDF satellites. They have some comm capability so they can talk to the deployment vehicle when it comes back looking for them. It's not a perfect solution, ma'am, but it's close."

"Very well. Send one of them out to do the flyby on our new find."

"Yes, ma'am."

"That'll have to do until we get the new non-hyperspace cargo shuttles."

"You've ordered those, ma'am?" Gannet asked.

"Yes. Finding more colony planets ups our advance payments from the government, and I'm not yet paying lease payments on *Star Runner*."

"That's excellent, ma'am. We'll have plenty of platforms for *Star Runner* then."

"And I should probably buy that adjacent location at the shuttleport and put up the warehouse we talked about so you have enough room out there."

Gannet nodded.

"It's not the flight ops, ma'am. It's the time on the ground in prep for these bigger missions. Moving the *Star Runner* effort next door would give us some elbow room."

"All right. I'll take care of it."

The fourth and fifth deployment vehicles returned the same week. One of the eight RDF satellites they carried had found a third new colony planet. JieMin added the seven negative bubbles for the unsuccessful satellites and the fixed bubble of a new colony planet to his map, and the unfixed bubbles shifted again.

A pattern was beginning to emerge.

Two weeks later, the sixth and final deployment vehicle returned to Arcadia. Three of its RDF satellites had located colony planets.

The last deployment vehicle to return had been the one JieMin was most interested in from the start. It came in last, despite having left at the same time as the others, due to its longer mission. A mission to where the stars were a little denser, and the most hospitable colony planets likely were denser as well.

They were still three thousand light-years apart from each other. That was a given. But that's how the RDF satellites had been deployed as well.

JieMin entered the one new negative bubble – the two hundred and forty-four light-year diameter volume they now knew held no colony – to the map, then added the three new colonies and their fixed three thousand light-year diameter bubbles.

The unfixed bubbles corresponding to possible locations of the remaining fifteen colonies shifted in his map, maintaining their distances from each other and the colonies they'd found. JieMin rotated the map first one way, then another.

And there it was.

The pattern he had been looking for.

JieMin made some adjustments to those unfixed bubbles' locations, based on the availability of G2 stars in their volumes. Looking over his work, he nodded.

JieMin sent a message to Chen Zumu requesting a meeting.

Once seated, and with tea served, Jessica guessed at JieMin's purpose.

"You have information on the new colony finds, JieMin?"

"Yes, Chen Zumu. May I have access to your display wall?"

Jessica nodded and pushed a temporary permission to JieMin's computer account. JieMin pulled up the bubble map he had been working on.

"This is a map of the colonies, enforcing a three thousand light-year distance between them. The bubbles with a green tint are the colony locations we know for sure now. The red bubbles are potential colony locations, and are allowed to float as more known colony locations are fixed."

As Jessica looked at the map, JieMin rotated it first one way, then another. At one point, Jessica gasped.

"Yes," JieMin said. "You see it, don't you, Chen Zumu?"

"Yes, of course," Jessica said. "It's very nearly a three-dimensional close-packing arrangement. Within the bounds of where habitable planets can be found, I suppose. One cannot simply cause a planet to exist where one wants one."

"I believe that is correct, Chen Zumu. In three clusters, one in the Orion Arm, one in the Sagittarius Arm, and one in the Perseus Arm. The variations are due to the granularity of finding suitable planets. But notice these also."

JieMin highlighted three colonies with a yellow tinge.

"Those colonies bridge the three groups together, JieMin. One between the cluster in the Orion Arm and the cluster in the Sagittarius Arm, and two between the Orion Arm and the farther Perseus Arm."

"That is correct, Chen Zumu. There is a minimum of three thousand light-years between colony planets, but it is possible to travel on a multiple-stop course from any colony planet or Earth to any other colony planet along a course where there is no transit between planets greater than eight weeks. Four thousand light-years."

"It looks like the colony planet locations were selected to facilitate trade among the colonies, once hyperspace travel became reality."

"As long as the six-week minimum transit period was maintained. I believe that is correct, Chen Zumu."

Jessica looked out her doorway at the statue of Matthew Chen-Jasic in her garden, a gift – and a message – from Janice Quant.

"She knew, JieMin. She did this on purpose."

"Of course, Chen Zumu."

"And Arcadia just happens to be the bridge between the Orion Arm and the Sagittarius Arm. Which makes us a natural transportation hub."

"Yes, Chen Zumu. We have a prime location as a trading center, at least between the Orion Arm colonies and the Sagittarius Arm colonies."

"Which are the two bigger clusters."

Jessica stared into the map for a few minutes. JieMin was content to wait.

"What are the odds that the hyperspace drive would be developed at such a hub?"

It was a rhetorical question, but JieMin had an exact answer.

"About twelve percent, Chen Zumu, if you consider the two colonies that bridge the Orion Arm to the Perseus Arm."

JieMin shrugged.

"I had to be born somewhere, Chen Zumu."

Jessica nodded.

"And if not you, someone else. Sooner or later."

JieMin nodded.

"Very good, JieMin. Thank you for briefing me on this. You need to inform ChaoLi as well. On this, at least. Janice Quant, though, must remain our secret."

"Understood, Chen Zumu."

The next day, ChaoLi began her day with a visit to JieMin's university office downtown, at JieMin's request.

"I need to show you something, ChaoLi, for which I need the big display in my office," was all he would say.

When they got to his office, JieMin waved ChaoLi to one of his guest chairs. They sat facing the display at the far end of his office.

"This is the current map of the colonies, known locations in green and possible locations in red."

JieMin rotated the map first one way and then the other.

"My God," ChaoLi said. "We're the hub of these two clusters."

"Yes. Whether through accident or design, we are at the crossroads of human colonies."

"Looking at that map, if I could choose anywhere to base Jixing Trading, Arcadia would be the best choice."

JieMin nodded.

"And so your question of where to locate your big freight transfer hub has been answered," he said.

"It sure has."

ChaoLi stared into the map, then shook her head.

"It's exactly the right place," she said. "Who'd've thought?"

# Deal

None of the news of finding other colonies had been made public. Rumors circulated from leaks out of the project, but there was no official confirmation. Rob Milbank and Jean Dufort were waiting for the precise moment when the impact of those discoveries would have the most salutary effect on their conspiracy against Josephine Sellick.

The perfect moment came when *Star Tripper* emerged from hyperspace and made its way to Arcadia orbit. *Star Tripper* took up a position twenty mile from *Star Runner*, far enough away to keep shuttle operations on the two ships from interfering with each other, but close enough to allow easy transfer of materials, tools, and personnel between them.

From the surface of Arcadia, you could now see the two ships orbit across the sky in formation, every ninety minutes.

What that second ship meant, though, was that *Star Runner* was not a one-off. It was just one of a series of ships that would be rolling out of the Beacon Shipyard, where *Star Gazer*, *Star Dreamer*, and *Star Dancer* were under construction.

"There's one more thing I think we should do, Rob," Jean Dufort said.

"What's that, Jean?"

"Recall your ambassador."

"What?" Milbank asked.

Dufort made a waving-away gesture.

"With the QE radios, Rob, Sasha can be in touch with us from Arcadia. After all these months, we have the relationships established now. And I think he wants to go home anyway. But it will be a kick in the teeth here for people. Not just a threat, but the actuality of being cut out of the colony trade due to one intransigent person."

"Well, we can certainly use the shuttle here. We have a whole bunch of colonies to investigate and contact now."

Dufort nodded.

"Exactly. You've mentioned the strain on your resources for getting all this done. So pull the shuttle back. And bring Sasha back home with it. Then I can handle this end."

Milbank nodded.

"All right, Jean. I would never do that without your buy-in, you know that."

"Yes, Rob, I know. But it will certainly bring things to a head here."

The *Star Tripper* orbiting Arcadia in tandem with *Star Runner* was hard to miss, especially in the dawn and evening sky. Along with that success, the government now announced the finding of six more colony planets. Identification of those was under way.

The Arcadia government also released JieMin's map, though only showing the locations of known colonies, and without the bubbles. Looking at that map, Arcadia's strategic location would be evident to some people, but Milbank's government made sure to point it out.

The Arcadia news wires went nuts.

Of course, all the Arcadia news wires could be picked up on Amber and Earthsea as well.

Valerie Laurent called Milbank to congratulate him on Arcadia's successes and to inquire about progress with Amber.

"We're not there yet, Valerie, but we're working on it. I hope all this news will get some things moving over there."

Laurent nodded.

"There's one more thing I should mention, Rob. In addition to QE radios on the colonies, I think we need to try mounting QE radios on those ships of yours."

"That would be a good move, I think, Valerie. Then ships could get in touch if they had problems and had to drop out of hyperspace out in the middle of nowhere. They could tell us where they were, so we could go rescue them."

"Oh, it's more than that, Rob. I think it's been everybody's assumption, but we don't actually know that QE radios don't work in hyperspace. Some people believe they will. That it would violate some rule of something or other if they didn't. Conservation of spin or parity or something."

That rocked Milbank back in his chair.

"That, that would be incredible," he said.

"Yes, rather than six weeks in transit out of touch with the universe, people could stay in touch, do business, attend meetings, all while in transit. You just couldn't go outside."

"That would change a lot, Valerie. We need to try it as soon as we can."

"I agree, Rob," Laurent said. "Whenever you can get a shuttle free. It doesn't even need power and cooling capability. For a simple two-channel rig, we have a self-contained unit."

"And that gives me justification for something else I need to do. Thanks, Valerie."

"You're welcome, Rob. Stay in touch."

The news out of Arcadia hit Amber like a brick upside the head. Josephine Sellick's strategy of delay, of putting together their own version of the agreement, or of building their own hyperspace ships, was backfiring. The promise of an Amber-designed hyperspace ship looked more and more hollow. By the time they had any such thing, even assuming they could duplicate Arcadia's breakthrough, it would be years down the road. Years of missed opportunities.

And then came the coup de grace.

The announcement on Arcadia came from Milbank himself, who walked into a press conference being held by his new foreign minister, Haruki Tanaka. When Milbank made his surprise appearance, Tanaka ceded the podium to him.

"Thank you, Mr. Tanaka. I have a short announcement to make. I will take no questions.

"It has become eminently clear to me over the last six months that Amber has no interest in entering a free-trade agreement with Arcadia and Earthsea. I can no longer justify the waste of resources our mission to Amber represents. We now have six new colony planets to approach with our trade agreement.

"I am therefore recalling our ambassador to Amber.

"Thank you, everybody."

Milbank ignored the shouted questions and left the press room.

Sellick was meeting with her faction in the majority caucus room of the Assembly. She was assuring them they could weather this storm. With elections coming up, they needed a lot of reassuring.

"This will all be fine. Don't you see? This just emphasizes how easy it is to build these ships, that they can just punch them out at six-month intervals like that. We just need to stick with what we're doing and–"

Bertrand Leland burst through the door.

"Madam Chairwoman. Arcadia just withdrew their ambassador. He's leaving, ma'am."

In the uproar of conversation that followed, no one heard Sellick's muttered, 'Oh, shit.'

The ambassador's departure was broadcast live on the Amber news wires. They smelled blood in the water now, and they were covering every nuance.

Ivanov, Moore, McKay and Costa all walked up the mobile staircase to the shuttle's cockpit door, carrying their small personal bags. The shuttle was on just one container, carrying their personal cubic for the trip back.

Whether Costa should go on this trip or not had been a question. But the plan was for the shuttle to go to Earthsea first, and pick up three of the two-channel self-contained QE radios. They would test one in hyperspace on the way back to Arcadia, then all three would be available for mounting on *Star Runner*, *Star Tripper*, and *Star Gazer*. Whether they worked in hyperspace or not, a way for a stranded ship to call for help was a good idea.

So Costa went along, which the news wires picked up on. Not only was Arcadia's ambassador leaving, but so was the one Earthsea representative on Amber.

The incoming message queues into the Assembly delegates exploded.

When the Assembly met the next morning, there was general bedlam as delegates sought to get permission to speak. Sellick pounded the gavel in futility trying to bring the meeting to order.

And then one loud voice bellowed and cut through the

chatter.

"Madam Chairwoman. The President of the Republic of Amber."

A hush fell over the chamber as Jean Dufort walked up the aisle toward the dais. Sellick sat back in her chair in shock. There was only one circumstance in Amber's constitution that allowed the President to appear uninvited before the Assembly.

To call for a no-confidence vote on the Chair.

Dufort walked up the aisle, onto the dais, and up to Sellick. He held out his hand, and, mechanically, she handed him the gavel and ceded the chair and the dais to him. She went down to the floor of the chamber and took the seat for her district. She looked dazed.

Dufort rapped for order and the chamber fell completely silent. The chamber's proceedings were always run live on the Assembly's video channel, but all the news wires cut live to this once they picked up on Dufort having appeared in the Assembly.

Not one to overdo it, Dufort kept his comments short.

"Delegates of the Assembly:

"For almost a century and a quarter, the colony planets have been isolated from each other. That period is finally coming to an end. We have been invited to join with our sister colonies in forming a trading network, to unite all the colonies in one trade consortium, pooling our resources and our talents and our products, for the benefit of all.

"We have been invited to join this trading network as an equal partner with Arcadia and Earthsea, and on the same terms. Another six colonies have now been found, and they will be invited to join as well. We stand to profit from much larger markets for our products, as well as from the availability of exciting new products from our trading partners.

"A large majority of Amber citizens support our joining this network. I believe a large majority of this Assembly does as well. But one person, out of a combination of petulance, politics, and prerogative, stands athwart this path to a brighter future for everyone, Chairwoman Josephine Sellick.

"Therefore I appear before you to call no confidence in the Chair."

The floor erupted in calls to speak. Dufort pounded the gavel to restore order, and, as the floor quieted down, one voice called out.

"I call the question."

"Seconded," yelled another.

Dufort had to restore order again. He spoke softly, forcing delegates to be quiet to hear him.

"The question has been called and properly seconded. We will vote by show of hands to limit debate. Ayes will vote to move to the question. Nays will vote to debate the issue further.

"Ayes?"

Dufort scanned the room for the Aye votes as delegates held up their hands.

"Nays?"

Dufort scanned the room for Nay votes.

"In the opinion of the chair, the Ayes have a two-thirds majority. We are voting on the question. 'Has the Chair lost the confidence of the Assembly.' For this vote, you must vote with the voting system, and your vote will be recorded and published. The vote will end in fifteen minutes."

Dufort sat back in the chair to wait out the vote.

Sellick sat stunned in her seat on the floor. It had all moved so fast. It had been engineered by Dufort, of course, to pick the perfect moment to spring, but that didn't matter. That was politics. It was a game she knew, a game she had played, and, very likely, a game she had lost.

With an election coming up, the news out of Arcadia, the recall of their ambassador, and the delegates' certain knowledge their votes would be made public, Sellick knew she stood no chance on this one. She had scanned the room, too, and Dufort hadn't tipped the scales. He'd had his two-thirds for cloture.

He would have no trouble getting a three-fifths majority on the no-confidence vote.

With the shuttle just approaching the hyperspace limit, and still in touch with the Amber network, Sasha Ivanov called Dufort that afternoon.

"Congratulations, Jean. Well played."

"Thank you, Sasha. It went well for us."

"And your faction leader is now Chair?"

"Yes, the first thing after the no-confidence vote was to move to the issue of electing a new Chair. Victor has been one of my lieutenants in the Assembly for years."

"Victor indeed," Ivanov said, chuckling. "Please pass on my congratulations to Mr. Brouwer when you have a chance."

"I will, Sasha."

"Will the Assembly now take up the trade agreement, Jean?"

"That is the first thing on Victor's agenda, and he now controls the agenda on the floor."

"Excellent. And you have the copy of the trade agreement I signed yesterday morning?"

"Yes, Sasha. I expect to be able to sign it tomorrow."

"Wonderful. Well, we are approaching the hyperspace limit, so I will speak to you again in six weeks, Mr. President."

"Bon voyage, Mr. Ambassador."

Deployment vehicles were sent out to perform flybys of the new colonies as they were found. As each came in they learned which colony planet it was, something about its governance, and a lot about how it had developed.

One of those colony planets stood out, though.

Rob Milbank was surprised to get a call from Chen JieMin. They had both sat in ChaoLi's meetings early in the project, and had become friends, but it was unusual for JieMin to call him in the middle of the business day, and to put a priority tag on the call.

"Yes, JieMin. What is it? What's happened?" he asked.

"The latest flyby results, Rob?"

"Yes?"

"We've found Olympia," JieMin said.

"Olympia?"

"Yes. Olympia was the twenty-first colony on the drop-off list. They know where everyone is. All the colony planets. All but three."

# Quant

Janice Quant had watched the situation unfold in Arcadia, Earthsea, and Amber. There were several things that had caught her attention.

Chen JieMin and Chen ChaoLi were definitely the up-and-coming power couple of the Chen-Jasic family. That was very good news for Quant. If she had to intervene in human affairs, she might be able to do it through them, from the sidelines, without exposing herself more widely to humanity and triggering conquered-culture syndrome.

That Arcadia had been the colony to develop the hyperspace drive had been a stroke of luck. Quant had searched hard for a suitable colony planet in the gap – not so much a true gap as an area of lesser star density – between the Orion and the Sagittarius Arms. That planet would be a natural hub for the interstellar colony traffic she had anticipated.

Quant had done the same thing with the other gap, between the Orion and Perseus Arms. That gap was larger and had taken two colony planets to bridge, but she had eventually found them.

While Quant had put concentrations of certain specialties on some of the colony planets, anticipating the trade that would develop, she had not done so on her bridge colonies. Big hubs were better off being generalists, she figured, and so she had given them a broad mix of colonists.

Quant had also placed the Jasic family on Arcadia, her primary bridge colony, on something of a whim. That had worked out, in a very big way.

The only thing still to worry about was war. War between colonies. War between the colonies, collectively, and Earth. Quant's big transporter was coming along nicely, though. Ahead of schedule. By the time she needed it, she would have it.

Quant had done nothing to interfere with what was happening on Earth. She didn't feel the responsibility toward Earth that she did toward her colonies. She had driven the colony effort, she had persuaded the colonists to emigrate. If they failed, that would be on her.

Earth was another matter entirely.

Please review this book on Amazon.

# Author's Afterword

After the discovery of hyperspace in Arcadia, the next book in this series would be about getting hyperspace exploration under way and finding the other colonies. That much was clear going in. And the first thing they would need was some means of propulsion that was consistent with the hyperspace they had found.

This is not the propulsion of the Childers series, nor of the EMPIRE series. This hyperspace was corrosive. Protecting the ship from hyperspace also meant those propulsion methods wouldn't work. It would have to be something else.

We solved that problem, my characters and I, first thing in this book. We could now go out and look for the colonies.

Galactic Survey didn't work out the way I'd originally conceived it when I started the series, however. I had thoughts of people in exploration ships spacing around, sort of like Star Trek, but without knowing where the other human settlements were.

That's not how it turned out. In Galactic Survey, they find the other colonies with analysis of star records for the first two drop-offs, and with unmanned probes for the others. That makes more sense to me now. Sending large manned ships out into space needs an income stream to support it. But interstellar trade cannot come until after finding the other colonies.

So the search for the other colonies comes down to unmanned probes, looking for their radiation signatures. Which means you need to get close enough to see them. Within the expanding sphere of their colony radiation.

During the course of this process, Chen JieMin stumbles onto the reality of Janice Quant, and Jessica Chen-Jasic contacts Quant to make sure they don't step outside whatever her rules are. Quant answers her, but obliquely.

One of the hardest parts of writing this book was figuring out what the other colonies were like, and why they were like that. Which got me to thinking about what Arcadia was like and why Arcadia was like that.

What opportunities for trade would there be? What frictions might develop because of their differences? How would they solve those?

A bigger question for the next book is, What are the other colonies like? Why are they like that? Twenty-one more times. I haven't answered those questions yet. And I won't deal with them in the detail I dealt with Amber and Earthsea here. That would be another ten books, and I couldn't maintain my own interest or yours.

And that doesn't include whatever is happening on Earth, another question I haven't answered yet.

For those who've read my other two series, this one will stand out a bit. There's no war. No space navy. No big space battles. At least not yet. I'm not sure there will be. There's a bunch of possibilities, but, since I haven't written the future of the series yet, I don't yet know where it's going.

But I'll have fun with it, and I hope you will as well.

Richard F. Weyand
Bloomington, IN
August 9, 2021

Made in the USA
Las Vegas, NV
07 February 2022